Voodoo Blues

Blue Moon Sacramento

Book 1

Alex Gates

&

Steve Higgs

Text Copyright © 2022 Alex Gates & Steven J Higgs

Publisher: Steve Higgs

The right of Alex Gates and Steve Higgs to be identified as author of the Work has been asserted by him in accordance with the Copyright, Designs and Patents Act 1988

All rights reserved.

The book is copyright material and must not be copied, reproduced, transferred, distributed, leased, licensed or publicly performed or used in any way except as specifically permitted in writing by the publishers, as allowed under the terms and conditions under which it was purchased or as strictly permitted by applicable copyright law. Any unauthorised distribution or use of this text may be a direct infringement of the author's and publisher's rights and those responsible may be liable in law accordingly.

'Voodoo Blues' is a work of fiction. Names, characters, businesses, organisations, places, events, and incidents either are the product of the author's imagination or are used fictitiously. Any resemblance to actual persons, living, dead or undead, events or locations is entirely coincidental.

Table of contents

Crushing Experience. Thursday, April 21st. 1237hrs.
Perfect Murder. Thursday, April 21st. 1301hrs.
Rabid Sasquatch. Thursday, April 21st. 1313hrs.
Into the Woods. Thursday, April 21st. 1423hrs.
Headed Back. Thursday, April 21st. 1856hrs.
An Unpleasant Surprise. Thursday, April 21st. 1942hrs.
A Ghostly Inheritance. Thursday, April 21st. 2003hrs.
Forgetfulness. Thursday, April 21st. 2111hrs.
Heart to Heart. Thursday, April 21st. 2236hrs.
Bump in the Night. Thursday, April 21st. 2351hrs.
Breakfast. Friday, April 22nd. 0617hrs.
Early Arrival. Friday, April 22nd. 0747hrs.
When Cows Fly. Friday, April 22nd. 0813hrs.
Distracted. Friday April 22nd. 0853hrs.
Home Visit. Friday, April 22nd. 0907hrs.
Cadaverous Company. Friday, April 22nd. 0923hrs.
Innocent by Disconnect. Friday, April 22nd. 0931hrs.
The Truth. Friday, April 22nd. 1027hrs.
An Unwelcome Visit. Friday, April 22nd. 1102hrs.
Slow Afternoon at the Office. Friday, April 22nd. 1212hrs.
Before the Birthday Party. Friday, April 22nd. 1637hrs.
Birthday Party Surprises. Friday, April 22nd. 1808hrs.
One More Surprise. Friday, April 22nd. 2159hrs.
The Cinnamon Challenge. Saturday, April 23rd. 0534hrs.
Sit and Wait. Saturday, April 23rd. 0803hrs.
The Showing. Saturday, April 23rd. 1011hrs.

Judgement. Saturday, April 23rd. 1017hrs.

What Next? Saturday, April 23rd. 1148hrs.

Breaking and Entering. Saturday, April 23rd. 1223hrs.

The Rest of the Day. Saturday, April 23rd. 1306hrs.

Four Real. Sunday, April 24th. 0011hrs.

Sunday Best. Sunday, April 24th. 0821hrs.

Getting Ready for the Date. Sunday, April 24th. 1301hrs.

Date Ruined. Sunday, April 24th. 1602hrs.

Stood Up. Sunday, April 24th. 1611hrs.

Double Date. Sunday, April 24th. 1647hrs.

Aftermath. Sunday, April 24th. 1707hrs.

Ghosted. Monday, April 25th. 0002hrs

Bigfoot Conundrum. Monday, April 25th. 1446hrs.

Saying Goodbye. Tuesday, April 26th. 0923hrs.

Knocking on the Door. Tuesday, April 26th. 1133hrs.

Author's Note

What's Next for August and Friends?

Books by Alex Gates

Books by Steve Higgs

More Books by Steve Higgs

Free Books and More

Crushing Experience. Thursday, April 21st. 1237hrs.

Randall sat straight in the cab with shoulders pinched back, staring out the windshield at Steele Hardware and daydreaming about purchasing the essentials—a hammer, a tarp, and a shovel.

All the while, his mother, Muriel Fincher, honked at him like an upset seal fighting for position on a warm rock. "Fat... worthless... idiot," she chastised, perpetually angry about something, perpetually releasing her pent-up steam on her thirty-year-old son.

Randall didn't listen to what she said, but he knew she insulted him. His mother was a lot of things, but not creative. Over the years, her barrage of verbal affronts had evolved into a steady and predictable stream, one which Randall often tuned out by fantasizing about different and violent scenarios in which he would shut his mother up for good.

"Did you hear me?" Muriel asked. Spittle beaded from her mouth like venom off the fangs of a snake, dangling from her lower lip. A dark-brown mole the size of a black widow spider grew on her chin just beneath the spit, a single hair twisting from it like a tentacle reaching from the depths of the ocean.

"I heard you," Randall said, opening the passenger door.

Muriel grabbed her son's collar with her thick, powerful hands. She jerked him toward her. "Don't disrespect me by turning away. You look me in my eyes. Now, what did I say?"

Randall had his right hand on the old Camry's exterior siding, ready to pull himself free of the stuffy vehicle.

Muriel was twice his size, though, and she held his collar and awkwardly twisted him, forcing him to look at her beet red, furious face.

Randall mentally scrambled to think of one of the predictable insults she may have uttered. He dropped his grip from the car's panel, returning his hand to his lap. An instant later, a violent gust of wind slammed the passenger door.

Muriel startled and screamed, releasing Randall from her grasp and covering her mouth.

Randall jerked and sharply inhaled—glancing back and forth between the now-shut door and his hand. He exhaled. "Look what you did! The door could have crushed my hand."

"Look what I did?" Muriel's voice rose to a screech, severed only by the solid crack of her palm slapping across her son's cheek. "Look what you did!"

Randall's face stung and burned, and tears rolled into his eyes, but he refused to let them fall and have to endure another round of mockery.

"We would have had to rush to the hospital," Muriel said. "I would have missed lunch—or worse, had to eat the cafeteria food. You nearly ruined our lovely day together. What do you say?"

Randall bit down on either side of his cheek until he tasted blood. He stared hard and lustfully at Steele's Hardware.

"What do you say?"

"I'm sorry."

"Look at me!"

Randall faced his mother, his face scrunched and trembling as he struggled against the sobs. "I'm sorry."

Muriel nodded, pleased with herself. She stretched her neck, raising her chin and checking her troll-like reflection in the mirror. "Well, apology accepted. We should grab lunch, don't you think?"

"Yeah." Randall remained rooted to his seat, staring longingly at Steele Hardware. They stocked hammers, chainsaws, hunting knives, shovels, pickaxes, screwdrivers, and so much more. He imagined purchasing every item in the store, and he fantasized of all the gruesome ways to rid himself of his mother.

The driver's door slammed.

Randall flinched at the sharp and sudden noise. He opened the passenger door and stepped into the parking lot.

Muriel hobbled across the street, heading toward Taco Bell. The violent gusts of wind plastered her long dress to one side of her body. Her gray wig struggled to remain stitched to her head against the conditions. Muriel didn't seem to notice.

"Mommy!" Randall shouted.

Muriel continued shuffling forward, but turned her head to glance at her trailing son. As she did, a horn blared. A truck swerved. The driver avoided slamming into Muriel and narrowly missed clipping a parked car. He shouted inaudible words out the window, punctuated with a single-finger wave and a cloud of black smoke.

Randall shrank to the size of a pebble as his mother recovered from the near collision and glared at him. "What were you thinking, you miserable excuse for a child? You fat, ugly, lazy, worthless boy? Were you trying to kill me? I should ground you. No. I should do worse than ground you. I should throw your gaming consoles and your computer and your phone into the fire pit and send them to the Devil in a burning pillar of smoke." Muriel's voice grew tight at the end as she ran out of breath. She panted like an enraged bull, ready to charge. "I should throw you in Confession for a week."

Randall shook his head. "It was only an accident. Your wig." He covered his mouth with both hands, swallowing the rest of his sentence.

"My what?" Muriel's voice had terribly softened.

"Your hair… the wind messed it up. I wanted to warn you."

Muriel drifted toward him. She pointed an arthritic finger at her adult son. "Do you have a job?"

"No," Randall whispered.

"Do you have money?"

"No."

"Can you buy yourself lunch today?"

Randall shook his head back and forth.

"Well, I guess you're not eating then. Get back in the car and wait for me to finish my meal. We'll continue this conversation afterward." Muriel made her way back to Randall, jabbing her index finger into his doughy chest. "Maybe my full stomach will save you from Confession. You can only pray."

"I'll pray." Randall fumbled with the passenger door handle, opening it and diving into the car. Muriel locked the door with the key fob, setting the alarm. Only unlocking the vehicle with the keys would disarm the system's alarm—not that Randall had any intentions of disobeying his mother.

He watched her cross the street, putting her shoulders down to battle the gusting wind.

"God," he said, closing his eyes and speaking aloud to pray, "help me." Much like his mother's repetitive insults, his pleading to God followed a well-worn path—one that obviously led to nowhere. Still, he had no other recourse but to pray. "Help me. I can't sit in Confession again. I can't, I can't, I can't. I'll die, and I've done nothing wrong. I shouldn't die. She should die. Kill her."

Randall opened his eyes as a wave of guilt cascaded over him. He had wished—no; he had prayed—for his mother to die. He had ventured off his trodden path of unheard prayers.

Through the side mirror, Randall saw his mother and the Taco Bell building and the old Taco Bell sign hanging loosely above the front doors. It rang silently, rocking back and forth. Unrelenting bursts of wind swayed it like a pendulum, and it counted down the last seconds of Muriel Fincher's miserable life.

Five.

Muriel stepped over the curb and onto the sidewalk.

Four.

She adjusted her wig, securing it atop her head.

Three.

She neared the tinted front door, reaching out to pull the vertical handle.

Two.

An especially petulant gale whipped the sign free from its perch, from its anchor, from its long-standing post.

One.

The Taco Bell sign plummeted in slow motion, end over end, plunging directly into Muriel's askew wig.

"Watch out!" Randall's warning went unheard from the car, and he offered it too late. He pushed on the door, but it didn't open. Muriel had locked the vehicle. Randall bumbled with the pin, finally pulling it and throwing it open. The car's alarm wailed as Randall screamed and sprinted to his mother. "Mommy! Mommy!"

Muriel, though, remained silent.

Perfect Murder. Thursday, April 21st. 1301hrs.

Officer Eddie Denier arrived on the scene first. After witnessing the carnage, he immediately rushed into the Taco Bell restroom, barely making it to the toilet before losing his lunch. He wiped his mouth with the back of his hand and stared at the bathroom floor. A layer of sticky liquid stood across the tile, holding strands of hair and crumbs in place. Eddie's stomach roiled at the sight. He stood, stumbled to the sink, and tossed cold water over his face.

When his stomach balanced and his nerves settled, he leaned into his shoulder radio and reported the scene. As he recited what he had observed, his innards somersaulted, and he had to grip the edge of the sink for support. After a few deep breaths and another splash of cool water across his face, Eddie exited the bathroom.

The unforgiving wind crashed into him as he secured the scene while waiting for emergency medical services and police backup to arrive. A sobbing man harassed him, pestering after him and asking ridiculous questions as Eddie stretched caution tape around the Taco Bell perimeter.

"Is she okay? Is Mommy okay? I saw her leg twitch. Is that a good sign?" The man had a receding hairline, but sported a ponytail in the back. He was short and chubby, and based on the translucence of his skin tone, Eddie wondered if the man ever saw light beyond the glow of a computer screen in a dark basement.

"Medical services are on their way," Eddie said.

"Does that mean she's alive? Are they going to save her? Please, Officer, tell me they'll save her."

"I'm not licensed or qualified to speak about the state of your mother. You'll have to wait for the EMTs to arrive." Eddie tied off the last of the yellow tape and faced the desperate man. "What's your name?"

"Randy. Randall Fincher."

"She was your mother?"

"Yes." Randall held his hands together at his chest, as if pleading or praying to Eddie. "Wait? What—what do you mean by, 'was?'"

A crowd gathered around them.

Eddie cursed under his breath. Where was his backup? He needed to speak to the Taco Bell employees, conduct crowd control, interview Randall and other potential witnesses, among a list of other tasks.

"Randall," Eddie said, reaching out and touching the man's soft shoulder. "We're going to figure this out. Once I know what's going on, I'll let you know. How's that sound?"

"Mommy hates hospitals," he said, as if he hadn't heard a word from Eddie's mouth. "She can't stand the food. It doesn't digest right in her stomach."

Eddie frowned at that revelation, considering she had intended to order from Taco Bell. How did the fast food digest normally, but not the hospital cuisine? He wrinkled his nose, squeezing the thought from his mind. He had more pertinent questions to ponder.

"We'll figure it out, okay? Now, follow me to my car." Eddie pointed at the squad car parked at an angle in the drive-thru, blocking potential traffic. "You could sit in the backseat and—"

"I'm not a criminal. I did nothing wrong. You can't arrest me."

Eddie rolled his eyes and stared at the sky, exhaling. "I know that." He needed to calm Randall down, deal with the growing crowd of people, and speak to the manager within the restaurant. Eddie licked his lips and stared directly at the panicked man. "I'm trying to help. That's all." Eddie's phone buzzed in his front pocket. He ignored the call, tightening his grip on Randall's soft flesh, squeezing his shoulder hard enough to leave finger-shaped bruises. "Now, you'll get in the car's backseat. You understand?"

"You're hurting me."

"Do you understand?"

"Yes."

"Good. I have a few other things I need to do. Once they're taken care of, we'll have a chat. Okay?"

"Am I in trouble?"

"Not at all."

"Will I have to sit in Confession?"

Eddie didn't know what Randall meant by that, but he didn't care enough to ask. "No, not if you do what I say." He released Randall's shoulder, leading him to the squad car and guiding the man-child into the backseat. Without another word, Eddie slammed the door.

He removed his phone from his front pocket, checking to see who had called him. Maya. What did she want? As he debated calling her back, a firetruck wailed into the parking lot, followed by an ambulance and another Sacramento Police Department squad car.

The EMTs worked methodically, clearing the sign from the woman's smashed and pulpy head, transferring her to a gurney and zipping her body into a bag.

From the backseat of Eddie's squad car, Randall pressed his face to the window, smearing his snot and tears on the glass as they wheeled his mother away.

"Who's that?" Officer Ted Wilson asked, nodding at Randall. Ted was a large, muscular man with a short temper and a hunger for violence.

"The old woman's son. He gave off some real-life Norman Bates vibes about his mom… or Mommy, as he referred to her."

"Why's he in the car?"

Eddie chuckled. "You talk to him for thirty seconds. See if you don't come up with something creative to shut him up."

Ted held his arm across his body, stretching his shoulder. "The bell rang her head, huh?"

Eddie glanced at the double doors leading into Taco Bell. Blood spatter and brain matter washed the cement. Caution tape surrounded the mess. Standing behind the tape, onlookers gawked, snapped photographs, and recorded videos.

"What do you think are the odds of something like this happening?"

Ted drummed his lips. "Man, never again will something like this happen. My guess, God punished that old hag for something evil. Either that, or someone cursed her. Where I'm from, we don't call something like this a freak accident, but a perfect murder."

"Louisiana?"

"New Orleans."

"You really believe someone cursed her, and that's why she died?"

Ted shrugged his broad shoulders. "There's no way that sign just," he smacked his bearish paws together, "falls on her. Splat! Not unless someone incited a curse and guided the happenstance."

Eddie rolled his eyes. "If murdering was that easy, we'd all do it."

Ted glanced at Randall. The man-child rested his forehead on the window and stared at the ambulance the EMTs had lifted his mother into. The muscular officer popped his lips and shook his head. "It takes a lot of emotional power to manipulate voodoo spirits. If we sat down and spoke with that guy, I bet he would have a few interesting stories to share with us. He's a thirty-year-old man calling his mom, 'Mommy'. If we take the time to hear him out, and you still don't believe he cursed her, I'll buy you a beer."

Eddie scoffed. "Easiest free beer I'll ever drink."

"Just you wait."

"First, if you want to run crowd control, I can speak with the Taco Bell manager about all this."

Ted cracked his neck. "I hope one of those gawkers crosses their little toes over that yellow barrier." Ted always opted for tasks with the least amount of talking and the potential for the most amount of shouting and fighting.

Eddie headed toward the double doors, toward the mess remaining on the sidewalk.

"The perfect murder," he muttered, shaking his head in disbelief.

Rabid Sasquatch. Thursday, April 21st. 1313hrs.

I plopped onto the rocky shore of Cherry Lake, untying my hiking boots and peeling off my double layer of socks. Once my overheated and blistered feet popped free of their humid prison, they plunged into the cold, shallow wake, steaming as they cooled. I sighed and stared across the sun-glittering mountain water. The view was simply breathtaking.

Beside me, a plastic bag crumpled. Fred, my assistant, sat to my right, tearing open a granola bar. At six-foot-six inches and a couple dozen pounds over two-hundred fifty, his body demanded a nonstop caloric intake. "Gorgeous, isn't it?" Fred asked, biting half of his snack in one go. "They don't make lakes like this anymore. Except Tahoe. Tahoe has a lake and a half."

I couldn't help but agree with his assessment. The water was clean, the location remote, the view splendid. Yosemite neighbored our position, and the granite cliffs rose on the horizon. Surrounding us at every side, old pines and furs from the Stanislaus National Forest jutted into the sky. Wilderness stretched as far as the eye could see, and it tempted the imagination—it persuaded one to believe crazy things, like the existence of Sasquatch.

James Connors stood off to my left. He looked like Colonel Sanders, if Colonel Sanders retired from the chicken business, grew his beard to his waist, forgot to shower, and spent his free time hunting Sasquatch.

"That's where I saw her," James said, speaking with a southern drawl, though he had lived in Northern California his entire life.

I craned my head to glance back at him. The stocky old man pointed across the lake, as if his finger highlighted the exact spot where he had spotted Sasquatch. "Right there?" I asked, pointing forward at nothing in particular.

"Right there."

"Wait," Fred said, planting his palms into the shore and looking back. "Wait, wait, wait. There?" He nodded where Connors' finger pointed. "As in, we still have to hike further to get there? Come on now."

"A seven-mile hike from my cabin," Connors said. "Don't you remember me saying that?"

"I thought that meant the round trip. Seven miles total." Fred opened his backpack and peered inside. "You're lucky I brought enough snacks to last me until dinner."

"It was dark," I said, righting the conversation. Connors and I had agreed to a consulting rate, where he paid me to drive to him and investigate his sighting. I had dragged Fred along in case Connors cared to lure me into the national forest to murder me. Part of the payment schedule included hiking, so I found no reason to complain about our terms. "You saw Bigfoot at night, correct?"

"I did," Connors said. "But it wasn't a trick of the mind, if that's what you're getting to. I know what I saw. She was right down there, crazy as a bat—swiping at the trees, foaming at the mouth, and snarling like a wolf. As you're most likely aware, Sasquatch doesn't call any attention to herself. Never."

"Did you go after her?" I didn't care to ask how Connors knew the gender, so I played along with his theory rather than challenging it. Agreeability often proved more successful when fishing for information, anyway.

"I looked down to unlock my phone and record the creature." He paused. "Do you have children?"

I frowned, unsure about the change of subject. "I don't."

"Well, good luck catching a child doing something impressive on camera. Soon as you hit record, they intuitively know, and they cease all action. That's what the Sasquatch did. She knew soon as I pressed the record button. When I looked up to film, she had disappeared." He snapped his finger. "Gone."

Plastic rustled beside me again. I tore my attention from the breathtaking landscape and glanced at Fred, who dutifully ripped through another wrapper, this time opening a bag of trail mix. I shoved my hand into my front pocket and removed a packet of gum, unwrapping a stick and popping it in my mouth. I chewed and sucked on the cinnamon flavor, savoring the mild burn and pondering my next steps. They would likely lead me to the obscure, shaded area Connors had pointed toward.

To introduce myself, I'm August Allan Watson. August for Auguste Dupin, the famed detective created by Edgar Allan Poe—the namesake of my middle name. Two months back, I formed a business investigating paranormal and unexplained mysteries, with one goal in mind. I wanted to find inarguable evidence through meticulous and truthful investigation to prove that the supernatural world existed.

Too many people claimed the same profession as I, but they dabbled in dishonesty and greed, doctoring documentation and planting evidence to garner attention, or to land a film or book deal. I didn't care enough about money to lie, and I enjoyed fame even less. My intentions were singular: to find legitimate evidence proving the existence of the supernatural.

I have approached every case, no matter the details, with skepticism. To acutely prove something exists, not only to yourself but the world, requires a scientific method—inquiry is false until purposely tested, criticized, corrected, and proven. So far, all my attempts at proving the supernatural have ended in the testing phase, as a mundane answer always rears its ugly and unwanted face.

I based the business in Sacramento, but I served most of the Northern California region, which included a whopping forty-eight counties.

My most recent case—a high-profile investigation involving a disgruntled scientist—hooked the attention of a guy named Tempest Michaels. He called me out of the blue one day, and honestly, I thought it was a prank or something.

He had a terrible fake British accent, at least to my untrained ear. It turned out that's how he actually speaks. Anyway, he had me look him up, then we switched our phone conversation to a FaceTime call. He was real.

Tempest is a Brit, a globally renowned paranormal investigator, and the owner of the Blue Moon Investigation Agency. Once I searched him on the internet, I realized he was a guy I had read about in some forums I keep up with.

It seemed he had kept tabs on me, too. Success had brought him opportunity, and he's on some kind of crusade to disprove the supernatural thing. He wanted to branch out, to open franchises elsewhere and, well, you guessed it, buy my firm and rebrand it from PARANORMALIZE to Blue Moon.

That all occurred six weeks ago.

I don't have the money yet, but it took less than a day to update my website and order new business cards. I still need to get around to changing the sign on the door, but who knows when or if that will actually happen? Maybe I'll ask Fred. Either way, my paranormal investigative career bears the credible Blue Moon name, though it has yet to bring my company much work. To generate income until the wheels found traction, I followed through with a Bigfoot sighting.

California constantly ranks second in Bigfoot sightings by state in all of America. If I investigated every supposed appearance, I would have to change my job title from paranormal investigator to Bigfoot hunter. Connors' story provided enough intrigue for me to pursue, though.

A rabid Sasquatch.

"Why were you that deep in the forest at night?" I asked, returning to my line of skeptical questioning. Had Connors been high? Afraid and paranoid? Did his over-imaginative mind see a shadow, a bear, a cougar, but wanted instead to see a Sasquatch and so had seen a Sasquatch?

Conners spat onto the ground. Though I didn't face the portly gentleman, I had witnessed him pack chewing tobacco into his bottom lip twenty minutes prior. "I was hunting squirrels and rabbits. Saw her in the distance. We stared at each other for a long second, then she went wild, tearing at that there tree. Like I said, I went to record, looked up, and she had disappeared."

"Were you drinking?"

"I don't drink," he said with somber conviction.

I touched my front pocket, feeling the edges of my sobriety chip. "I'm going on two years sober."

"Ten years for me," Conners said, snuffling. "An entire decade. Drunk driver sideswiped my wife. He lived. She died. That's how it goes, though—the righteous and the innocent suffer the crimes of the guilty. I couldn't drink without getting sick to my stomach after that."

"I'm sorry for your loss," I said.

"Ten years is a long time for a lot of things, but it's not long enough to get over someone you loved. I don't think there's enough time in eternity for that. That's why I pray, though. Three times a day, like Daniel did. Maybe my suffering will get me somewhere one day, and maybe I'll get to hold Shelly again."

"Were you high?" Fred asked with a mouthful of food.

"I know what I saw," Conners said. "I wasn't high or drunk or frightened. I live in these woods. I know this forest day and night. It's not my first Sasquatch sighting either, but it's the only one that made me uncomfortable. I think if we don't find her, she could hurt or possibly kill someone."

"Do you often hunt at night?" I asked.

"That's when it's most quiet," he said. "Peaceful. Absent of people. Besides, I can't sleep anymore. Too many demons haunt my mind and torment my thoughts. I've tried the marijuana and the pills. I've tried it all, but nothing works. So, I don't sleep until my body can't handle the stress, and I conk out for an entire day, only to start the cycle over."

That sounded eerily familiar to my personal struggles. I didn't care to share all my faults with a stranger, though. Instead, I shouldered my backpack off and unzipped it. In the pack, I carried a few ghostly repellents and weaponry—a cross, a wooden stake, a carton of salt, a silver-bladed fruit knife, a lighter, an iron horseshoe, a can of tactical pepper spray, and a Taser gun. None of it could slow down a rampaging Sasquatch, but I removed the Taser gun, clipping it to my belt, and the canister of pepper spray, sliding it into my pocket. After zipping up my backpack, I stood and faced Connors.

"Those won't stop her," he said. "Doubt they'll do much of anything."

I shrugged and smirked. "I don't carry a gun, but I have a winning smile and elderly women think I'm charming—though I'm sure they're mistaking my devilish good looks for charm."

Fred slapped his leg, chuckling. "You going to seduce the beast?"

"It wouldn't be the first time."

Connors regarded me with pure worry spread across his face. "We're all gonna die."

Into the Woods. Thursday, April 21st. 1423hrs.

Connors stopped hiking, spinning a slow half-circle. "Here," he said. "I spotted a squirrel in that tree." He pointed to his right at one of the umpteen pines congregated together. "Like I mentioned, Sasquatch thrashed and snarled, and my attention shifted her way." His index finger lowered, pointing to an obscure location in the same direction as the squirrel. "She was right there."

"Where exactly?" I asked.

"Come on." Conners spurred himself into gear, trekking a hundred yards in the direction he had pointed. "Right here. Even from this far away, I smelled her back at where we stood. She stank like Hell's sewer system."

I carefully studied the area. No oversized footprints stamped the ground, but to my amazement and disbelief, slash marks raked across the tree trunks—deep, jagged scars. I reached out and touched them, to prove to myself they existed. "Fred, you see this?"

"Yeah," he said, his voice distant.

"Are there bears out here?" I asked.

"Black bears," Conners said.

"And they're awake this time of year?"

"Usually they emerge from hibernation in April, though sometimes May. But I know what a black bear looks like, and I know what Sasquatch looks like, and I didn't see a black bear that night."

I turned to Fred. His attention skittered around the forest. "What do you think?"

"I think we should leave. Skedaddle." His wavering eyes fixed on me. Sweat beaded his brow and dripped down his face. "Let's get out of here and discuss it, I don't know, back in Sacramento. I told you I don't do forests or wildernesses or nature of any kind."

"We're fine," I said. "With you around, nothing is dumb enough to attack us."

"You think I'm fighting a Sasquatch? You're out of your mind."

"Sasquatch wouldn't fight none of us," Connors said. "She would keep her distance, remain hidden. Of course, that's a normal Sasquatch. I didn't see no normal Sasquatch. The girl I saw was mad." He tapped his head with his knuckles. "Rampaging from her rabies."

Fred dropped his snack—a serious and unnatural accident. His eyes impossibly widened and his jaw dropped. He breathed in staccato gasps. "Behind you."

I tilted my head, admittedly confused by his suddenly erratic behavior. "What?"

Fred gulped and whispered, "Look behind you."

"Don't panic," Connors said. "Whatever you do, don't run."

Now a little nervous, I slowly rotated around. A black bear stood fifteen feet from us. Instinctively, I backed away a step.

Connors snapped his hand out, grabbing my arm. "Don't retreat. We have the advantage with Fred."

"What's that mean?" Fred asked.

"You're big. You're probably bigger than the bear standing at full height."

"Don't mean you have an advantage with me. I'm a man. That's a bear. Do you know what bears can do?"

"Step forward and make yourself as large as possible," Connors said, his voice oddly calm. "Then you'll make as much noise as you can, waving your arms and stomping your feet and hollering. August and I will do the same, but from behind you."

"From behind me? No way," Fred said. "Not happening. Why do I have to stand in the front?"

The bear stared at us, growling from deep within its broad chest. At that close distance and down on all fours, the creature was nothing like Sasquatch. But at night, a hundred yards away, clawing at a tree while standing on its hind legs, a hunter could easily mistake the two beasts.

"It's more scared of you than you of it," Connors said.

"I doubt that," Fred said. "I highly doubt that."

"I'll buy you steak," I said.

"What?"

"From the steakhouse of your choosing. No price limit." I cringed, wishing my fear hadn't spoken for me. Fred could eat a wealthy man out of business. I was far from a wealthy man. "Do what Connors says, and I'll buy you a steak."

"Keep eye contact," Connors said. "Slowly step in front of us and make yourself as big as possible. Get loud as possible. We will do the same. The bear will turn around and explore safer territories."

Fred swore under his breath and stepped in front of me. He raised his hands over his head, hesitating for a second. Then he performed a series of jumping jacks, shouting each repetition as loud as possible.

"One! Two! Three!"

Connors and I followed his lead, flailing our arms and screaming and shouting.

The bear wisely thought twice about hanging around. It grunted and pivoted, loping deeper into the forest.

Fred stopped counting, breathing hard. He bent over, planting his palms on his knees. "Do you think... do you think he went to get friends?"

"He's gone," Connors said.

"Can we be gone, too?" Fred asked, not removing his eyes from the direction the bear had fled.

I snapped a few photographs of the claw marks, the tufts of hair clinging to the tree trunk, and the ground.

We headed back to Connor's cabin. As we hiked, I kept pace with the old man, wanting to share my thoughts with him.

"You hired me to gather evidence and find a rabid Bigfoot before it harms someone. Often, my job leads me to mundane and ordinary answers that have nothing to do with the supernatural."

Connors halted. "What are you getting at?"

I cracked a few knuckles. "We just had a bear encounter in the exact location you spotted a rabid Sasquatch." I raised a finger to silence the old man, figuring he might consider interrupting me right then. "I have a simple yes or no question for you. Is it possible that someone walking through the forest at night could mistake a black bear a hundred yards away, standing on its hind legs and clawing at a tree for Sasquatch?"

Colonel Bigfoot hunter said nothing, which said everything I needed to know.

"Do I get that steak tonight?" Fred asked from behind us.

"Yes," Connors said.

"Yes? To the steak?" Fred asked.

"Yes, to August's question. It's possible someone could mistake a bear for Bigfoot. Not me, though. I know what I saw. A creature taller and more violent than any black bear in this forest. It didn't run off, either, galloping through the woods, but it vanished. Poof! Gone. Now you agreed to help me find this Sasquatch and to stop it before it could hurt anyone. So, will you do as you advertised and promised?"

I sighed. "Connors, a contrary opinion of what you believe doesn't mean I didn't do my job. You didn't hire me to agree with you, but to locate the creature you saw. Based on the obvious evidence, I think we found that creature."

"The obvious evidence is what I know I witnessed."

"To ensure my deductions, I'll send the photographs to a cryptozoologist, along with your story and our encounter with the bear."

"A second opinion hurt no one," Fred said, biting into an apple.

"I can't pay you for a complete job until I see what the cryptozoologist says. I also want the name of the person you use so I can confirm their credibility."

"They're as valid as any cryptozoologist out there," I said.

"Well, believe me when I say I've met a few quacks in my time."

Considering my failed attempt at sarcasm and the subject, I wasn't sure how to proceed with the conversation. I continued hiking back to Connors' cabin, wondering where I would find a cryptozoologist, let alone a credible one.

Headed Back. Thursday, April 21st. 1856hrs.

Fred reclined the passenger seat so far, he nearly laid down in the car. He nursed a bag of pistachios, throwing the shells out the open window, humming along to a country song, and bobbing his head rhythmically.

"I love this song. Kelsea Ballerini," the big man said, pointing at the radio.

"What happened back there?" I asked, driving along the swerving mountain roads. We had a little over two hours left of the three-and-a-half hour drive.

"Back where?"

"With the bear. You freaked out."

"It was a bear. Of course I freaked out."

"You played in the NFL and you're afraid of a bear?"

"Those two comparisons don't correlate. I once knew a man, I won't say who because you'll recognize the name, afraid of dogs. Three-hundred pounds of pure muscle, but if he saw a chihuahua, that boy is climbing the fence, the house, the tree, anything to avoid that yapping puppy. Fear is like that, though. Irrational."

Fred had a point. I considered it for a few seconds. "Does fear explain Connors' stubbornness? He's afraid of, I don't know, being wrong about what he saw, so he's doubling down despite the evidence of a bear?"

"You really think he just saw that bear?"

I twisted my wrist, cracking it. "You think he saw Bigfoot?"

Fred went back to the song and pistachios, ignoring my question.

As the car devoured the miles, the sun dropped in the sky, and we eventually returned to civilization. My phone found service for the first time in hours, and my lack of notifications proved I had never taken part in any popularity contests. More depressing, it showed my flailing business and Connors' Bigfoot sighting had something very much in common—their questionable existences. Still, I had two voicemails to boast about, though my mom left one of them. I hit play, and her voice came through the car's speakers.

"Gussy," she said, "just calling to check on you. Fred told me about your Bigfoot case, and I've heard stories about cannibals dressing up as Sasquatch to lure people into a trap and eat them. Call me when you can. Love you."

I glanced at Fred.

"What?" he asked, smirking.

"Since when do you talk to my mom?"

"You never call her back, and she worries about you."

"So, what, you took it upon yourself to ease her worries by talking to her?"

"I'm your assistant."

"For business-related situations."

"She's your mom, and she's concerned. Rightfully so."

"What's that even mean?"

"You're a paranormal investigator with no paying customers. You work a second job at a used bookstore, and you don't have a girlfriend. Also, she thinks your haircut—or lack thereof—makes you look homeless, and she actually thinks you might not have a place to live."

"Stop talking to my mom."

"We're double-dating tomorrow night."

"What?" I asked, exasperated. "Who is?"

"Daphne and me with Kim and Jason."

I gagged, coughing from my disgust. "First, don't call parents by their real names. Second, don't go on a date with them. What's wrong with you? Do you talk to my dad, too?"

"We text occasionally, but not about you. Usually about the game or some movie."

My mind exploded. My thoughts burst into fragments of shrapnel and lodged into my brain, hemorrhaging any possibility of me forming a sentence to respond.

"We had dinner last week at their house," Fred said, speaking even though no one asked him to. "They showed me some baby pictures of you." The big man chuckled, a deep, reverberating sound. "Kim claims you grew, but I don't know, buddy. You were tiny." He held his index finger and thumb close together. "She had to point it out to me. At first, I thought you were Rachel." Rachel being my sister.

"I'm going to vomit," I said. A wave of humid heat filled the car, making me sweat. "Why were you looking at my naked baby pictures? How do you know my sister's name? Wait... do you also talk to my sister?"

"Occasionally, when she comes by."

"When she comes by?"

"Her and Daphne hang out together. They're tight. Like, legit friends, you know?"

"Nope. I don't know any of this."

"Well, they often schedule hair and nail appointments together, get massages… girl things. Sometimes Rachel and Jake will come over for dinner and games, but we haven't done that for about a month now."

I cracked my knuckles one by one and mouth-breathed, winded and dazed, as if I had finished a double marathon.

"I can shoot Kim a text right now to let her know we're out of the forest and safe." Fred scrolled through his phone.

"I don't want that." Operating from a state of pure shock and impulse, I returned my mother's call.

As if she spent the entire day staring at her phone, waiting for my call to come through, my mother answered before one complete ring. "Gussy," she said, her voice bleeding through the speakers.

"Hi, mom."

"Where were you? I couldn't get hold of you."

I rolled my eyes. "Don't pretend like you don't know where we were. Fred confessed. He told me everything. He's right here, too."

"Fred, you weren't supposed to tell him."

"He's impossible to keep a secret from," Fred said. "It's what makes him such a brilliant detective."

"Investigator," I corrected.

"Paranormal investigator," my mom said, harboring a hint of disdain.

"Why did you tell me you were a private investigator?"

"Technically, I am, except I specialize in the paranormal."

"You don't believe all that devil nonsense, do you?"

"No," I said, scowling at Fred.

My mom ranted about demons and the devil.

So, I muted the call. "After this debacle, no steak for you. I don't care how many bears you scared away with your aggressive jumping jacks." I unmuted the call. "Mom," I said, cutting her off. "The supernatural doesn't exist. Most of these people are whackadoodle, kooky—they've done too many drugs, drank too much booze, are old and losing their mind, or are naturally gullible. These cases always end with a simple, grounded explanation. A safe one."

"Is that why you don't go to church anymore?"

"What?" I was incapable of keeping up with the twisting conversation.

"Because you don't believe in God, because he's supernatural and all-powerful. Instead, you think there's a simple, grounded explanation for all His many miracles?"

I rubbed the back of my neck and mouthed, "I'm going to kill you," to Fred.

The big man flashed a broad, amused grin in my direction.

I had no energy to spend on a religious-themed conversation with my stubborn and worrisome mother. She was semi-right, though—my faith had faltered over the years, and I no longer believed the Christian God, or any deity at all, existed.

My mind worked through sludge, desperate for a reply, but I didn't have a proper response. I couldn't admit I had lost my faith to my mother—at least not on the phone with Fred in the vehicle. I couldn't lie to her either. I despised the act of lying, even small, white lies. So, I remained quiet and hopeful she would move forward with the conversation.

"You should come to church with us this Sunday. There's a woman who attends every week. She's your age and is single. Beautiful, too. I think it would do you good to attend a service. Maybe you'll find God and a girlfriend. A thirty-year-old man shouldn't live alone."

"Thirty-two." I cringed after the admittance, realizing I had furthered her point.

"Even worse. You should have a wife, two or three children, and a reliable job with a steady income. I'm just worried you're not happy. Will you hate me for that?"

"I'm plenty happy and I could never hate you," I said. "But I have to make another call now."

"See you Sunday?"

"Maybe," I said, the closest I could come to saying no without actually refusing her request. "Quit hanging out with Fred. It's weird."

"It's not weird," she said.

"It's weird."

"It's not weird," Fred said.

"Love you, mom." I ended the call before she could dig herself into another lecture. "What is wrong with you?"

"Me?" Fred asked, rolling up his half-finished bag of pistachios and lifting his reclined chair to a more naturally seated position. "What's wrong with me? What's wrong with you? Hang out with your family more often. What else you doing with your time off?"

"Why, do you go to church with her?"

"I went last weekend for Easter. She even introduced me to the woman she mentioned. Cambria. Pretty girl. Your type, too." Fred cupped the air in front of his chest, portraying what he found pretty about the girl.

I played the second and final voicemail, that one from Maya Adler.

Maya and I worked together at the bookstore, but like me, she had greater ambitions. Currently, she freelanced for the online tabloid, *Here and Now*. They reported similarly to *World News Weekly*, though they only covered regional ridiculousness, not worldly. Maya aspired to become an investigative journalist for a legitimate national media firm. Her life goal was to report unbiased and fact-driven news void of political or corporate agendas.

"Hey, call me back when you can," she said in her voicemail.

To avoid dealing with Fred and my familial situation, I called Maya back.

"Where have you been?" she answered.

"Stanislaus National Forest, hunting for a rabid Sasquatch."

"I have my pen and paper out. Any juicy details for me to report? My boss said the next freelancer to pen a viral story will receive a contract for a full-time job. Before you get weird about me going full time there, remember, I need this experience to land something bigger."

"Sasquatch was nothing more than a brown bear," I said. "Confirmed."

"Unconfirmed," Fred said, lending his unwanted opinion.

"Boring." Maya yawned.

"Worst part, the guy who claims to have spotted Bigfoot won't pay me unless I actually find his Bigfoot, and he won't take the bear we encountered for an answer."

"The bear I scared away," Fred said. "Quit leaving out details."

"Well, as impressive and brave as you are, Fred," Maya said, "I have extremely exciting and day-saving news."

"Day-saving? My hero. What is it?"

Fred stuck out his tongue as if disgusted. He pointed a finger into his mouth and faked gagging.

"I have exclusive access to a case that will spark me a viral article and also attract for you a little more attention to the business."

"Continue," I said.

"I spoke with Eddie."

"Officer Eddie Denier?" I asked, glancing at Fred and finger-shooting myself in the head. Officer Eddie Denier and Maya had dated for a little over a month now, and he was, in polite language, a tool—at least in my humble and well-received opinion.

"Get this," Maya said. "A Taco Bell sign—you know, one of those giant bells? Well, it blew off the wall and landed on an old lady earlier today, crushing her skull."

"Gross," Fred said, tossing a handful of M&M's into his mouth.

"Yeah, gross for sure." Maya's pace quickened, as it did when she grew more excited about the story. "That's not the craziest part, though. Her son was with her, and he saw the entire thing happen. Freak accident, right? Like, what are the odds? Well, the son goes home and finds, lying on the counter..." Maya trailed off. I could nearly feel her grinning through the phone.

Fred slapped his knees in quick succession, making a drumroll affect.

"What did he find?" I asked.

"A voodoo doll on his counter. It had a pushpin shoved through the top of the doll's skull. Randall—that's the son's name—said he had never seen the doll before. He doesn't know where it came from or how it got there."

"When did this happen?" I asked.

"About six, seven hours ago. Eddie told me everything when he came home from work, joking that I could write about it for my promotional article."

"Dead by the Bell, or Crushed by the Bell," Fred said. "Crushed by the Bell isn't really too bad, is it?"

"What?" Maya and I chorused.

"Brainstorming titles for your article. I'm thinking you should incorporate a voodoo mention. Prime the reader, you know?"

Maya ignored him, continuing to speak. "The police are ruling the death as accidental, of course. Why wouldn't they? They claim the voodoo doll was nothing more than coincidence. Magic doesn't exist, right? And it can't kill people, especially through dolls. At least, what prosecutor will take on a case and try to convince a jury the defendant is guilty of magical murder?" Maya giggled. "Salem Trials all over again, right?"

"Right."

"But what if it did?"

"What if what did?" I asked.

"You and I, August, we don't work by the same rules as the police. They deal in What Is—cold, hard facts. We deal with What Ifs—exploring the possibilities of another explanation, and only eliminating that explanation when proven false. So, I implore you to ask yourself, what if the mysterious appearance of the voodoo doll is somehow connected to the woman's death?"

I bit my lip, enticed by the question, if only by Maya's energy and optimism. "I can't."

"Or you won't?"

"I won't. We need work that pays, not work that might lead to paying customers in the future. We tried that with the Living Gargoyle case, and it hasn't panned out."

"Yet." Fred tapped my shoulder. "Hasn't panned out yet. Only a few weeks have passed."

"You want to look into the voodoo doll?" I asked him.

"Voodoo Doll Killer." Fred bit his lip and shook his head. "No. We need a word that rhymes with voodoo to make it sing."

"Doo-doo," I said.

"Kangaroo," Maya said.

"No, no, no. You two don't help at all. It'll come to me. Just let me think."

"What do you say?" Maya asked.

"You're looking into it?"

"I need a story."

"And you think this one has bones?"

"I think this one has meat. Wait until I tell you about the son-mother relationship. I'm talking about Norman Bates on steroids. If I had to guess, Randall dabbled in the occult and cursed his mom to die."

"Cops not looking into him?"

"Of course not. He's not even a suspect."

"So, there's no chance he'll pay me to prove his innocence in a murder charge. The police won't contract with me to find a supernatural plausibility connecting Randall to a potential murder. In other more precise and factual words, I would do this for free."

"You're doing it to help a friend land a crappy job which will eventually lead to her dream career. Or does that not matter to you? You don't care how many hearts you have to break, how many souls you have to crush, how many dreams you have to destroy to get your measly, material, replaceable money."

"Speaking of dreams, did Alina tell you she starts her internship on Monday?"

Maya had conned me into hiring her high school aged niece as an intern so she could gain investigative experience for her dream job of becoming a detective.

"What? No! That girl doesn't tell me anything. I'm so excited I can scream!" Maya did. She screamed.

"How about this?" I asked, willing to compromise for a friend. "I'll assign Alina to look into the voodoo doll case. You two can work it together. That's my best offer."

"Fine. I'll take what I can get from you."

Fred's face illuminated, and his mouth opened. I covered it, sealing whatever inappropriate joke he had locked and loaded and ready to fire.

"See you Saturday night?" I asked, referencing our shared second job at the bookstore.

"See you then."

The call ended. Fred snapped his fingers. "Got it! The Boy who Played with Voodoo Dolls."

An Unpleasant Surprise. Thursday, April 21st. 1942hrs.

Fred spent the last leg of our drive splitting his time between singing along with country songs, brainstorming headlines for Maya's article, of course eating, and convincing me to look into the voodoo doll case. His energy, though a lot, proved infectious.

My singing talents rivaled that of a screeching cat getting tortured, but I belted the lyrics to the few songs I recognized. I also joined in with spitballing a few titles, though my creativity lacked compared to Fred's endless well of drawing catchy titles. My mind stuck to voodoo hoodoo or hocus pocus, or some variation thereof, neither creative and both tired. As for Fred's pestering about tackling the newfound case, I held steadfast and repeatedly refused to entertain another free investigation.

"It won't hurt, will it?" Fred asked, digging through the backpack at his feet, foraging for more food. "And it's not like we have any other business to attend to, unless you count setting up those ant traps around the office as business." He found a bruised banana and peeled it from the bottom.

I hugged the road's shoulder as I drove along the highway and cruised in the slow lane, exiting into downtown Sacramento. Our office space was only a few minutes away now. I could taste freedom, the liberation from this conversation.

"You still haven't set up the ant traps?" I asked. "I asked you to do that a month ago. It's your food that's attracting them, so it's your job to rid the office of them. Also, I'm your boss, you're my employee."

"I don't get paid."

"Would you like to?"

"No, I enjoy working for free. It makes my life so much more unpredictable and exciting."

"Well," I said, pulling my attention from the road to glance at him, "your contract states you get paid a percentage of what we make from each case."

"Which is why we should tackle as many cases as possible to gain popularity. Oh, wait, I forgot, you don't understand how popularity works."

"Do you know what a percentage, any percentage, is of free? Zero dollars. That's being optimistic. Most likely, we lose money we don't have on free cases. It's hard to pay employees when the company doesn't have any cash flow. So, no more free cases, including the voodoo doll."

Fred finished his banana in silence.

The big man had a cushy pension from his years spent in the NFL, and his wife, Daphne, had a high-paying job at a tech company. Fred floated through life without having to worry about money at all, which was why he stayed with me at Blue Moon. He enjoyed chasing monsters. I couldn't blame him, though. I enjoyed it, too.

"You excited for Alina to join us?" Fred asked, rolling down the window to toss the banana peel into the street.

I popped a knuckle. "She's sixteen, so not particularly. Teenagers, from my limited experience with them, are emotional, unreliable, and, for lack of a better word, idiots."

"I was an idiot as a teenager."

"Me, too," I said. "I would hate to hire teenage you or me to work with the adult versions of us."

"Why? You're still mostly an idiot. I don't see what has changed."

I pulled my car to the side of the street, parking parallel to the curb. I leased an old office space from an old, multi-tenant brick building. A restaurant, Frank Fat's, took up the ground level, and four stories of office space sat above it. We had a 300 square-foot office on the third floor.

A woman sat on the single step which led up to the double glass doors into the building. The sun sat low in the west, the last of its dim rays shining directly on her radiant face. She wore a denim button-down top and skinny trousers, along with black pumps.

Fred's hand touched my chin, propping up my jaw. "You're drooling, and not in a good way."

I wiped my mouth with the back of my hand. "There's a good way to drool? Never mind. I don't want to know." I stepped out of the car and padded toward the woman. "Hi," I said, though much too softly. I barely heard myself speak, so I doubted she had. After clearing my throat, I tried again. "Hey."

The woman jumped to her feet. Her eyes darted both ways, most likely determining her best chance at escaping from the dirty, sweaty man who had parked before her and stepped out of his car to greet her in a more than creepy manner. Also, a gigantic ogre sat in the passenger seat, face smashed against the window as he watched with eager anticipation for me to crash and burn.

I raised a hand. "I don't bite." Said every serial killer ever before kidnapping, butchering, and devouring their prey. I had to break the ice. "He might, though." I nodded back at Fred, just in time for the oaf to open the passenger door and step out of the car with a smile bordering on psychotic rather than amused.

My poor attempt at humor didn't land well. The woman backed into the cubby, pressing against the glass doors.

"I should have recorded this," Fred said, "and sent it to Kim. She would finally understand why you don't have a girlfriend, and probably never will. You give off serious murder vibes."

The woman shoved her hand into her purse, holding it there. "I have… a gun."

I doubted she had much of anything beyond a wallet and gum based on the way she hesitated to think of what weapon she possessed.

"This is a colossal misunderstanding," I said, interlacing my hands behind my head. "Fred and I work in those dingy offices up there." I pointed upward.

The woman's eyes remained fixed on me.

"We are just getting back from a job. I'm dropping him off. That's all."

"Can we help you, ma'am?" Fred asked, his demeanor far more calm and poised and less sweaty and frantic than mine.

The stunning woman licked her lips, and the tension semi-melted from her shoulders, but her hand remained in her purse. "Do you know August Watson?"

Fred and I exchanged a look.

"That's me," I said, smirking. "We're closed for the night, though. You'll have to—"

"What my colleague means to say," Fred said, shouldering me aside and stepping forward, "is that you'll have to forgive us for scaring you like we did. If you're comfortable, we can head into the office and discuss what you need, or we can remain out here in the public. I quite prefer the fresh air. Our office smells like a cat used grandma's attic as a litter box."

"You're sure?" she asked, slowly removing her hand from the bag.

"We're sure," Fred said. He held up a finger. "Can you excuse us for a second?"

The woman frowned. "Sure."

Fred's massive mitt grabbed my arm and pulled me toward him, dragging me a few feet away from the woman. He whispered, "What are you doing?"

"What do you mean?"

He threw back his head and growled at the sky. "Are you an idiot?"

"I don't know what you're talking about."

Fred rubbed his big, bald head. "August, she's a potential customer, and you about tossed her aside like expired food because it's too late, and we're closed. Since when is it ever too late for you to work? Also, don't we want to make money? Double also, she's gorgeous and your age, and you can't string together a sentence that makes a lick of sense or doesn't sound like you want to bury her in your backyard. Get your wits together!" He yelled the last part loud enough for the pedestrians six blocks over to hear.

I glanced over my shoulder at the pretty lady, embarrassed. She looked right back at me, smirking. I darted my eyes elsewhere. My stomach twisted and my mind blanked.

"Do we want paying customers or not?" Fred asked.

"Yeah, sorry. I've always struggled to speak with cute girls I don't know."

He narrowed his eyes and shrugged. "This is some revelation? I've known you since you were, what, twelve? Get over it. She's a client, not someone who you might eventually make sweet, passionate love to." Again, Fred didn't bother to lower his voice.

To make up for his obnoxiousness, I whispered. "Client or not, it's… I usually avoid speaking to women. That's why you're here. To handle any potential clients, especially the attractive females."

"You're a moron. You and Maya talk all the time."

"That's different."

"How? She's smoking hot with a banging little body."

"You're married. Why do you talk like that?"

"I appreciate beauty of all kinds, and Daphne knows that about me, and she loves that about me."

"Tolerates it."

"Excuse me," the woman said. "I don't know if you think I can't hear you, but I can. And though I'm flattered that you think I'm attractive, I need your help, not a drink or a lay."

If I felt awkward before, I now felt like a slug sliming its way across the dinner table—someone was going to vomit or eat me, and I desired neither scenario.

"He and I have a lot of boundaries to reestablish," I said, glowering at Fred before pivoting, slapping a forced grin across my face, and stepping toward the woman. "My apologies. How can we help you?"

A Ghostly Inheritance. Thursday, April 21st. 2003hrs.

We agreed to conduct the business over dinner, because according to Fred, he had hadn't eaten enough and needed calories.

"I haven't had a bite to eat since lunch." That was his exact quote, even though he had done nothing but eat since we had stopped for lunch.

The woman, who had introduced herself as Glacia Vasquez, agreed, though. There was an old diner open all night long two blocks away from the office building, and that's exactly where we headed.

We sat in a booth in the back. Glacia had eaten dinner already, and like a normal person with a normal appetite, she wasn't hungry. I actually hadn't eaten since lunch, so I ordered a grilled chicken sandwich, no mayonnaise, and a side of fries. Fred ordered an appetizer, an entrée, two sides, and a dessert.

"Again," I said, facing Glacia as the waiter walked away, "I apologize for frightening you earlier and for dragging you to dinner."

Glacia reorganized the silverware set before her. "It's not entirely your fault. I've been more on edge recently, which is why I found a paranormal investigator to help me." She laughed, a tic some customers established when admitting they needed help from someone like me, someone who could solve their supernatural problem.

"I hate to do this, but we should discuss my rates before you tell us what's happening." I needed to wedge a payment plan into the conversation before my nature took over and I accepted her case for free—a knight saving the damsel in distress. Though I struggled to speak to women when first meeting them, I made up for it with grand romantic gestures.

After we established a fair and agreed-on price, one I discounted to the disapproving head shake of Fred, Glacia shared her ghost story with us.

"My grandmother, Nana, passed away a few weeks back." She paused after the initial statement to drink water. "I had a rough childhood. Nana brought me into her home, provided me with stability, and raised me like her own daughter. Before she died, she must have written me into her will like one of her own children. She left all of her possessions to her two children—my mother and uncle. Everything except for her house, which she left for me. Her home was the only thing she owned worth anything at all, especially since she had lived there her entire life. She had no mortgage on it, and it's now worth a small fortune."

"So Nana's daughter and son received her clothes and trinkets and… knickknacks?" Fred asked.

"Her bank account," Glacia added. "Which had nothing in it. They also received her old car, worth pennies now, and her jewelry, which, again, is not worth much."

"You received the house?" I asked.

Glacia nodded, twisting her hair around her finger. "Unfortunately."

"Unfortunately?" Fred asked, glancing over his shoulder at the kitchen. "Unfortunately doesn't mean inheriting a million-plus dollars. It means my food hasn't come out yet. I ordered appetizers. What are they doing in there?"

"I live out of state, in Oregon. Now that Nana has passed, I have no reason to come down here, and I don't care for the headache of owning and managing a house five-hundred miles away. So, I listed it." She adjusted the silverware again and tucked her hair behind her ear, staring at the table. "I don't know. It sounds silly to admit, to say aloud, but... the house... it's haunted."

"Haunted?" I asked.

"I don't mess with ghosts," Fred said. "Bigfoot is one thing. I can see the hairy bugger. Ghosts, though." He clicked his tongue and shook his head. "I humbly bow out. I'm not a man afraid to admit to his fears."

"What about the bear?" I asked.

"What do you mean, what about the bear? It was a bear. A bear! A giant, massive black bear! You asked me to go toe-to-toe with it, as you stood behind me, shaking. I said nothing out there, but since you brought it up, I'm pretty sure I saw a puddle near your feet. What about the bear?" Fred exhaled, drumming his lips.

I grimaced, turning to Glacia. "We encountered a bear today, but I didn't pee my pants." I returned my attention to Fred. If he feared ghosts because he couldn't see them, but not Bigfoot because he could see the 'hairy bugger,' why was he afraid of the bear? His argument contradicted itself. "Also," I said, ready to debate his plot-holed story. I bit my lip instead, remembering I had a client sitting across the table from me. "Never mind. Glacia, I apologize. Please, continue."

"My real estate agent told me about the ghost. Whenever she showed a client the home, weird things happened."

"What kind of weird things?" I asked.

"Doors and cabinets slamming shut. Windows opening. Banging on the walls in other rooms. I didn't believe Susan, of course. Ghosts don't exist, right? Well, it kept happening. So, I scheduled a trip to Sacramento, planning to stay a couple nights in the home."

"Something happened?" I asked.

"Of course something happened," Fred said. "Why else do you think she's here?"

"I heard strange noises, like moaning and footsteps in the attic."

"You didn't look?"

"What kind of dumb question is that?" Fred asked. "Who's going to check on a ghost?"

"I couldn't get into the attic. There's no ladder, and I didn't bring one with me, or a chair tall enough so that I could climb through the ceiling. Anyway, I don't believe in this kind of thing. But I don't know what else to believe right now. I think my grandma's spirit remained in her home after she passed, and now she refuses to let a stranger buy it. I know that sounds ridiculous, but I don't know what else to think."

The tired, pimple-faced waiter appeared, sporting a lazy smile and carrying a couple of plates and my cup of coffee. "Mozzarella cheese sticks," he said.

"Here," Fred said.

"Nachos."

"Here," Fred said.

"And the coffee is yours." The waiter set the cup before me. "Can I get you anything else?"

"No, thank you," I said, smiling with closed lips. When he left, I returned my full attention to Glacia. "You're staying in the house tonight?"

"I booked a hotel room."

"Why didn't you call us and schedule an appointment, rather than waiting all evening?"

"I called a few times, but it always went straight to voicemail. I couldn't convince myself to speak the problem aloud, at least not over the phone. I don't know. This has been the strangest two days of my life."

I raised the coffee mug to my lips, blowing on the steam. "I never sleep. Instead," I sipped from the mug, "I renew my strength through this black elixir. With your permission, I can stay the night at your grandma's house to observe any ghostly activity."

Fred swallowed his mouthful of food loud enough to draw our attention. "Well, I'm not staying with you. I have a wife to get home to and a ghost to avoid. Are you okay staying alone? I mean, I know you get scared at night, especially in the dark. If you really want me to, I will gut it out and stay with you."

I narrowed my eyes, thoroughly confused. "I live alone, so I think I'll be okay."

Beneath the table, Fred kicked my ankle. He cleared his throat. "You don't live in a haunted house, though. What if something spooky happens and you're all alone?"

Glacia chuckled. "I'll hang out with August and protect him from any ghosts. Does that work for you?"

Fred beamed. "That will help me sleep worry-free."

My face flushed with heat and my innards floated as if in zero-gravity at the thought of spending all night with Glacia. "You don't have to do that. Though the idea of ghosts and spirits is exciting, I doubt they actually exist. I'm sure I'll be safe alone, and I'm sure that oaf will sleep just fine."

"Do you have a car?" Fred asked.

"I grabbed an Uber."

Fred kicked me again. "Well, I'm sure August wouldn't mind saving you a few bucks and giving you a ride to your hotel."

"Yeah," I said, silently hating Fred. "I can do that. We would have to stop by my apartment, though. I spent the day hiking, and I need a shower and a change of clothes. Also, there's some ghost hunting equipment I need to grab."

"That's my wife," Fred said, showing us his phone. He beckoned the waiter over to our table, requesting all his food to-go. "My wife's here, and she hates waiting." The big man reached for his wallet, removed a twenty-dollar bill, and tossed it on the table. "You two kids have fun tonight. And be safe!" He slid out of the booth, turned away from us, and walked toward the exit, yelling, "More importantly, have fun!"

"What about his cheeseburger?" Glacia asked.

I shrugged. "He'll be back for it. I doubt his wife is even here, yet. She's probably calling from the office, asking why he's not out front." I shied my gaze away from Glacia, awkwardly chuckling at the fact that all I could think about was the many ways to murder Fred when I saw him next.

Forgetfulness. Thursday, April 21st. 2111hrs.

I lived in a studio apartment—a wide-open expanse of nothing but a bed, a table, one chair, and a dresser. My life occurred outside those four walls, though, and I preferred to minimize temptations that might keep me alone in the loft.

Sobriety wasn't an effortless task, and my thoughts, when left unattended, balanced on dangerous, self-harming lines. I preferred staying busy with work and exercise, preventing any chance of falling off the wagon or allowing my mind an opportunity for a hostile takeover. A few minutes of idle thought might convince me to walk into a liquor store and drown what lived in the dark recesses of my mind.

Not only did my apartment appear scant, but it lived up to the stereotype of a single bachelor incapable of caring for himself. The drawers to my dresser were in varying states of open, vomiting clothes. My bed was a ball of tangled sheets. Crumbs from old food covered the kitchen counter and dishes heaped in a sink that smelled more like an outhouse than a place to prepare meals.

I prayed to God Glacia wouldn't ask about the last time I had vacuumed or dusted because I didn't know the answer, and I begged every pantheon known to humankind that she wouldn't step into my bathroom. Not even I knew what she might find in there—a lifted toilet seat covered in an assortment of unflattering stains and a hair-clipping monster rising from the grimy sink were two of many possibilities.

I didn't enjoy living in filth. It actually disgusted me, which worked to my advantage, repelling me from ever being alone at home. While at the apartment, I could wallow in the sanitary disaster I had created, or I could leave and stay busy.

Forethought kept me alive and surviving.

"You live here," Glacia said, entering the extravagant mess.

"I mostly change clothes here, though I occasionally sleep. When I'm desperate and in a pinch, I convince myself to step into the shower. But only with shoes on."

"Where do you shower otherwise?"

"The gym," I said.

"Gross."

I scratched the side of my neck and twisted my wrist enough to pop it. "Unfortunately, not as gross as what's behind door number two." I gestured to the bathroom. "Avoid entering that dungeon at all costs."

"Dungeon, huh?"

"It's wet everywhere, stinky, and always, for a reason I'm unsure of, humid." I ventured across the loft to my chaotic dresser situation, not bothering to close or open a drawer. I snatched a pair of boxers dangling over the front, snaked my hand through the open space and clawed out socks—the pair didn't match—and swiped a pair of jeans splayed atop the dresser. "I would say make yourself at home while I shower, but…" I trailed off, glancing around my barren, sloppy place, "Maybe just avoid touching anything."

"I'm way ahead of you," she said.

I showered, realizing halfway through I hadn't grabbed a towel. My bathroom didn't have a linen closet, so I stored the two towels I owned in the kitchen pantry on the top shelf.

Panic zapped through my body. For a second, maybe an hour—I lost time during that period—I shut down, considering my options. Either I tromped naked out of the shower, soaking wet, to grab a towel, or I hollered for Glacia to brave my bathroom and bring me one. Both options hugged the line of a nightmare. Forget about Sasquatch or voodoo dolls or ghosts. This was truly terrifying—and real.

Oh, so real.

Impersonating Matthew McConaughey, I chanted, "Alright, alright, alright," over and over and over, hoping the words might anchor me from spiraling out of control and spur a brilliant idea into my mind. No luck. Instead, my fortunes continued to have their fun at my expense.

A terrible knock sounded at the door. "You okay?" Glacia asked. "You've been in there for quite a while, and I think there's a family of rats living in your sink. I don't feel safe here any longer." Her tone carried a hint of amusement and sarcasm, but I'm sure she wasn't comfortable standing around waiting for me to take the world's longest shower.

"I'm fine. It's just… uh, I don't have a towel."

"Can I get you one?"

"Please." I scrunched my face, cringing. "They're in the pantry. Top shelf."

A few seconds spiraled down the drain. Glacia returned to the door, knocking. "I found two towels, but they have holes in them and they're frayed on the ends."

I closed my eyes and planted my forehead against the wall. I nearly asked myself how anything could be more embarrassing, but I buried the thought, not daring to tempt fate. "That's them."

"I'm going to open the door and toss the towel in. Does that work?"

"I locked the door," I said, turning off the water and sliding open the stall.

I stepped onto the bathmat, wiping my feet to dry them off a little, then tiptoed to the door, opening it and angling an arm through the narrow slit. Glacia shoved the towel into my hand, and I quickly accepted it, slamming and locking the door once again, sealing myself in the steamy, warm, stinking bathroom.

After drying and stepping into my boxers, pants, and socks, I exited the bathroom shirtless, stepping out of the humidity and into the cool loft.

Glacia leaned against the refrigerator door and glanced up from her phone. "Does that often work for you?"

"What's that?"

"Walking out of the bathroom without a shirt, looking like that." She waved her hand in the general vicinity of my body.

When not working, I exercised. I ate mostly healthy, naturally not interested in sugar or sweets, and I didn't drink alcohol. My body had gained a muscular physique over time, one I wasn't necessarily proud of or cared to show off—but a byproduct of my lifestyle.

Instead of feeling proud or sexy, embarrassment flushed over me. "I forgot my shirt. That's all. I rarely have women in my apartment."

"I wonder why. It's a beautiful place." Glacia continued to stare at my pecs and abs with overtness, not bothering to disguise her gaze. "You forget things often?"

"What do you mean?"

"You forgot a towel and a shirt."

"Habit, I guess. I don't think of those things when I'm alone."

"Lucky me you forgot, then." She smirked. "Put a shirt on, Channing Tatum, we have a place to be and ghosts to see."

Heart to Heart. Thursday, April 21st. 2236hrs.

Maria Luna, or Nana, had lived her entire life in the rural community outside of Sacramento. She grew up there with seven siblings. They all had a job around the property, tending to the hens, milking the cow, caring for the couple of horses, feeding the pigs, and weeding a garden. Maria's father worked as a laborer, as did her brothers when they came of age. Her mother, her sisters, and herself sold their fresh produce on a road-side stand. Eventually, Maria married and had two children—a boy and a girl. Her parents eventually passed away, and their home fell into her possession, where it had remained until the day she died a little over a month ago.

Glacia directed me to turn onto a gravel driveway, and my car's headlights illuminated a green yard, lavish, lively trees, bushes and hedges, and a thriving garden off the side of the wood-paneled home. The meticulous care, even beyond her death, unnerved me for some untold reason. To see the world so obviously continue after a life ended rattled me, I guess.

Glacia must have noticed my shoulders tensing, or my hands tightening on the steering wheel. "She had help with the yard and the garden. Nana had arthritis in her hands, and she struggled to dress, let alone tend to her plants. But those plants had brought a sense of stability into her childhood home. They saw her family through so many uncertain times, and I think Nana refused to let them fade away, despite her ailments."

"Her landscapers still show up, even after…" I trailed off.

It felt rude to finish that sentence, mentioning her death. I had never excelled in social situations, mostly because I never knew what to say. After parking the car a few feet from the front patio, I reached into my pocket for gum.

"I pay them, at least until I can sell the place. If I can sell the place, that is." Glacia hugged herself and shivered.

The interior lights had dimmed in the vehicle. The headlights had cut away, and the night surrounded us. A half-moon burned through a portion of the night, casting enough light to create shadows. They danced across Glacia's face, drowning her in mystery.

"Don't feel obligated to stay the night," I said. "You can take my car back to your hotel room and pick me up in the morning."

"If it's okay with you, I think I want to stay and learn the truth."

"That's fine with me."

"Do you think Nana doesn't want me to sell her home, and so she's haunting it?" Glacia cringed after asking the question. "That sounds so stupid, doesn't it?"

"It doesn't sound stupid. She grew up here, built a family here, struggled and thrived right here. Her soul lives in those walls. It's not farfetched to say her spirit does, too."

"You believe she might be a ghost haunting the house?"

I cracked a knuckle and shook my head. "I would like to believe that, or at least the idea of something like that—that we continue to exist after death. In my experience, most of these things have a simple explanation, though."

"I'm not the only person who experienced the spirit. Susan did, too, and another real estate agent, along with any potential buyers they showed the house to. They all witnessed unexplainable things here." Glacia touched my hand. Her fingers felt warm and soft, sending a chill down my spine. "What if I'm making a mistake? What if Nana's telling me not to sell the house?"

"I'll help you find that answer." I pulled my hand away from hers and opened the driver's door, stepping onto the gravel, walking toward the three wooden steps leading to the porch.

The energetic wind from earlier in the day hadn't exhausted itself. It thrashed against me, slammed into the home, howled through the gutters, and rustled the tree branches.

Glacia unlocked the front door, opening it, and a wild gust grabbed the door and threw it against the entry wall. She hurried into the home, flipping on a light, and I followed, grabbing the door and forcing it closed, turning the deadbolt for added resistance against the wind.

I leaned against the door as the gusts threatened to break it down and sweep through the ranch home. "Nana made entering the home interesting."

Glacia placed her tongue against her upper teeth and grinned. "You think she directs the wind? If she had that kind of power, what we experienced… that's nothing. The woman had a temper on her. If she wanted to make herself known with something like the wind, we would have had to wade through a tornado."

I surveyed the entryway. "Anyone else have a key to the house?"

"Only Susan, my real estate agent."

No photographs hung on the walls, no visible furniture stood in the halls or the rooms from where I stood.

I frowned. "Where is everything?"

"My mom and uncle."

"They already collected what belonged to them?"

"They had this place emptied a day after learning their mother passed away. A week later, they were counting the money they made after selling the furniture, clothes, and jewelry."

"I'm sorry," I said.

"It is what it is. I lost any respect for my mother long ago. She only cared about two things in life—making a quick dollar and buying a quick high." Glacia stared at her feet for a second, then she bolted upright, wearing a beaming smile. "But I have wine in the cupboards, untouched. After experiencing the ghostly emergence of Nana last night, I decided alcohol wouldn't pair well with a potential haunting. So, I didn't drink it. But that means we have wine for tonight. You want a glass?"

"I don't drink," I said, patting my pocket to feel the sobriety chip, feeling nothing but my phone. I had left the token in my hiking pants. "Sober. Almost two years now."

"Congratulations."

"Thanks."

Glacia looked at me, lips slightly parted, then glanced over her shoulder down the hallway. "I don't mind standing by the front door all night, if that's what you want to do, but we don't have to, either. There are snacks in the kitchen, and a couple of folding chairs to sit on. I also brought my laptop so we can stream a movie."

"You care if I walk around for a sense of the layout?"

I reached into my backpack with all my monster hunting gear and removed an EMF meter. The device supposedly detected energy changes and proximity to alert the user of a spectral presence and track the source. It was the cheapest item I could find for identifying ghosts, and it served mostly as a prop to build credibility with clients. Success is all about dressing to impress.

"Do those things actually work?" Glacia asked, nodding at the EMF meter.

"Nope," I said. "It's all for show. There are apps on your phone that do the same thing. But what paranormal investigator worth his salt will wave around his phone when he could spend thousands of dollars on equipment?"

"Why do you have one, then? To impress me?"

"Most people expect to see something like this, and they doubt the investigation if I don't play the role."

"Okay Venkman, do your thing. I'm going to pour myself a glass of wine." Glacia left me alone to perform my preliminary investigation.

With the truth revealed to Glacia, and knowing I wouldn't need the meter, I returned the device to my backpack and leaned the bag against the entry wall.

The home was quaint and cozy—two bedrooms, two bathrooms, an office, a kitchen and dining room, a living room, and a garage with hookups for a washer and dryer. Twelve-hundred square feet on a little over an acre of land.

When I completed my self-guided tour, discovering nothing of paranormal interest, I found Glacia in the kitchen. She sat on a folding chair, sipping wine, looking splendid and tasty. I buried my baser instincts and sat on the empty chair across from her. She had poured me a glass of water, placing it on the ice chest between us.

"Thanks," I said, drinking.

"Find anything spooky?"

"Other than the wind ripping off the tree branches, nothing stood out."

"That's good."

"How much you selling the place for?"

"To you, a bazillion dollars. I saw your apartment, remember? I couldn't bear to see this place undergo the same transformation as your studio."

"For a friend."

Glacia mentioned the ludicrously high price, which matched the current market. "I'm not trying to profit off Nana's death. I just... I can't care for the house like it deserves. Not from Oregon. I thought about renting it, but renters—case in point, you—don't really care for things as they would their personal possessions."

"If he made an offer, my friend, would you consider it?"

"Depends on the offer. I'm not trying to profit, but I don't want to give it away either."

"It's haunted, though. Don't they offer haunted discounts on these transactions?"

Glacia smirked, tipping back her wine glass. "Earlier, when you removed your little ghost gadget, you said you had it for show." She went silent, staring out the dark nook window at the gales bending trees sideways.

"The manufacturers create those things with faults and misreadings in mind. They don't work, though. And if they did, there's no way I could tell the difference between a false reading or an actual identification of ghostly energy."

Glacia's eyes cut into me. She twirled the wine within her glass and recrossed her legs. "You don't believe any of this, do you? Earlier, you said you would like to believe it, but you don't. That's strange, considering your profession. You're a paranormal investigator, but you don't believe in the paranormal. Isn't that like saying I'm a homicide detective, but I don't believe in murderers?"

I rocked my head back and forth, considering her rhetoric. I had always complicated my lack of belief in the paranormal, but Glacia provided me with a simple explanation—well, a long-winded explanation, as we soon discovered.

"I see what you're saying," I said. "Your example, though, is flawed."

"You're telling me I'm wrong?"

"Just not right." I smirked. "A good homicide detective will work in a pattern. Problem, or the homicide comes first. He finds and collects and uses evidence to narrow suspects and identify the murderer. It should always work in that order. Homicide. Evidence. Proven perpetrator. Now, some homicide detectives, whatever their reasoning may be, work under less honest circumstances. They come across a homicide. Instead of allowing the evidence to guide their investigation, they decide who's guilty, and they find evidence, or they plant evidence, to sustain their suspicions. Their equation looks like homicide, suspected perpetrator, and then evidence."

"Okay," Glacia asked, leaning back and smelling her wine.

"Most paranormal investigators fall under the same umbrella as the corrupt homicide detectives. There's a mystery. They plant evidence, or they fabricate evidence—using something like the unreliable EMF meter—to convince themselves and others that the supernatural exists. Then, they use their faulty evidence to write a book or star in a ghost-hunting TV series, or to speak at conventions. They leverage their lies to manipulate others and profit off their gullibility."

"But not you, oh knight in shining armor."

I licked my lips and cracked my knuckles. "Not me. I follow the natural pattern. Mystery. Evidence. Solution. Every case I've investigated has provided evidence that points to a simple, mundane, and natural solution." My attention dropped to the tile floor, and my tone lowered. "That's not to say I don't want to believe, because I do."

"You want to believe the supernatural exists, but you don't?"

"I didn't enter this business to secure a book or film and make millions of dollars tricking my audience to believe my doctored videos. I entered to find legitimate evidence, real and unadulterated evidence of the supernatural." I raised my eyes, looking into hers. "It makes little sense, I know. But I want reliable proof of the paranormal. That's why I'm never in my apartment, even when I don't have an active case. I'm researching and looking into unsolved mysteries, seeking evidence that proves the problem fell into the realm of the supernatural."

The wind howled, and neither of us said a word for some time. I don't know why I had opened up like that to a virtual stranger. Maybe my subconscious needed to shed some buried weight, and I knew I wouldn't ever see Glacia again, so sharing with her felt safe. I don't know.

After a minute, she finished her goblet of wine and poured another glass. "Why?" Glacia asked, her voice so soft I barely heard it above the screeching gusts of wind.

"Why, what?"

"Why to a lot of things? But first, why do you need to prove to yourself that the paranormal or the supernatural, or whatever you want to call it, exists?"

I coughed one of the awkward laughs that possessed not a single hint of humor. "Well, that's a question that reaches far into the hornet's nest."

"We have all night, don't we?"

I scratched the back of my head and chuckled again, humorlessly. "It's a sad story."

"I already shared my sad story. It's your turn."

"Okay. Well, I joined the police force out of college. The Galt Police Department. A small, rural community where I had grown up, where my parents and siblings still live." I ran my tongue over my lips. "I spent five years on the job, serving the community as a patrol officer. I responded to emergencies." My voice droned as I avoided what came next. My insides melted into hot liquid. I stared at the wine bottle, beyond tempted to wet my mouth.

"What happened?"

"I murdered someone." My eyes squeezed shut, and I flinched as I reimagined the gunshot exploding through the crisp afternoon.

"August." Glacia leaned forward.

"I murdered a kid."

In my mind, I no longer sat in the dark, empty room of a haunted house. I had returned to the hot, sunny park. The boy lay on the asphalt basketball court, bleeding a halo of blood around his body. Apart from my therapist, I had never uttered those words aloud to a single, living soul. They cut deep, and they hurt.

"It was an accident, and the court deemed it as justifiable, but..." I couldn't continue. I had nothing to say other than excuses, and excuses did nothing for healing or improvement or accountability.

Glacia reacted stoically, rooted to her chair in a stiff, unmoving posture. She stared at me, as if seeing me for the first time. "How old?"

"Nineteen."

"Why?"

"Is there really a reason other than it happened?"

"There's a reason for everything."

I laughed again, not finding anything funny, but not knowing how else to react. "Not to his parents. My reason doesn't revive their son. It doesn't excuse what I did."

"I want to know."

I swallowed back a bitter taste. "I responded to a call. Kid at the park had a gun." I paused, remembering how I felt when arriving on the scene. Not scared, but angry. "An officer was shot and killed in Sacramento the night before. Everyone was on edge—angry and scared. The kid stood alone on the basketball court. He held a gun, pointing it at the sky and shouting nonsense. I demanded he drop his weapon. He looked at me with a terrifying hunger, and he pointed his pistol in my direction. 'Boom!' the kid shouted." I stared at the wine bottle, knowing the alcohol would, temporarily, erase the memory. "I shot him once. He fell, and I ran to him, applying what little first aid I knew. It didn't work. He died before the EMTs arrived on scene. You know the worst part? He had an air soft gun, the orange tip painted black. Still, I should've spotted the difference. I should have, but didn't. I didn't because I didn't want to. I was angry, and I wanted vengeance, and I enacted it."

An eerie, heavy silence, punctuated by the cascading windstorm, filled the emptiness for a few seconds.

"That's why you don't sleep?"

"What?"

"In the diner, you mentioned you don't sleep, but you recharge through coffee. That's why."

I slowly nodded.

"How long do you go without sleeping?"

"Never more than a day. I usually sleep a few hours every night. My body crashes, and I pass out."

"Be careful with that habit. It's dangerous to your mental and physical health. If you starve your body of enough rest, you'll face several side effects, including psychosis and hallucinations. In this line of work, investigating the paranormal, where you're constantly thinking of monsters, you might see them, believe they're chasing you, and... and you might end up hurting someone else."

"My therapist said the same thing."

"Well, she's probably worth her money." Glacia offered a sad smile. "I'm a psychiatrist, and I work with the criminally insane. I've seen people murder others because they refused to sleep, their mind snapped, and they believed monsters wanted them dead. So they retaliated, not killing monsters, but innocent people."

Anger rose within me. Had I not just explained to her I didn't sleep because I had quit drinking, and I had only drank so much to sleep? It was insomnia or alcoholism for me, and I had chosen the lesser of the two evils. I breathed through my frustration, calming myself.

"I quit the force," I said, steering the conversation. "I took to drinking heavily and far too often. I abandoned any ideas of hope or faith I once entertained, replacing them with dark, harmful thoughts. I lost three years of my life to alcohol before I sobered up and found another job." I finally averted my gaze from the wine bottle, turning it to Glacia. "As long as I remain busy, the tormenting thoughts remain quiet. I need to silence them forever, though. I need to find proof that there's something more to this life—that the supernatural exists. So, I created this business, which allows me the opportunity to stay busy while seeking the answers I crave."

"If you find your evidence?" Glacia asked. "Then what?"

I shook my head. "I want to apologize to Aaron. That was the kid's name. Aaron Brooks. I want to apologize knowing he can hear me. It sounds ridiculous, I know, but... I need him to know I'm sorry."

Glacia finished her goblet. "My Nana had these wise little sayings she would share with us. I'm going to butcher this, but I'll paraphrase to the best of my ability. People often mistake mirrors for windows, and they only see ghosts standing before them as a reflection of what is actually behind them." She chuckled, shaking her head. "See, I already screwed it up. To continue slaughtering her words, she would finish by saying something like, 'a window partly serves a reflection, allowing you to never forget what's behind you, but it mostly permits you to see forward, to see the world, to see that there's something brighter and clearer and more.'"

I softly smiled at her.

A rambunctious noise sounded from above us, like cymbals crashing to the ground. Glacia flinched, tipping her wine glass into her lap. Luckily, she had emptied it already. I launched from the chair, kicking over my glass of water and staring at the ceiling. The chandelier hanging in the nook swayed back and forth.

"What was that?" Glacia asked, staring upward.

Bump in the Night. Thursday, April 21st. 2351hrs.

Glacia, Glacia's Nana, and Nana's parents had all lived in the farmhouse. I'm not sure, and Glacia didn't know—not that it mattered too much—who had owned the house before Nana's family. If I had to guess based on the structure and design, despite a few obvious remodeling attempts throughout the years, the original owner had built the home in the early 1900s. The bones were ancient, and they creaked.

"I remember as a girl," Glacia whispered from behind me as we tiptoed to the attic's access door, "the house would talk to me all night long, every single night. Even in the dead of summer, with no wind or rain or anything, it made crazy sounds." She grabbed the back of my shirt, tugging on it. "Right there."

I stopped in the middle of the hallway and glanced upward at the ceiling, noticing the hatch. It was a cover someone had to push up and over, not one a built-in staircase unfolded out from. We needed a ladder, or—

"Want to do something dangerous?" I asked.

"Always."

"Come on."

Glacia and I hurried back to the kitchen, collecting the ice chest and a chair before returning to the hallway. With the ice chest situated as the foundation, I placed the chair on top of it.

"Secure the chair so I don't fall." I climbed onto the cooler, then onto the chair. It wobbled slightly, but Glacia grabbed it, steadying my makeshift climbing apparatus.

I reached up and popped off the access hatch, sliding it to the side. I gripped the edges of the hole and pulled myself up and into the attic. Thankfully, I worked out often and had the strength to perform the feat.

As I sat on the ledge, feet dangling in midair, I finagled my phone from my pocket and turned on the flashlight. It shined over a mess of tangled spiderwebs. Center of them, a thick, furry, black spider, the size of a golf ball, stared back at me. The unnaturally sized insect scurried away into the dark, disappearing as the light revealed it.

I squealed and leaped out of the attic, landing on the unsecured chair, toppling it, losing my balance, and falling into Glacia. My momentum and weight proved too much for her to sustain. We crashed to the ground. Luckily, she broke my fall. Well, her breasts broke my fall. I face-planted directly onto her chest.

"Get off of me," she grunted, shoving me to the side and scrambling to her feet. "What's wrong with you? You could have broken your neck. You could have broken my neck."

I rolled onto my back and crunched into a seated position, staring upward at the black hole in the ceiling to make sure the giant spider hadn't crawled out to chase me.

"What did you see?" she asked.

"A spider," I said, immediately wishing I wasn't so obsessed with speaking the truth. "A big, black spider covered in hair."

"You screamed like a little girl, blindly jumped from the attic, and motor-boated my tits because you saw a spider?"

"A giant, black, hairy spider."

"Are you an idiot?"

"I'm on that spectrum," I said.

"Next time you decide to grope a woman, do it the old-fashioned way and kiss her first." She half-chuckled, shaking her head. "Now, did you see anything else, like a ghost that might have made a crashing noise, or should I climb up there to investigate?"

"I can do it," I said, immediately regretting my words.

Everyone has their irrational fears. Mine included anything arachnid. I squirmed when watching videos with spiders in them, let alone coming face-to-face with an actual eight-legged monster.

"I can do it," I said.

"You're sure? Because I can also do it."

"You hired me to investigate, so I'll do just that." I swallowed, standing and reasserting the chair on the ice chest. "Besides, they're more afraid of me than I am of them, right?"

"Probably not," Glacia said, grinning and biting her lip.

"You're not helping any." I stepped onto the chair and hesitantly grabbed the edges of the hatch again. Closing my eyes, I waited for the spider's legs to scurry over my fingers.

"What's taking so long? Put those big, sexy muscles to use already."

I knew she was making fun of me, but I hardly cared. I focused on breathing and calming my nerves, settling my mind in case I saw another spider. I pulled myself upward, realizing as I sat on the dark perch that I hadn't grabbed my fallen cell phone.

"Can you hand me my phone?" I asked, glancing down to search for it. "It's right there." I pointed.

Glacia picked it up and handed it to me. "Careful up there. I think there are big, black, hairy spiders."

I shined the light into the attic. A wall of cobwebs straight ahead prevented me from exploring any further in that direction. Shifting my body around, I shined the light in the opposite direction.

"Holy smokes," I said.

"What do you see?"

The cobwebs in that direction lay on the wood planks like fallen leaves. Someone or something had cleared a path from the hatch and through the attic. I swallowed back some nerves. Honestly, I would have rather gone toe-to-toe with James Connors' rabid Sasquatch than explore any more of the spiderweb-covered attic. But I had a job to do.

"Someone cleared the webs away," I said.

"What's that mean?"

"There's thick cobwebs from floor to ceiling in every direction but one, and in that direction, someone knocked down the webs."

"Someone did, or something?"

I cracked my neck and scooted fully into the attic, dealing with the goosebumps sprouting all over my body and the overwhelming impulse to drop back into the house and quit investigating the paranormal forever. I crawled forward on my knees.

"There are blankets up here," I called back, shining the light on a bundle of bedding that appeared reasonably new—not covered in dust or webbing, intact and whole. A pillow lay on the blankets, and surrounding them, a heap of empty takeout boxes and wrappers. "There's also food."

"What do you mean?" Glacia asked.

I shined the flashlight on the back wall, centering it on an old fireplace set that had toppled. The iron tools had spilled across the wooden floor. They lay scattered about the cobwebbed floor, intermixed with shards of glass. A shattered window allowed the screeching wind to blow into the attic. An especially strong, well-timed gust had most likely broken the glass and knocked over the fireplace set, alerting Glacia and me as we sat in the dining room.

"The wind blew over an old fireplace set," I called out, turning my head toward the hatch so she could hear.

"A what?"

"Like one of those metallic stands that sits on the hearth. They come with a poker, tong, and shovel."

"How did the wind blow it over?"

"Broken window." I scooted back, went to camera application, activated the flash feature, and snapped a few pictures of the attic before returning to the access door and sliding out of the attic.

Glacia steadied the chair, preventing any more falls and accidental boob landings. As soon as my feet touched the floor, I pried off my shirt, held it with one hand, and beat it against the wall, dislodging any lingering webbing or spiders from the material. I brushed off my jeans and ran my fingers through my hair.

"Are you okay?"

My entire body trembled from a spell of chills. "It feels like spiders are crawling over every square inch of me."

Glacia stared at my stomach. "Lucky them."

I shook my shoulders again, believing I might feel squeamish and skittish for the next few hours. "Did your Nana have anyone staying with her?"

"No." Glacia refused to meet my eyes. "Even if she had, though, why have them sleep in the neglected attic? There's a spare bedroom." The woman stepped forward, nearer to me. "There's a spiderweb right," she touched my chest with the back of her fingers, "here." Her hands moved across my body, around to my back, down my ribs, sliding over my abdomen.

Another current of chills rushed down my spine again, though no longer from the sensation of spiders crawling over my body. I stepped away from Glacia and pulled my shirt back over my head, considering—at the last second—the possibility of spiders nesting within the material. I pushed away the nonsensical ideation.

"I'm sorry," I said. "But I can't. Professionalism and all that ethical nonsense, you know?"

"I'm sorry," Glacia said, holding her hand as if she had burned it. "It's been a long time since I've spent the night with a man. The wine, the emotions… everything… I got carried away."

"It's okay. Honestly, I'm more afraid of women than of spiders." I cleared my throat, half-snickering. "But I think we should further explore the idea of someone living here with or without your Nana's knowledge. They could be the one acting as a ghost, haunting the place to scare potential buyers away from their temporary home."

"Did you see receipts amongst the food?"

"What?"

"Receipts."

I mentally chastised myself for not thinking to look through the styrofoam boxes and other trash for a receipt. "I took some pictures. I'll look through those and glean what I can, then go back into the attic." I frowned at the thought of returning up there. "Sometimes, when shock or fear doesn't blind you, you can expect what's happening, and evidence emerges that previously remained hidden."

"You plan on staying up all night, then?"

"Most of the night."

"Can I make you coffee?"

"I'd love nothing more than a cup of coffee." Maybe to fall into her breasts again, but that couldn't happen under the circumstances. Going bump in the night while under her employment expanded my professional resume to a sex worker. Off the clock, I decided, after the investigation had concluded, I would ask her out. First, though, I had to figure out who haunted her Nana's old house.

Breakfast. Friday, April 22nd. 0617hrs.

The sunshine flooded into the living room through two picture windows overlooking the back yard. I rolled away from the bright morning, grabbing the pillow Glacia had provided me with, and shuttering it over my face. It was difficult to sleep on the first attempt, impossible on the second. After three hours of rest, I was awake.

I peeked at the clock on my phone—which warned of less than ten percent battery life. 0617hrs.

"Go back to sleep," Glacia said from beside me, her voice groggy. "It's too early."

We had slept together, but we hadn't slept-slept together. We had chilled and watched a little Netflix, but we hadn't Netflix and chilled. Glacia hadn't expected to have a sleepover with a man while visiting California. She had brought a single pillow and a couple of blankets. We shared the blankets and a warm cuddle, but I allowed her exclusive use of the only pillow. I rested my head on one of her rolled-up sweatshirts. It smelled like a spring meadow, so I had little to complain about.

Not that I enjoyed the pleasant fragrance long. I had burned away most of the night's oil in the attic, riffling through the trash and old food, searching for clothes or toiletries, and writing notes of everything I found.

1. A cleared, semi-cleaned space inside the otherwise neglected attic—a neglected and filthy space within an immaculate home.

2. Broken glass scattered along the attic floor. Had the wind broken the window? Had someone else?

3. A tipped over fireplace set, which had originally alerted us to the scene. Most likely, the wind blew that over.

4. Clean bedding, not covered in dirt or cobwebs and not moth eaten or frayed. Someone brought it up here recently. Who? Why? When?

5. Chip bags, takeout food boxes, candy wrappers, water bottles, soda cans. Not a lot, though. Two bags of chips. A half-dozen soda cans. A one-gallon water bottle. Four empty boxes of takeout. Why so little food? Did the squatter usually eat away from the house? Had they only moved in within the past few days? Where were they now?

I reviewed the notes, adding information and questions to it throughout the night, always landing on two. Why? How? Why would someone crash in the attic? Why would they pretend to haunt the home? How did they perform their ghostly routine? How did they move throughout the house and property without being noticed, especially since the only way into the attic was climbing through the access door without a ladder?

After rubbing the sleep from my eyes, I sat up in our makeshift bed, basking in the morning's warmth. Outside the open windows, the world stood serene and still. The wind no longer snapped the trees in half, whipped against the house, or threw leaves and debris across the yard.

I climbed to my feet and tiptoed into the bathroom, careful not to wake Glacia fully from her sleep. I relieved myself, washed my face, and wandered into the kitchen, searching the refrigerator for food.

In the refrigerator, I found a carton of milk set to expire in two weeks, along with fresh meat and produce. I massaged my stiff neck, staring at the minimal amount of new groceries. Had Glacia purchased them for her temporary stay in Sacramento? She had mentioned nothing about food in the refrigerator, meaning she either hadn't opened the door and noticed or she had placed it there herself.

I thought back, straining my exhausted mind. What had she said?

Glacia had arrived at the house, stayed half of one night, and she left for a hotel room. Would she have stocked the kitchen upon her arrival, expecting to stay there a couple of nights, or was she more of a takeout girl? Would she have opened the refrigerator during her brief stint alone in the house? I noted each of those questions on my growing list.

Grabbing my car keys off the kitchen counter, I snuck out of the house and drove into town. I bought two coffees and a half-dozen bagels of varying flavors with a selection of spreads before returning.

As I pulled into the gravel driveway, my phone buzzed—Fred. The time on my screen showed 0700 on the dot. Fred's alarm had sounded, waking him, and he immediately called me. I had half a mind to ignore him, because I knew he called for only one reason.

"Good morning," I answered, parking in the same spot as last night.

Fred chuckled, unable to contain his excitement. "So?"

"So."

"How did it go? Did you catch any ghosts, perform an exorcism, experience any paranormal phenomena?" By the tone of his voice, it was obvious his words had double-entendres, though they made next to no sense at all. "Did you stake a vampire?"

"That last one was a little on the nose."

"I didn't know if you were catching what I threw at you."

"You make it more than obvious, especially since your subject of conversation always revolves around two topics. Sex and food."

"Not in that specific order. But the suspense is killing me. Did you or did you not find evidence of ectoplasm?"

"I'm going to go now."

"Wait!"

"What?"

Fred exhaled into the phone, created a whirlwind of static in my ear. "Don't forget that today is your grandma's birthday. You should call her. She turns eighty."

I tapped my fingers against the car's dashboard. "I don't want to know how you came across that information."

"Kim invited Daphne and me to Bam's birthday dinner tonight. The entire family will be there."

I closed my eyes, imagining myself anywhere but in this conversation with Fred. "Thank you for the reminder." I had completely forgotten about both my grandmother's birthday and her big party. "I'm uninviting you to the party, though."

"Kim said Bam would love to see me."

"I'm uninviting you. Stop calling my mom Kim, and how do you even know my grandma's nickname? Why would she love to see you? Actually, no, don't answer any of those questions. I don't want to know. Some things are best left a mystery."

"I'm sorry, Buddy, but unless you're going to fire me from my unpaid assistant job, I will not disappoint Bam. Or Kim. We have to face the bitter truth—this could be her last birthday. Imagine my regret if I skipped out because you felt weird and awkward. I wouldn't forgive myself. So, I'm going, as is Daphne, and we hope to see you there."

"Work begins in an hour. Don't be late."

"Wait!" Fred called through the line as I went to hang it up. I didn't bring the phone back to my ear, but I strained to listen to what he had to say. "Did you and Glacia slay any—"

I disconnected the line and stepped out of the car.

Glacia lay propped on her pillow, scrolling through her phone. She glanced at me and smirked. When she noticed the food and coffee, she beamed and bounced to her feet, hustling to me. She wore an oversized shirt and nothing else. A primitive urge propelled me to grab her and lift her onto the counter, to kiss her and strip her and... I bit my lower lip and cracked a knuckle, stifling the desire. Circling into the kitchen, I placed her coffee and bagels on the table.

"I didn't know how you liked your coffee, so I got it black. There's milk in the refrigerator, though. Did you buy that?"

Glacia frowned, glancing at the refrigerator as she dug into the bag and removed the bagels and cheese. "I only brought wine. Red wine, too. No refrigeration needed."

"The milk expires in two weeks. There's also fresh produce and meat in there." I sipped from my coffee. "That makes little sense, no?"

"What do you mean?"

"We initially assumed a squatter lived in this home, and they scared potential buyers so they could continue squatting." I opened the notes on my phone, reviewing them. "Bedroom in the attic to remain hidden. Food they're too afraid to throw away and create evidence."

Glacia found a plastic knife and dressed the bagel with a jalapeno cream cheese. "And?"

I cracked my neck and stole a few seconds to think. "It doesn't make much sense."

"What doesn't?"

"Bear with me. I'm thinking aloud here." I stole another sip of coffee. "If the squatter wants to remain hidden, why store groceries in the refrigerator where anyone could find them? All the trash in the attic was from styrofoam boxes or brown bags. Nothing homemade. Why the produce and meat, then?" I scratched my head. "Something feels off." I moseyed over to the refrigerator, opened the door, and peered inside. Who would feel comfortable enough to stock the refrigerator with food, believing no one would open these doors to find the meat, produce, and milk? "You have a contact number for your real estate agent?"

Glacia snickered, swallowing her bite of bagel. "I already told you, I'm not selling you the house."

"I know, but I want her to show it to me as if I were a client."

She cocked her head and eyed me with suspicion, mouth full of another bit of food. After chewing, she said, "You know something."

"I suspect something."

"Can you share?"

I licked the back of my teeth. Could I trust Glacia wasn't a part of this? Probably, but probably wasn't a definitive yes.

"Not yet." I glanced at my phone and checked the time.

"When?"

"After the showing." I grabbed my coffee and keys.

"Where are you going?"

"I have work, and if Fred beats me to the office... well, I lose a bet. Shoot me your agent's number. I'm going to contact her and get myself a viewing. I'll call you later tonight and let you know what I learn."

"Hold on." Glacia dug through her purse and found her real estate agent's business card. She handed it to me. "What do I owe you for breakfast?"

"I'll include the cost in your bill."

I exited the house, taking a detour from my car by walking to the side yard, searching for the broken attic window. It overlooked the garden. A wrought-iron trellis covered in flowering ivy leaned against the wall.

I moved toward it, inspecting the foliage and finding the leaves and vines crushed. Establishing a foothold on the lattice-work trellis, I stepped up, climbing the design. It held my weight without bending. I could have ascended it with ease to the broken window, pulling myself through into the attic. That answered a few of the How questions. How did the squatter move around the house without using the access door? How did they perform their routine without getting caught?

"I got you," I said, dropping back onto the cement flatwork.

Footsteps stamped around the corner, bare feet slapping on the warm cement. Glacia appeared in her oversized shirt, breathing hard and smiling, her tongue resting on her lower lip. "Hey."

"Hi."

"I don't have a car."

"Right." I checked the time on my phone.

She must have recognized the indecision on my face—I often wore my emotions like a mask. "Actually, don't worry about it. I know you have to get to the office, and I still need to get ready for the day and clean up the house a little. I'll call an Uber."

"You're sure?" I asked, simultaneously feeling guilty and relieved. "You'll be okay here, alone?"

"Ghosts only come out at night. I'll be fine and dandy."

I walked forward, stopped a foot before her, leaned in, and kissed her on the cheek. "Thanks."

Glacia touched her face. "Go get 'em, tiger."

Early Arrival. Friday, April 22nd. 0747hrs.

Fred Rogers didn't own a vehicle. He relied on his wife, Daphne, to transport him to and from the office. Luckily for him, Daphne worked remotely and had a flexible enough schedule to drive her husband to his job, where he made no money.

"Yet," Fred always emphasized, holding up his massive finger, whenever Daphne mentioned he had zero income. "No money, yet. August, though, with his beautiful face and charming smile, will attract business."

Daphne didn't care either way, as long as Fred vacated their house while she worked. It's not that she worried about money. Daphne loved her job. It gave her purpose and meaning. If neither of them desired to work, neither of them had to. Fred's NFL retirement helped them, though the investments he made while earning a full salary would support them forever. Not that it mattered too much. Daphne's income would have kept them well above water.

They worked because they loved to work, not because they needed to.

Daphne, though, fought with Fred to purchase a commuter vehicle, if for anything, to ease her schedule. Fred refused. He, A, hated to drive, and B, despised driving in the city. The Rogers lived too far out of town to make public transportation a legitimate option. Fred declined to wake up earlier than 0700hrs., and for the light rail to benefit him, he would have to set his alarm for 0600hrs. He had dabbled with Uber, but that strategy had proven ineffective, as drivers weren't readily available that early in the morning in his rural location. So, he and Daphne continued to bicker about buying a vehicle versus having her drop him off at the office, and they would probably bicker about that for years and years to come.

I pulled up to the building, parking in my preferred space. With no manner in which to determine if Fred had arrived before me, I called him.

We had a long-standing bet. If he ever beat me into the office, I would have to go on a blind date with a person of his choosing at a place of his choosing. That doesn't sound too terrible on the surface, but allowing Fred that kind of power over my life would prove nothing short of catastrophic. Most mornings, I had no worries about losing the bet. I cheated by accident, often falling asleep in the office. On the rare occasions where I risked sleeping in my apartment, I arrived at work before Fred's third alarm finally dragged him out of bed.

Today, though, I had pushed my luck.

"August," Fred answered, a smile audible in his voice.

"Want me to grab you some coffee?" I asked.

The big man chuckled like Santa. "You would risk everything to buy me coffee?"

"Purchasing breakfast and coffee would negate the bet."

"You're running late, aren't you? You're looking for a way to weasel out of owing up to your side of the bet."

"You want some coffee? How about donuts?"

"Don't you tempt me with donuts. That's not fair." Fred cleared his throat. "How about this? If you provide me with some insight into last night and bring me donuts, we'll suspend the bet for one day."

"Deal."

"That quick?"

"That quick."

"Is that what you're sharing about last night?" he asked.

"No." I rolled my eyes. "Nothing happened last night, other than me doing the job she hired me to do."

"Nothing at all?"

"Nothing at all."

Fred sighed. "I want a half-dozen donut holes, one maple bar, and one chocolate bar. Also, I'm a married man, and you're my only single friend. Do you know what that means?"

"No."

"I live vicariously through your sexual exploits. You serve as the window into the world I can no longer explore. You know what, though?"

"I really don't want to."

"You don't provide me with any kind of view other than dreary boredom. I get more action out of my ten-year marriage than you receive as a single man. It's depressing for the both of us. Mostly for you, though."

"Six donut holes and a maple bar?"

"And the chocolate bar. And a coffee. Black with four sugars."

I ran to the nearest donut shop, purchased Fred's ransom donuts, and returned to the office. When I entered a little after 0800hrs, the place was still empty. Fred hadn't arrived yet, making him late... again. The man had played me for a sucker and pocketed a few treats in the deal.

I set his donuts and coffee at his desk and shuffled to mine, plopping into my chair and turning on my laptop to check emails. Nothing new other than spam.

I considered calling Tempest Michaels and asking when his advertising dollars would flex and the potential customers would flock to me, but I didn't. Advertising would only go so far, anyway. I had to establish a credible business and build a reputation. So, instead, I researched Sasquatch sightings in the Stanislaus National Forest.

Apparently, a high concentration of Bigfoot sightings occurred in the Sierra Mountain Range, which stretched four-hundred miles through California and Nevada. The Bigfoot sightings mostly occurred in Tuolumne County, where James Connors had met with us. No other recent reports of Bigfoot sightings showed from that specific county, though, further complicating my investigation into Connors' claims.

While on the subject, I performed a quick Google search for local cryptozoologists. No legitimate results. Scratching my head, I sighed, knowing I would have to perform a little legwork to find a cryptozoologist within the area. I needed to find a contact in that field anyway, considering my line of business, but I had more pressing matters to concern myself about.

I switched gears to something more practical and lucrative. I laid the real estate agent's business card on my desk and dialed the number.

"Susan Owning speaking. How may I help you?"

"I'm August Watson, a friend of Glacia Vasquez. I'm interested in buying her grandmother's house." I cracked my knuckles as I waited for a response.

At first, Susan said nothing.

I pulled the phone away from my ear to make sure I hadn't lost her through poor service.

She remained on the line. "Has she told you about the...?" The woman paused, most likely hesitant to admit the paranormal activity.

I filled in the blank for her. "The haunting? Yes, I'm aware. Luckily for you and her, I don't believe in that sort of thing. I'd like to see the home whenever you have the availability to show it."

"Glacia suspended all showings until further notice. I'm sorry."

"Suspended all showings?"

"She hired an investigator to look into the disturbances occurring on the property. Once she has an answer, she will resume the sale of the house."

I didn't want to reveal I was that investigator, as I wanted a legitimate showing—one with a ghost involved. "Could you call her and confirm? I believe she will make an exception for me. Again, my name is August Watson, and she's expecting for you to show me the house."

Again, Susan hesitated before responding. "I'll call her, but even if she allows this to happen, I don't have an availability to show the home until Monday."

I scratched at the stubble on my chin. When did Glacia fly back to Oregon? I hadn't asked. "Susan, if you can work with me on this, it'll prove beneficial for all parties involved. If you can't accommodate me, I'm sure it won't take much to find an interested agent willing to show me the house."

"Is this the best number to reach you at?"

"It's the only number to reach me at."

"Let me contact Glacia to confirm you can see the house. I'll call you back."

"Very well," I said. "I'd like to see the house today, and I'll make sure that happens."

"We'll talk soon."

I placed my phone on the desktop and sighed, grabbing my coffee and drinking.

Fred burst through the door, wearing an uncharacteristic frown. "Uh, boss. Good morning and thank you for the treats and all that, but... were you expecting someone this morning?"

"I expected you to be early for once."

"No one else?"

I scowled. "No."

"Interesting. Well—"

"Hi." A girl, no older than sixteen, popped around the corner and entered the small, dingy office barely big enough for Fred and me. She sniffed the air and grimaced. "It smells like... old feet or, like, a clogged drain in here."

"Who are you?" I asked.

"I'm Alina Mylene Moore, and it's a pleasure to meet you finally. Maya said nothing about your office being so small or dusty or stinky." She hurried to the third-story window overlooking the street and ran her index finger across the glass. "Gross. Have you ever cleaned in here?"

I glanced at Fred, who stared at me with his mouth ajar. Returning my attention to the young lady, I said, "You're not supposed to work until Monday."

"I skipped school today. Well, not really skipped. It's a minimum day for testing periods six and seven, but I have study hall at those times, so there's nothing for me to test."

"But you don't start until Monday."

"Did you not hear what I said? I had the day off." Alina put finger quotes around the word off. "I figured why not get the full experience? I mean, from Monday until summer break, I'll only intern a few days a week for a few hours a day after school, right? That's boring. I want the full day. The whole enchilada."

"Enchilada sounds good," Fred said, biting into a donut. "You want to get Mexican food for lunch?"

"You're fourteen," I said, ignoring Fred and tackling one problem at a time.

"Sixteen."

"We had a schedule approved by your parents and school. I have the emails documenting all of it. Want me to show you?"

"Nope," Alina said, moving from the window to the metallic shelf of books stocked with paranormal literature. She pried a book free and flipped through the pages.

"Neither your parents nor the school approved today as a workday, so you legally can't be here."

The girl shrugged. "Technically, none of my days are workdays, since you're not paying me."

"That's what I tell him when I show up late and he complains," Fred said.

"Would you rather me wander the streets of Sacramento alone?" Alina asked. "Think what kind of danger might find a sixteen-year-old girl?"

"I have your parents' numbers on my computer. Should I call them?"

"Call Aunt Maya. She approved."

"What do you mean, she approved?"

"Well, she recommended it. I told her I had the day off. She said you had a case for me to investigate, one where her and I could work together. She recommended I swing by and get all the information from you."

"Maya sent you here."

"That's exactly what I said." The girl smirked, closing the book in a small poof of dust. She coughed.

"Where did we land on Mexican food for lunch? I'm really craving enchiladas," Fred said, shoving more of the donut into his mouth.

I bit my lip, preventing myself from screaming in response to the chaos. I hadn't even finished two cups of coffee, usually having downed four by this time. "Fred, Mexican food for lunch sounds amazing. I'm partial to that taco truck, but we can also sit down somewhere if you prefer."

"Doesn't matter to me, boss, as long as they have enchiladas."

"Alina," I said, turning to the girl. "I'm calling Maya. Sit down in that chair and stop touching things."

"I wasn't planning on it. This place is disgusting. I hate when stereotypes and factuality collide. You two prove men can't take care of themselves. You need a womanly touch in this office, and I'm here to help with that. What's the decorating budget look like? I'm going to buy you some plants to spruce this place up. And some cleaning supplies. Don't worry, it's all deductible on your taxes."

My jaw dropped as I attempted to keep up with her. "There's not a budget for anything," I said three whole seconds after she had finished speaking. "We currently have one paying customer, and one customer refusing to pay unless we substantiate the impossibility he believes he saw. Without reliable income, we don't have a budget for plants or cleaning."

"Plants and cleaning would make this place not only look professional, but successful, and people gravitate toward success. To play the role, you need to look that part."

"I'm calling Maya," I said, dialing her number.

Maya answered immediately. "I know. I know. I know. But I'm not sorry."

"You could have warned me."

"You wouldn't have allowed it."

"I'm still not allowing it. She's skipping school."

"She has the day off," Maya said.

"I have the day off," Alina said at the same time.

"I scheduled her to begin on Monday," I said.

Maya sighed. "Just... brief her on the voodoo doll murder and let her loose. She's very ambitious and self-motivated."

"I know nothing about the voodoo doll murder other than what you told me. Why can't you have her tag along with you today?"

"Don't you think it's worthwhile that she learns the ins and outs of your office and how you operate before beginning? I mean, you won't have to iron out wrinkles on day one."

"Not happening. Come pick her up. I have things to do."

"You have big, important client?"

"Maya," I said.

"You're breaking up. I can't hear what you're saying. August, you there?"

I exhaled and hung up the phone, staring in defeat at a grinning Alina.

"Voodoo doll murder, huh?" the girl asked, slipping her backpack off her shoulders. She opened it and pulled out an iPad with an attached keyboard. "I'll have a ten-page report on your desk before 1500hrs. on all things voodoo. Don't worry about me joining you two for lunch, but if you don't mind, I'd like a vegetarian burrito with the spiciest sauce they can offer. And a Sprite. Also, a side of carrots and peppers. Make sure they're spicy, though."

"Don't leave any papers on my desk. We can't afford to print, especially not ten pages of anything. Email me."

"Of course," Alina said. "You remember my order for lunch, or should I email that to you?"

"Text it. I don't have an email set up on my phone."

"Why?"

I closed my eyes and shook my head. "I don't know. At one point, I had a legitimate reason, but now it's more out of habit. I don't know, okay?"

"Okay." Alina popped her lips. "Mr. Watson?"

"Call me August."

"August, why don't you ask my aunt on a date?"

Fred suddenly grew a tongue and involved himself in the conversation. "That's a brilliant question. Why don't you ask Maya out on a date?"

My phone buzzed in my hand, saving me from having to take part in their probing inquiries. "August Watson," I answered.

"It's Susan Owning, the realtor."

"Hi."

"I can show you the house tomorrow at ten in the morning."

Slightly frustrated at having to wait an entire day, I bit my tongue and opted not to say something regrettable.

"Mr. Watson, are you still there?"

"You can't get me in today?"

"I'm sorry. Today is not a possibility."

I could have returned to the farmstead at any moment I wished, but the hauntings had mostly occurred during real estate showings. With that in mind, I had to ask myself a few simple questions.

Who had a key to the home? Glacia and Susan.

Who had a reason to be at the home consistently, especially now that it was empty of all valuables? Susan.

Who would know where to locate a nearly hidden attic window to climb into and hide? Susan, most likely.

Who would feel comfortable enough to stock food for the ghost living in the attic? Well, again, Susan seemed likely.

Susan and the ghost most likely worked together, and the ghost probably wasn't available to haunt anything until tomorrow morning.

"Tomorrow works," I said, hanging up the phone and staring at Alina and Fred. As I parted my lips to chastise them, my phone buzzed again. I didn't recognize the caller ID, but I answered the call, hoping for a potential client rather than a telemarketer or spammer. "August Watson."

Bated breaths for a few heartbeats.

"Hello?" I asked.

"I," the voice on the other end of the line said before breaking into sobs. It sounded halfway masculine, but I couldn't be sure. "I killed... her. I killed my Mommy!" The voice blurted the last bit. "Help me!"

"Slow down," I said, sinking into my desk chair. "Who is this?"

"Randall... Fincher. It's my... fault!"

Randall Fincher. Randall Fincher. How did I know that name? I grabbed a pen out of my desk drawer and scribbled his name onto a piece of paper, sliding it across the desk, showing it to Fred and Alina. They moseyed over, glancing at the name.

"What about him?" Alina asked.

I shrugged and mouthed, "Who is he?"

"The boy who played with voodoo dolls," Fred said.

"Muriel's son," Alina clarified. "He was at the scene when his mother died. He found the voodoo doll on the counter when he got back home."

Randall continued to speak incoherently through sobs, mostly confessing to his mother's gruesome and unlucky death. "I cursed her. I killed her."

"Randall," I said, speaking slowly and calmly. "I'm headed to your house right now, okay? I'm going to help you." I collected my keys and my coffee and stood, crossing the small office to the front door. I snapped my fingers and pointed at Alina, gesturing for her to follow me.

She obliged without hesitation.

I muted the phone. "Grab the voodoo case files."

Alina skidded to a stop and rushed back to where she had placed the files, grabbing them and returning to me. "Am I going with you?"

I unmuted the phone. "Randall, my assistant and I are leaving the office now. We'll be at your house soon. You're at home, right?"

"Yes."

"I thought I was your assistant," Fred said. "The girl has already replaced me?"

"Stay here and field any calls," I said, turning to Fred. "And get us lunch. I'll have Alina text you."

"What?" Randall asked.

I had forgotten to mute the phone. Too much occurred at once, and I could only juggle so many tasks. "Sorry. Randall, we're heading to your house now. Stay calm, okay? Stay where you're at."

"Hurry, please. Help me."

When Cows Fly. Friday, April 22nd. 0813hrs.

Gilbert Tonyan drove his Honda Accord eastbound on Highway 50, staying in the slow lane. Not that it mattered much where he drove. Every lane was the slow lane. Sacramento traffic had worsened the past few years with the increasing population and the perpetual roadwork construction.

Gilbert had left his house two hours early to ensure he arrived at the interview on time. When his wife asked why he needed to leave so early, Gilbert cooly explained he wanted to sit in a cafe, drink a coffee, and enjoy the morning sun. Though his excuse aligned with the truth, it wasn't the truth.

He had left two hours early to meet with Christopher Steele, his true love. They had spent an hour together that morning, first tangled and sweaty, then wet and soapy, then dried and clothed and on the hotel balcony, enjoying room service coffee and basking in the early sun's refreshing warmth.

Unfortunately, Gilbert had lost track of time while with Chris. He had seventeen minutes to make his interview and twenty minutes until he reached his destination.

Gilbert Tonyan had never been late for anything in his life. He lived by a strict philosophy—on-time equaled tardy. So, he showed up to everything at least fifteen minutes early.

The only time he dared arrive late to anything was for an interview that would promote him to a Store Director.

Gilbert felt his lungs compressed, crushing his heart. He had to make the meeting, even if that meant breaking a few traffic laws. Clicking on his blinker, Gilbert creeped into the passing lane, though it barely moved any faster.

A semi-truck hauling dead cattle drove in front of him, obscuring his vision and dropping flakes of dirt from the trailer onto his windshield. Taking his rebellion one step further, Gilbert slid into the carpool lane.

His stomach now sat in his throat, making it difficult to breathe. The traffic on the far-left side of the highway moved considerably quicker than the other two lanes, though, and the estimated time of arrival already dropped an entire minute.

Gilbert's phone rang, chiming throughout the car and startling him. For a terrible moment, he thought California Highway Patrol had spotted his illegal activity and signaled to pull him over. Instead, Greta, his wife, called.

"Hi, honey," he answered in a small voice.

"You okay?"

"Nervous. Traffic is unbelievable today, and I'm running late."

"Gill, I'm sure they'll understand. You left two hours early. That's not your fault."

"I should have left earlier." He thought of sitting on the balcony and enjoying coffee with Christopher. He should have left the hotel earlier. "I mean, I knew this kind of thing could happen."

"Listen to me. You'll do amazing. No one deserves the position more than you. No one has a better track record than you. You're always present, on-time, and efficient, right?"

"Yeah."

"So what if you're a few minutes late because of traffic? They'll understand. Don't drive crazy. Drive safe and smart."

"Yeah, you're right."

"I bet if you canceled the interview, they would still hire you. Alright?"

"Okay."

"You got this."

"I know."

"I love you."

"You, too."

Ultimately, Gilbert knew she was right. He had spent the past twenty years building a flawless resume of commitment and consistency. If he called the store now, informed them of his situation, they would understand without repercussion. The Store Director job belonged to Gilbert, whether he showed up thirty minutes early or thirty minutes late.

He glanced down at his phone and scrolled through his contact list, searching for his boss's name. When he glanced back up at the highway, red taillights flashed. He slammed his brakes, screeching to a sliding, swaying halt, barely avoiding rear-ending the vehicle in front of him. The near-collision, the tardiness, the affair, the unrelenting nerves tormented his mind and body. He panted, as if he had finished sprinting a mile, and his chest burned.

When he calmed a little, he tapped his boss's contact.

"Gilbert," Janine answered in a cheery tone. "Good morning."

"Hey," Gilbert said, less enthusiastically. "I'm sitting in dead-stop traffic. My navigation predicts my arrival five minutes late. I'm sorry. I left early and everything, just... not early enough."

"You're fine. Doug just called. He's in the same traffic. He said he's running a little late, too. Just drive safe and make the interview."

"Thanks," Gilbert said, ending the call and exhaling a sigh of relief.

As the weight and worry shed off his shoulders, destiny responded in kind. The traffic gave way, returning to normal speeds. Gilbert laughed, pressing the gas pedal.

After a few miles, the carpool lane ended. He merged back into the center lane, somehow finding himself stuck behind farm truck hauling a dead cow in an uncovered trailer. Drifting to the dotted lines separating the two lanes, Gilbert peeked ahead to see if he could pass the slow-moving truck. A line of traffic slammed on their brakes to navigate an approaching offramp.

Gilbert jerked his car back into the fast line, directly behind the dirty truck. He tapped his fingers on the steering wheel and bit his lip, practicing patience the best he could but failing when a beat-up Camry cut him off.

"Come on!" He cursed under his breath, but calmed himself by mentally reverting to the balcony, living in a more calming moment to settle his nerves.

Then it hit him.

He should call Christopher. Hearing his voice would help steady Gilbert's anxiety. He grabbed his phone, staring at the screen to unlock it.

That's when he heard a Pop! An explosion.

Whipping his attention to the highway, Gilbert saw smoking tires as vehicles locked their brakes and veered to the shoulder. The farm truck rested on its side in the middle of the highway, and Gilbert's skidding vehicle came to a stop inches before crashing into it.

In a split-second—in a fleeting space of time—he saw, arcing through the sky like a black-and-white eclipse blotting out the sun, a dead holstein cow plummeting toward his windshield.

Distracted. Friday April 22nd. 0853hrs.

"Eight-hundred square feet," Alina said, staring at her iPad. "One bedroom and one bathroom." She glanced across the car's cab, out the driver's window at Randall's house.

Potted plants withered and browned along the entry walkway. Weeds had long ago overtaken the yard, and they grew in the cement joints and the cracks.

"Only one bedroom," she said again, scrunching her face in disgust. "Do you think they, like... you know?"

"Shared a bed?" I asked.

"Ew. Gross. Don't say it out loud. But do you? Based on what Maya tapped from Eddie—pun intended. Get it? Maya, Eddie, tapped. We can even circle it as the mom-son relationship with Randall and Muriel, tapped that is."

"Aren't you too young to get that?"

Alina chuckled. "Please. I've already forgotten way more than you'll ever know. Not the point. Maya learned from Eddie that Randall and Muriel lived together, and they had a very Norman Bates relationship with each other. Did you ever see that show? *Bates Motel*?"

"I watch little television."

"It shows."

"What's that mean?"

"You're like, what, thirty-something?"

"Thirty-two."

"But you act like you're fifty-six. Maya says it's because you've been through some stuff. I think it's because you're boring, and you're boring because you don't watch television, so you're not aware of the popular culture. If you don't know popular culture, how do you connect with people on a basic level? What would you have in common? Favorite food? Blah. Favorite pets? Gross. Pop culture bridges one life to another."

"Why are you and Maya talking about me?"

"That's what you learned from what I said?"

"Answer the question."

Alina tilted her head and smirked. "We're girls. We talk about girl stuff."

"And I'm girl stuff?" I asked.

"I'm going to make you a list of must-see movies and TV shows, and I'm going to add all my streaming service usernames and passwords so you can log in and watch them. We need to spruce you up a bit. I mean, you're handsome in a… Henry Cavill way. But you're missing pizazz."

"I don't have time for this conversation, or for movies."

"We live in the twenty-first century, dude. People have more free time in their days than in all of history. Don't tell me you don't have time. You just waste it with nonsense."

"Like my job?" I shook my head, cracking a finger. "I'm not arguing with a twelve-year-old."

"Sixteen."

"Same difference."

"Same difference? You're one of those people, huh? Listen, respect your youth, man. I had a birthday last week, and I'm still getting used to the nightmare of having aged another year. Youth is so fleeting. Though, I guess, wisdom outclasses beauty any day of the week—at least to anyone worth much of anything at all. If you come across someone who cares more about physical appearance than," she tapped her skull, "you need to run for the hills, or at least not trust that person."

"Do you ever slow down to breathe?"

"I don't breathe."

I drummed my lips and glanced out the driver's window at Randall's house. "He and his mom were uncomfortably close, possibly sleeping together, considering the house only has one bedroom." I turned and faced Alina. "How do you know that, by the way? The floor plan and square-footage?"

"Internet. I can find about anything I want. Dude, you're thirty-two, meaning you're a millennial. You should at least know how to work the internet."

"I do."

"Then why did you ask how I knew that?"

Because I had never thought to look up house plans online. Also, I needed to have a long chat with Maya for not warning me about the firecracker that was her niece.

"What else do you know about Randall?"

Alina hummed, setting her iPad on her lap and trading it for the case files. "According to Eddie, Maya's boyfriend—"

"I know who Eddie is. You don't have to keep saying Maya's boyfriend."

"Woah, sorry. I didn't realize you were so sensitive about it."

My face flushed with heat. "I'm not."

"According to he-who-must-not-be-named—that's a *Harry Potter* reference, by the way. Harry Potter was a boy wizard created by J. K. Rowling."

"I know about *Harry Potter*."

"Did you read them?"

"No."

"See the movies?"

I glared at her.

"You haven't read the books or watched the movies?"

"We don't have time to discuss this."

"We're having a movie marathon. A *Harry Potter* movie marathon. Should I invite Maya?"

"What did Eddie say about Randall?" I asked, tempted to rip my hair out and scream until my voice gave way.

"He interviewed the man at the scene."

"Man… not boy?"

"Randall is, like, old. Your age."

"I'm not that old."

"You're exactly twice my age. Relatively, that's pretty stinking old. Anyway, instead of acting like he's twenty years older—such as you do—Randall acts like he's twenty years younger. Seriously, you belong to a messed up generation."

"Stay focused," I said.

"Eddie interviewed Randall, acquiring very little information. Now, whether that's from Eddie's incompetence or Randall's erratic behavior or a combination of both, we'll never know. If I had to guess, I would say Eddie's incompetence."

"You really don't like him?"

"He bought me a Barbie for my sixteenth birthday."

I narrowed my eyes, confused. "Do kids not like dolls anymore?"

"What about me makes you think I want to play with Barbies? I would rather discuss the portrayal of racial and social inequality in the movie *The People Under the Stairs*."

I shrugged. "But you're also weird for a sixteen-year-old."

"How many teenagers do you know these days? Times have changed, bucko. Gone are the days where a kid only wished to get drunk and laid."

"Or play with Barbies."

"Nothing about me, other than I'm a girl, hints that I enjoy Barbies. Besides, not all girls like Barbies, do they?"

"I played with Barbies as a kid, and I was a boy."

"I believe that about you, and I'm sure that was an acceptable gift for your aunt's boyfriend to buy for you. Not for me, though. I've hung out with Eddie multiple times. We've had conversations—well, what one might consider a conversation between an intelligent human and a snail."

"You're the snail in this example?"

Alina rolled her eyes. "I don't like him because he doesn't like anyone but Eddie. Would you have bought me a Barbie for my sixteenth birthday?"

"I would have bought you, I don't know… a book, hoping it might shut you up for a few seconds."

"Exactly! I love books. Not Barbies. And you've only known me for an hour. Now, don't let that go to your head, me saying you're better than Eddie. The wart on my foot is better than Eddie."

That one tickled, and I laughed. "The wart on your foot, huh?"

"Have you ever met him?"

"Maya doesn't bring her boyfriends around me."

Alina smirked, smug and knowing, as if she had a secret and refused to share.

"What's that look?" I asked.

"No look, but I'm going to set up a double date with you and Eddie and Maya."

"Good luck with that. Maya won't go, and even if she would agree, I don't have a date."

"You're handsome and jacked. I'm sure we can find someone interested, at least for a night. Just… don't talk too much."

"I'm not sure I feel comfortable with a fourteen-year-old commenting on my physical appearance."

"Get over it. That's all fourteen-year-olds do. Lucky for you, I'm sixteen and have a little more control, though not much." She winked at me. "Hormones are pumping through us teens like crazy."

I had to regain control of the conversation and steer it back to the center. Alina's nonstop jabbering didn't help me focus on the matter at hand. "Did Eddie gain any useful information?"

The girl flipped through the folder, skimming the information provided by Maya—the information I had conveniently ignored until now. With Randall calling and requesting my help, I could charge him and make some money, something the business desperately needed.

"Weird relationship with his mom," Alina said. "Voodoo doll found on the counter with a pin poked through the head." She clicked her tongue. "Nothing helpful. I searched for him on Facebook and other social media sites, but he has no online fingerprint. If I had to guess, I'm thinking this is a *Carrie* situation. Who knows, maybe he even has some power like her that released after years of pent up anger from the abuse he suffered."

"You think his mom abused him?"

"I don't know. Probably, at least mentally and emotionally. Why else would a thirty-year-old man sleep in the same bed as his mommy?"

"Fair point. But he doesn't have power, and he didn't curse her."

"Explain the voodoo doll, or him calling you and claiming he murdered his mother."

I couldn't—I couldn't even come up with a logical guess.

"Your silence says it all," Alina said, opening the passenger door.

"Where are you going?" I asked.

"To interview Randall."

"No, you're going to wait here, in the car, while I interview Randall. Like you said, he might have supernatural powers, and I can't have you getting hurt on a day you're not even supposed to be here."

"I won't sue you. I promise."

"You're not leaving this car."

"You assigned me to the voodoo doll murder case. So, I'm just doing my job—a job that I'm doing for free. So, either we work on this together, like complying coworkers, or I'll wait in the car until you disappear into the house, then I'll hop out and join you. Either way, I'm interviewing the man-child."

I cracked my neck, annoyed that a little girl had bullied me into a corner. "Fine. But I ask the questions and you take the notes. Understood? Not a single word from you."

Alina ran her fingers across her mouth, zipping her lips.

Home Visit. Friday, April 22nd. 0907hrs.

Randall Fincher stood slightly taller than Alina, maybe flirting with five-foot-seven, but he weighed twice, if not three times, as much as her. He waddled when he moved, holding his right hip at all times.

The man ushered us into his small home and sat us at the messy kitchen table. The house didn't have a living room. The kitchen was a single counter, a sink, refrigerator, and a microwave—no stovetop or dishwasher.

"Can I get you some water?" he asked, his voice shaky.

"No thank you," I said, reaching into my pocket for a stick of gum.

"Do you have Sprite?" Alina asked.

"Sorry. Mommy believed soda was a gateway to alcohol."

"Okay," Alina said. "That's okay. I should probably cut the sugar out of my diet, anyway. The problem is, I have a sweet tooth like you wouldn't believe. Luckily, I'm young and active and God blessed me with a great metabolism, so I abuse my privileges while I still can."

I glared at her and zipped my lips, shrugging.

Alina sucked her lips into her mouth and widened her eyes. "Sorry," she mouthed. "I forgot."

Randall poured himself a glass of murky tap water and sat beside us at the circular table. He stared at the center, where the voodoo doll lay—a pin still stabbed into its skull. Someone had cut burlap into a rough impersonation of the human form, stuffing it with straw and sewing it shut.

"Did you make the voodoo doll?" I asked.

"I don't remember."

"You don't remember?" Alina asked. "Do you often drink alcohol into a state of forgetfulness?"

"I don't drink alcohol. Mommy doesn't or didn't allow alcohol in the house. It's of the devil. It weakens our morality and our minds, and it invites demons into our hearts."

"Do you sleepwalk?" Alina asked, still asking questions and speaking, despite my instruction for her to not say a word.

"When I was little," Randall said, holding the glass of water in both hands, as if it anchored him in place amongst the storm that had taken over his life.

"Have you had other fits of amnesia, then?" Alina asked.

"Some."

"Can you explain?"

"When Mommy has me go into Confession, I lose track of time. Days might pass, but it only feels like hours, and I can't remember what I did in there."

"In where?" I asked.

"Confession," Alina said, scowling at me, as if I was the one who had agreed to remain silent and not interrupt the line of questioning.

"Where's Confession?" I asked, glaring at the girl. I needed to speak with Maya as soon as possible to discuss the very real idea of Alina volunteering her time anywhere else but with me.

"In the backyard," Randall said.

"What did you do during Confession?" I asked. "What do you remember?"

"I prayed to God. I confessed my sins to Him."

"For days at a time?" I asked.

"Sometimes."

"You didn't leave Confession for days?"

"No."

"Did you eat?"

"No."

"Did you drink water?"

"No."

"Where did you use the bathroom?"

"Where I lay."

"You laid down the entire time?"

"Yes."

I leaned back in my chair, cracking my knuckles. "Could you have made this doll during confession?"

"I don't know."

"Did you have the supplies? Burlap. Straw. Needle for sewing."

"No. But sometimes, while in Confession, especially the times that lasted for days, I prayed God would kill her. That He would strike her down. Yesterday, I wished her dead again, and as I wished her to die," Randall freely cried before us, "that sign crushed her. I prayed for it to happen, and God answered my prayer. I'm the reason she's dead." He lowered his chin to chest and trembled as he sobbed.

"Did you ever see this voodoo doll before yesterday?" I tapped the table near where the doll rested.

Randall shook his head back and forth, wiping snot and tears from his face. "Mommy prevented anything associated with the devil into our home."

"Is Voodoo associated with the devil?"

"Yes," Randall said, nodding. "Mommy said so."

I would have paid the man every penny I possessed to stop calling his mother Mommy.

"Will you help me?" Randall asked.

"Help you with what, exactly?" I asked.

"Exorcise the demon within me. Remove the curse from my body. I prayed to God that He would murder my mother. I prayed for God to sin, and that request has darkened my soul. It allowed a demon to possess me. That's how the voodoo doll arrived at my table. God placed it there to tell me I'm cursed. I need you to remove the curse. To heal me."

I shifted my attention to Alina, who stared right back at me. Thankfully, she interpreted my intention without me having to ask, taking over the line of questioning.

"Randall," she said.

"Yeah." He lifted his head, looking at her.

"We want to help you, but we're not priests. We're not associated with the church. Do you know what that means? We don't have the power of God to compel the demon possibly possessing you to leave your body and mind. Also, unlike the church, we don't operate for free. We can help you, though. In fact, we can probably provide more help to your cause than any priest or bishop or pope could. However, we need to know that you can afford to help yourself?"

Randall blinked a few times. "I couldn't ask a priest, anyway. He would tell me what I already know—that God abandoned me, allowing the demon to take over. Without God by my side, the church can't help. I will pay whatever you ask, as long as you can help."

Alina reached across the table and grabbed Randall's hand, massaging it with her thumb. "I promise you, we'll help. You can afford to hire us?"

"I believe so. My Mommy spent none of her money, claiming it a sin to desire material items. I saw her bank accounts, though—all the money she had stored away. Hundreds of thousands of dollars. I believe I can afford your rates."

"You have access to her money?" I asked, feeling halfway sick to bargain with a mentally ill and traumatized man who had lost his mother a day before.

"Yes."

I went over my rates with him, and we agreed on a fair price, one he would pay as soon as I cleansed his body and mind of the curse, or the demon.

"The first thing I'll need to investigate," I said, after we had come to our agreement, "is where you confessed your sins."

"Confession?" Randall asked, licking his lips. He glanced over his shoulder at the kitchen window, staring into the backyard. "Do I have to go out there?"

"Do you not want to?" I asked.

"No."

"Do I have your permission to explore your backyard?"

"Yes."

I pushed back the chair and stood. "Alina, you'll wait here with Randall?"

"No." She jumped up from her chair, emphatically shaking her head. "Nope."

I smiled at Randall with my lips and stepped to the side, beckoning Alina toward me. I whispered, "Let me rephrase the question into a statement. Alina, you'll wait here and keep Randall calm while I investigate Confession." As I shared my command, I heard it for the terrible idea it was.

"You would leave a teenage girl alone with a mentally unstable man who claims to have murdered his mother, who claims a demon possesses him? What kind of irresponsible person are you?"

"Well, we can't leave him in here alone."

"Why not? He's not going anywhere."

I bit my lip, unable to think of a legitimate excuse.

"Because he might attack us?" Alina asked. "If he does, we'll see him from a mile away. He's not the most graceful human I've ever met."

I sighed in defeat. "Mr. Fincher," I said, stepping away from Alina, "my intern and I will head into the backyard to check out the Confession and make sure it's not... infected with evil spirits." I ran my hands through my unkempt hair. "Do you have any questions for us?"

"Be careful. The curse of the Lord is over the house of the wicked. Once God curses someone, everything they own reaps that curse. The Confession is no longer hallowed ground, but holds great evil—evil that I spawned and brought forth into this world."

"Okay," I said. "Um, yeah. We'll..." I cleared my throat and reached into my backpack, removing a travel-sized bible and a cross. "I brought these precautions to ward us against any potential evil."

"Good. You'll need them."

Alina and I exited through the back door, stepping into the backyard. It had fallen into a further state of disarray than the front yard—the weeds grew to knee height, and trash and debris lay across the ground like detritus in a landfill.

"What's wrong with you?" Alina asked as I shut the sliding-glass door.

"What?"

"We'll make sure evil spirits aren't infecting the Confession? What's that mean? And why do you have that backpack filled with ridiculous props from a costume store? You really think that if we came across a demon, a plastic cross and a bible you've never opened will defend us?" She scoffed. "That's the most ridiculous thing I've ever witnessed... and I once watched Eddie attempt a five-hundred piece puzzle."

That elicited an amused laugh from me.

"I'm not being funny."

"These clients—those who hire me, a paranormal investigator—have certain expectations. It doesn't do any harm to say I'll investigate the very thing they're hiring me to investigate. Of course, we won't find cursed or haunted ground, but if we appear prepared, our clients will believe our investigation and trust our conclusion of non-paranormal activity."

"If you say so. Seems a bit much to me."

"You've been on this job for one hour. I've done this for…" I trailed off, not caring to admit my short tenure in the profession. "For far longer than you."

"Just put your costume kit away and look at this." Alina nodded toward the center of the backyard, filled with nothing more than overgrown weeds and collected trash.

"What am I looking at?"

"That." Alina pointed.

I followed her finger, squinting against the morning sunshine, seeing for the first time what she had noticed right away. Buried beneath the refuse and weeds, barely exposed, stood a chipped and weathered headstone. I crossed the overgrown foliage, avoiding split lumber with rusted nails and barbed wire and metal scraps—why they had such an array of garbage was beyond me.

"Careful," I said, glancing back at Alina.

"What does that even mean?"

"What does careful mean?"

"Yeah."

"To be careful."

"You can't define a word by using the word. That doesn't help."

I stopped and rotated to her. "You don't know what careful means?"

"Of course I know what careful means, but why do adults say that to kids? I mean, what do you think I'm going to do, sprint through this trash-heap yard with a blindfold around my face?"

I shook my head and pivoted around, dodging a long sheet of metal lying over the ground and kneeling before the tombstone.

"Why do teenagers have an answer for everything when they know next to nothing?" I asked.

Alina laughed, her humor infecting the dreary landscape with a slice of hope. "I like that." She squatted on the other side of the sheet metal, bent the weeds away from the stone, and read the epigraph on the marker jutting from the ground. "Phillip Fincher. May he find God's love." The girl cocked her head, looking at me. "No dates defining his lifespan? No accomplishments, like father or husband or anything? Just a name and a little quote that's possibly not even hopeful?"

"Those are your questions?" I asked. "Not why is there a headstone in this backyard?"

"Are home burials not legal?"

"Not in California, unless you jump through a lot of inconvenient and expensive hoops."

"Do you think there's a body buried in the ground? I mean, this could easily be a memorial or a shrine, no corpse."

I knocked on the sheet metal with my knuckles. "Have you seen an area to confess back here?"

Alina's gaze dropped to where I had rapped, shifting away quickly and settling once again on the tombstone.

I stood and shuffled to the end of the thin piece of metal, bending over to grab it. "You still want this internship?" I asked, dragging the scrap away from the headstone.

Cadaverous Company. Friday, April 22nd. 0923hrs.

I'm lucky enough to never have experienced the tragic loss of someone I love, and I'm still young enough that time hasn't caught up with any of my close family, including my grandparents.

My singular experience with death revolved around my brief employment as the reaper, the one who brought the all-ending blackness.

The air stank that day—not of blood or gunpowder or anything stereotypical like that. My encounter with Aaron Brooks occurred in a park on a hot, hot summer day. A muddy creek—one more sludge than liquid—cut through the park near the basketball court. On that sweltering afternoon, the muck exhaled a fetid, rancid stench that crept onto the molten asphalt like a rotting entity.

The sound, stuck perpetually in mind, wasn't my sidearm firing or the bullet plunging into Aaron's chest, or even his body thumping against the ground. Like time haunting the near-dead, ticking away their last seconds, I heard a tap, tap, tap bouncing across the basketball court. A yellow airsoft BB bounced toward me.

A halo of blood surrounded Aaron's body, as if God had already claimed him as an angel. Everything had seemed so distant and blurry, everything but the stink and the BB bouncing and the dark blood absorbing into the dark, porous blacktop.

From ten yards away, I knew the kid was no more. He appeared like a sick rendering of a human—a waxen display from an artist creating a mockery of life from cadavers. In the space of a single BB bouncing across the ground, Aaron ceased to exist, and I saw that, even as I drifted a thousand miles away.

When I slid the sheet metal away from the headstone in Randall Fincher's backyard, I uncovered a casket laying in a shallow grave, holes punched into the lid—like poking holes in a jar to allow a captured insect air to breathe.

Alina covered her mouth at the implication, back stepping, tripping on split firewood, falling into the high stickers. She remained seated in the weeds, wide-eyed and unmoving.

I rushed over to her, careful not to trip on any hidden debris. "Are you okay?"

Her lips parted, moving up and down as if she meant to speak, but couldn't form the sounds.

"Let me take you back to the car, okay? You don't need to see anymore of this."

"I do," she whispered. "That's why I'm here. It's just... do you really think..." Alina's gaze never strayed from the closed coffin.

"Yes, I think so."

My mind reeled as I struggled with the moral and ethical responsibility of how to proceed. Alina was sixteen. Was she old enough to witness what existed beneath the coffin's lid? Was I in a position to determine that? Should I call her parents? Should I call Maya? What would I have wanted, what would I have needed, or have done in that situation at sixteen? If she interned with me, would I always have to shield her from the hard realities of the job? What would she learn if I protected her, especially since she wanted a career as a homicide investigator?

"Alina," I said.

"Yeah."

"You'll have future opportunities to see messed up things—things you'll never forget, though you'll want to. You don't have to dive into this today. You can slog your way into the water. I'll walk you back to the car. I'll come back here and take pictures, and you can look at the pictures."

The girl shook her head. "It's not your job to censor what I experience, but to allow me the full experience of this job."

"I'm not sure that's correct. You're an intern, remember? I should have never brought you into the field."

"I'm fine. I really am. It's just… I've never seen a corpse, and I've never even thought of something like this." Alina nodded at the coffin. She knew what we would find after sliding off the lid. "August?"

"Yeah."

"I know, according to our coddling culture, I'm only a kid. Not only that, I'm a girl. You, as a male adult, feel a tremendous urge to protect me. Please, do us both a favor, and bury that urge. It's not your job to shelter me from the world—not even from this dark corner of the world. I'm not going back to the car. I'm not sitting in an office and staring at walls. Do you know why I wanted this internship?"

"To investigate paranormal mysteries?"

"To have the freedom to investigate actual cases. If I applied for an internship with law enforcement, they wouldn't allow a sixteen-year-old girl into the field. I'm here for the full experience. You're not paying me, but you can at least let me get something from this." Alina stood, brushing the dirt and pollen and thorns off her jeans. She shuffled toward the coffin, grabbed the lid, and pushed, hinging it upward.

An absurdly foul stench burped outward like cartoonish green gas. I gagged, dizzying into nauseousness. Alina coughed, choking on the assaulting odor. She lifted the collar of her shirt over her face, holding it there with one hand, and she leaned over the open coffin. I shoved my way through the noxious cloud, forcing myself close enough to peer into the casket.

'Yellowish, decaying bones rested inside the wooden box, pushed off to the side. Enough room remained for another human to lie inside the coffin with the skeletal remains.

"That's Daddy," said a shaky voice from behind me.

Alina gasped, lurching back.

I startled, wheeling around, a little unsteady and on edge.

Randall stood framed in the sliding glass door, watching us uncover his father's remains.

"What?" I asked.

"It's Confession. Daddy was a priest. Whenever I sinned, Mommy made me confess my sins to Daddy. I would lie in there with him. Mommy would shut the lid, but she at least poked a few openings so I could breathe fine."

Earlier, Randall had mentioned he would stay in Confession for hours or days. Had Muriel forced her son to lie in a coffin with his dead father for days on end? What kind of nightmare had I stumbled into?

"Daddy, who lives with Jesus and speaks to Him directly, would absolve me of my sins." Randall slapped himself in the face. "Until I invited evil into my heart and cursed his resting place, cursed his name, cursed this family. Mommy is dead because of me. Daddy isn't in Heaven anymore, all because of me." He slapped himself in the face again.

"Randall," I said, drifting toward him. "Hey. I know a priest—a very good, reputable priest. I'll get you in contact with him. You can speak with him, okay?"

"God abandoned me!" Randall yelled, spraying strings of spittle off his lips. "The church won't help me! They'll tell me they can't help those who God won't help."

I couldn't leave Randall alone in the house. He would hurt himself, or possibly worse. I couldn't babysit him, either—have him tag along with me throughout the day. He had called me. He claimed to have murdered his mother through a curse, and he needed me to release him of his curse, or prove his mother's death had nothing to do with him and everything to do with bad timing. Easy-peasy.

"Randall," I said, "based on my initial investigation, I have sensed no evil, no curse—there's no lingering negative energy or a dark aura or anything like that. Not here," I glanced at the casket, "and not emanating from you. Please, don't blame yourself or beat yourself up. Allow me to come up with a conclusion, to find out what's really happening."

"You think there's a chance this isn't my fault?" An invisible weight slipped away from Randall, and he stood a little straighter. "Do you really? I prayed for her to die. Prayed for God to murder Mommy. I invited a demon into my soul."

"Listen, I know a priest who will speak with you. Will you meet with him? Maybe you're right, and he can't do anything to help. But maybe you're wrong. Have you thought about that? Have you thought about the prodigal son? Do you know that story?"

Randall nodded.

"God's children leave Him, right?" I asked, working hard to recall my

Sunday school lessons. "But He doesn't leave us. He searches for us when we stray, and when He finds us, He welcomes us back into his family and home. Randall, meet with the priest and talk to him. Can you do that?"

Randall nodded twice—two subtle drops of his sunken chin.

I rotated away from the man-child and pulled the casket's lid down, hiding Phillip Fincher's remains, and I dragged the sheet metal over the casket.

Alina watched me, eyes wide, mouth slightly parted, but she didn't speak. I wondered how long it would take for her bubbly, constant chatter to respawn.

"Let's go back inside," I said.

Innocent by Disconnect. Friday, April 22nd. 0931hrs.

Randall and Alina sat at the kitchen table, across from each other, staring anywhere but at one another. Alina had her iPad out, furiously typing on the keyboard. Randall sipped his water, set it on the table, lifted it again, sipping, repeating.

I opened the front door and stood on the porch, leaning against the paint-chipped door frame to monitor Randall in case he lost what remained of his sanity and went after Alina. From halfway outside, I called my mother.

"August, are you okay?" She always answered my calls as if I were in grave danger, lying on my deathbed, and only her worrying could save me.

"Yeah. How are you?"

"I spoke with Fred. He told me you went to interview a potential murder suspect. What are you thinking? You're not the police. Why would put yourself in danger like that? Why would you put that little girl in danger?"

I closed my eyes and massaged my head. "To protect the privacy and safety of my clients, I can't discuss open investigations with you. I'll need to remind Fred of our policies as well."

"Who's the little girl?"

"I need your help, Mom."

"With a case?"

"With a case, yes. I can't pay you for the information you provide, but I can make you a deal." I cracked my neck, regretting my inability to abandon someone in need, especially someone like Randall, whose mother had destroyed any shot he had of a normal life. Had I simply cared less, I could have left Randall to whatever fate he, the world, or his God had in store for him. Unfortunately, that wasn't the case, and I feared, if left alone, Randall might snap and harm himself or others. He needed help, and I had the connections to help him.

"What's the deal?" My mom asked.

"I'll go to church this Sunday."

Pregnant silence followed that statement.

"Mom, are you there?"

"You'll go to church? Okay. Yeah, deal. I'll do anything. Anything at all. What do you need?"

"It's my client… he needs to speak to someone, and I thought Lloyd Henderson could be that person. Could you text me his number?"

Lloyd Henderson was the only man I knew who led a church congregation. He preached at my parents' small Baptist church every Sunday, and he had done so for the last thirty years.

"Yes, of course. I'll send it over right away."

"Thank you."

"Gussy," she said.

"Yeah?"

"Please shave before Sunday service. Also, make sure you wear something nice. You'll be stepping into the house of God, standing in His presence. Make yourself presentable."

"Yeah… okay. I will."

"I love you."

"Love you, too."

A second later, my phone vibrated. Lloyd Henderson's contact appeared in my messages. Without hesitation, I called him.

The phone rang three times before his raspy, cheery voice answered. "Good morning, this is Lloyd."

"Mr. Henderson," I said, referring to him by his formal name out of childhood habit. "This is August Watson, Kimberly's son."

"How's it going? It's been a while since we last spoke."

I hadn't stayed in contact with many people from my parents' church since the shooting. Truth be told, I hadn't spoken with many family or friends since the shooting, other than my parents.

"I've been busy," I said.

"Well, I'm glad you called. What can I do for you?"

"I don't know how much my mom has divulged to you about my current life, but I'm not policing anymore."

"She mentioned you started an investigative business, like a private detective."

I bounced my head back and forth and flexed my wrist. "Something like that. Anyway, I have a client who desperately needs to speak with someone who has… religious authority. My client blames himself for his mother's very accidental death, claiming he cursed her and caused her fatal end."

"Oh my," Lloyd said.

"The man's name is Randall Fincher. I'm sure if you Google his name, his mother will appear in the headlines. Anyway, I'm afraid if I leave him alone he might hurt himself. It's," I licked my teeth, not sure what information to reveal, "it's a strange situation, and he could use a lot of guidance—guidance that I'm not qualified to provide."

Lloyd sighed into the receiver. "Of course I will help. Where would you like to meet?"

He and I worked out a safe location, deciding to meet within the hour. Lloyd lived in Galt—a rural community thirty minutes outside of Sacramento where my parents had raised me. He needed time to prepare for the meeting and commute into the city.

As I stepped back into the small house, my phone buzzed again. Maya's name flashed across the screen. I stepped back onto the front porch.

"We have a lot to discuss in terms of your niece," I said, answering the call. "You failed to disclose a lot of important information about her personality."

"You're the adult, she's the kid. Figure it out."

"I'm not a babysitter."

"You're her boss."

"Does the term 'boss' apply to an establishment not earning an income to pay employees?"

"Alina spots weakness like a pride of ravenous lions on the hunt. If she's getting to your ego and confidence, if she's in your head and under your skin," Maya clicked her tongue. "It's too late. You're devoured. Eaten. Dead."

"Thanks for the warning."

"Eddie called."

A beat passed. "Okay... are you updating me on your boyfriend's call log now?"

"He's on duty today. But! But he didn't respond to the call this time. He heard about it through a coworker who responded to the scene."

"Heard about what?" I asked.

"Another freak death."

"What do you mean?"

"Apparently, a farm trailer somehow tipped, shooting a cow corpse into the sky. Don't ask me how. I don't know that answer. I heard the story from Eddie, who heard it from a coworker. The telephone game, you know? In whatever way the accident happened, the cow shot a few dozen feet into the air and slammed into a vehicle—like falling from the sky and crashing through the windshield. The force obliterated the driver, crushing the man."

"A Taco Bell sign killed someone yesterday and today we get a flying cow?" I hesitated to ask the next question, but it flitted off my tongue. "What's going on here?"

Maya snickered. "Voodoo magic."

"Voodoo magic?"

"Yup. Voodoo magic."

I rolled my eyes. "Let me guess, they found another voodoo doll at the victim's home?"

"Ding, ding, ding, we have a winner."

"You're not making this up to mess with me?"

"If I could make up a story that crazy, I would write novels. It happened. In real life. In our city. Two freak accidents in two days, and two voodoo dolls found in the victims' homes. What do you make of it? Do we have a magical serial killer on the prowl?"

"Absolutely not."

"How do you explain it, then?"

I couldn't—at least, not yet. But I knew magic didn't exist, and someone wasn't using the arcane arts to murder people. "What was the driver's name?"

"I don't know. With the second doll involved in another freak accident, I have a legitimate story for my editor, though. Eddie knows this case could launch my journalist career, and he's promised to help me by sharing any information he can without jeopardizing a potential investigation."

"That's so sweet of him."

"That's so sweet of him? Why do you say it like that?" Maya asked, her tone turning sour.

"Like what?"

"All sarcastic. I don't understand why you don't like him. You've never met him."

I turned my palms skyward, shrugging. "When did I say I didn't like him?"

"All the time."

"I've never once said that. Alina has mentioned how much she dislikes him about every chance she can, but not me. I'm team Eddie."

"Sarcasm."

I ran my hand through my too-long hair and sighed.

"Before judging him, you guys should meet and get to know each other," Maya said.

Why did people always want me to meet other people? My mom wanted to introduce me to the church lady she knew. Fred always annoyed me about a blind date. Now Maya wanted me to meet Eddie. I barely liked the people I liked enough to hang with. Why would I want to meet strangers?

"What about a double date?" Maya asked.

"What? No. Absolutely not."

"Why?"

"First off, I don't have a date." Glacia crossed my mind. A double date might prove an easy excuse to ask her out.

"Sunday night. Eddie doesn't work Sunday or Monday, so it's perfect. We can get drunk, sit around a fire, sing bad karaoke. Who knows, maybe swing a little? Wink, wink."

Her last statement deserved zero recognition. "I work both Sunday and Monday," I said. "It's the curse of working for yourself. Days off don't exist."

Maya chuckled. "Yeah, okay. Well, I'll share any information Eddie sends to me about the voodoo doll stuff."

"I told you, I'm not working the case unless I'm paid. Share it with Alina."

"Sure. Whatever you say. See you tomorrow night at work? We can talk more about Sunday's double date."

"There's no double date."

"August, you saying no to me is like a dad saying no to his little baby girl. It's just a word you say to say, not one you say to mean."

"You're literally the worst."

"Kisses and hugs, darling. Tell Alina to behave." Maya hung up the phone.

I turned into the doorway and rested my forehead against the doorjamb. Another freak death and another voodoo doll. Coincidences like that don't happen. The two incidents had a connection with each other. I wondered if Randall knew the latest victim. If he did, that tied him to two voodoo doll deaths. If he didn't know the latest victim, that painted a picture absolving him from his mother's murder and the self-diagnosed curse.

The larger question was, did I investigate the voodoo doll case in its entirety now? I still had no one offering to pay me, but with two dolls tied to both accidental deaths, this case would attract media attention. More importantly, it would attract the attention of conspiracy theorists and those who believed in the paranormal—my target audience. If I could insert my face and name into the investigation, I might churn some legitimate business.

"You okay?" Alina asked.

"Just thinking," I said.

"Well, can you think inside with the door closed? I'm not sure Randall has air-conditioning, and it's getting hot in here."

I entered the small home, shutting the flimsy door behind me. Neither Randall nor Alina had moved since I stepped outside.

My phone buzzed again. I glanced at the screen. Maya had made good on her promise, sending me the name of the most recent victim.

"Randall," I said.

"Yeah?"

"The priest I told you about, he said he'll meet with you."

"Did you tell him I invited a demon into my heart?"

"I told you him you believe you cursed your mother, causing her untimely death."

Randall flinched at my words, grimacing. "He's still willing to meet me?"

"He's a good man. He will help you. Do you think you can help me, though?"

"With what?"

"Do you know a Gilbert Tonyan?"

Alina shifted her attention to me, narrowing her eyes and tilting her head. She chewed on a fingernail like a dog gnawing on a bone.

"I've never heard that name," Randall said.

"Well, a man named Gilbert Tonyan died this morning in another freak accident. When police went to his home, they found another voodoo doll. Do you know what that means?"

"The demon I released... it's preying on other people now. I'm responsible for another life." Randall covered his mouth with a trembling hand, gasping for air.

"No. Unless you knew and wished death on Gilbert Tonyan, having created a doll for him, I can confidently say you didn't cause his death, and you didn't cause your mother's death. Randall, you're not cursed or possessed. The priest you're going to meet with, he'll back that up, too."

"They found another voodoo doll in someone else's house?" Randall asked.

I nodded, confirming his question.

Randall pushed back his chair and lurched to his feet. He pulled at his thinning hair. "What if I didn't invite a demon into my heart, but into this world? What if that demon is murdering people and leaving the doll behind as a... a... calling card?"

"That's not the case," I said.

"How do you know? None of this happened until I wished for her to die."

"Okay. Alright." I stepped forward, reaching out a hand and touching the man on his arm. He recoiled, and I brought my hand back to my side. "I'm sorry. I'm sorry. But listen, I found a priest who's willing to help you. Okay? Talk to him before you jump to any conclusions. He'll know what to do."

Randall collapsed back into the chair, pressing his meaty hands over his face and sobbing. "I'm so scared. I'm just so scared."

I kneeled beside him. "Me, too. I'm scared, too. Every single morning I wake up terrified of what the day will bring. Okay? You're not alone. We're all afraid, but we can all be afraid together. We can fight together and help each other. Right?"

Randall looked at me, nodding with beady, wet eyes.

"Okay," I said. "So, let's head to my car. I'm going to drive you to the priest, and you're going to talk to him. While you're with the priest—his name is Lloyd Henderson, by the way—while you're with him, I'm going to investigate Gilbert Tonyan and the latest voodoo doll. Alright?"

"Alright."

"We'll figure this out. We're in this together."

"Okay."

I assisted Randall to his feet and ushered him through the kitchen door, pausing on the front porch. "Do you have everything you need?"

He swallowed. "Yeah."

"House keys?"

"In my pocket." His voice hiccuped as he spoke, like a toddler's after throwing a tantrum.

"Can you hand them to Alina? She's going to lock your door while I lead you to the car."

Randall dug into his pocket and handed a keyring over to Alina. She grabbed the keys from him, shutting the front door and locking it. I escorted Randall to the car.

The Truth. Friday, April 22nd. 1027hrs.

I dropped Randall off at a church with Lloyd Henderson. Lloyd assured me they would be okay, and he would call me once the conversation ended and they had a plan of action to help Randall.

Once comfortable enough to leave the two men alone with each other and not having to worry about anyone's safety, I drove Alina back to the office.

Giovanni, a paralegal who worked in the small criminal law office across the hall from my rented space, stood on the sidewalk and smoked. He held the cigarette in a scissor grip against his opposite shoulder. Smoke drifted into the sunny morning sky. With his free hand, he scrolled through his phone.

"Good morning, Gio," I said, pausing beside him, though upwind of his smoke. We had a smoke-break relationship. I didn't partake, but I chewed gum and enjoyed his easy-going company. Giovanni didn't fear conversational silence, so we often found peace between each other in mutual quiet.

"Dr. Watson," he said in his best British accent, which was quite terrible. "How's your morning?" Giovanni often referred to me as doctor, alluding to Dr. John Watson from Sherlock Holmes, in his awful accent.

"My morning? It's something. I thought you quit smoking?"

"You know what they say about quitters? 'Winners never quit, and quitters never win.' I don't know about you, Mr. Watson, but I prefer to win. So, I quit on quitting." Giovanni inhaled, holding the smoke for a few seconds before exhaling.

"People who consistently smoke less than one cigarette a day have a sixty-four percent risk of earlier death than a nonsmoker," Alina said, crossing her arms.

Giovanni batted his eyes at my new intern. "Who are you?"

"Alina Mylene Moore. I'm Mr. Watson's new intern."

"I didn't know twelve-year-olds could work on school days?"

Alina scrunched her face. "You really should stop smoking. Your breath smells like old hard-boiled eggs, and your clothes smell like the grimy sweatshirt of a high school dropout."

"Alina," I said, pausing there, not knowing what to say next. Did I chastise her? Ground her? The parenting-slash-supervising gig wasn't fitting me too well. I faced Giovanni. "I'm sorry about that."

"I'm not," Alina said, shrugging her shoulders. "I'm an advocate for human lives, even if that means speaking brutal truth and hurting some feelings. If Mr. Skin-and-Bones cares so much about his physical appearance to have apparently stopped eating, I'm sure he'll also care to know that he stinks like the inside of a shower drain, and maybe that knowledge will inspire him to quit smoking. If that doesn't work, maybe he would like to know his hair looks like strands from a frizzy wire brush. Maybe that will get him to quit, and if so, you're welcome that I spoke so abrasively. My honesty, though painful, might save lives."

I stretched my wrists. "Gio, my apologies. Tell Sarah I said hi."

Sarah was Giovanni's employer—a criminal defender who dedicated her life to defending those wrongly convicted of crimes.

Giovanni frowned, dropping his cigarette on the cement and crushing it beneath his toe. "I will."

Alina and I entered the office complex and ascended the stairwell.

"You can't speak to people like that," I said.

"Why?"

"It's rude and hurtful."

"Of course," Alina said, rolling her eyes and jogging ahead of me up the stairs.

"Of course what?" I said, calling after her.

"Of course you find honesty rude and hurtful."

"False. I've made a point not to lie to people, but I don't go around criticizing others in the name of truth."

"No, you avoid lying by omitting information, not by speaking honestly. There's a difference."

I ran my fingers through my hair, annoyed with myself for stepping into yet another argument with a teenager. "For the sake of our relationship, I'm your boss and you're my employee. If I tell you to shut your mouth and not insult anyone, no matter how well-intentioned, then you shut your mouth."

She and I leveled onto the third floor in silence. I opened the office door, allowing Alina into the small space and following behind.

Fred hadn't moved from his desk. He smiled at us as we entered. "How did it go?"

"Awesome," Alina said, plopping into the client chair in front of my desk. "Apparently I'm supposed to lie now. So it went great."

Fred narrowed his eyes and frowned at me. "Went that well, huh?"

I pulled open my desk drawer and ripped the plastic off a new gum packet, bending a stick into my mouth and chewing. The burst of minty juices calmed my firing and agitated nerves. I slouched in my chair and pinched my temples. "Another voodoo murder."

"What?" Fred asked, standing from his seat and leaning over the high counter between us. "Another voodoo murder? What happened?"

"Apparently, a cow flew into a car and killed someone. They found another doll on the dining room table of the victim's house."

"Do we have a true-blue, real-life serial killer?" Fred asked, excitement splashing across his face.

"What?" I asked, pinching my skull. A headache formed behind my eyes—whether from the lack of sleep, the three cases I juggled, the teenager I managed, Maya and my mom's persistence for me to do things I didn't want to do, or the litany of other triggers, I did not know. My head throbbed, though.

"A serial killer. Do we have a serial killer?" Fred asked.

"We need three murders for a serial killer," I said.

"Well, two deaths in two days points to a strong likelihood of a third," Alina muttered.

"And there's an established pattern, or MO," Fred added. "The voodoo dolls."

"No, there's not," I said. "There's two freak, impossible accidents resulting in two deaths. A serial killer couldn't pull off those murders." I clambered out of my seat and paced to the back table, grabbing the carafe of coffee. It was infuriatingly empty. Biting back a tirade of swears and curses, I started brewing a new pot.

"What if it's a serial killer using voodoo dolls to kill the victims?" Fred asked. "He's flexing by leaving them behind. A calling card, of sorts."

"And James Connors really saw Bigfoot?" I asked.

"Why not?"

"Why not? Because Bigfoot doesn't exist. Voodoo doesn't exist, nor ghosts. Remember, it's not our job to corroborate the stories people share with us and hire us to investigate. It's our job to find the truth." I glanced at Alina. "Truth and conspiracy or imagined fears or monsters don't align. There's no such thing as a Bigfoot. There's no such thing as ghosts. There's not a voodoo serial killer cursing people to die. Period. It's our job to find the simple, normal answer to those problems."

Fred, like an elusive mole, dropped below the height of the counter. A second later, the tap-tapping of fingers sounded as his fingers flew over his keyboard. The coffee machine churned and dripped. Alina remained in the chair, staring at her phone. I leaned against the wall and closed my eyes, catching my breath and waiting for the coffee to finish.

A minute later, Fred cleared his throat. "Gilbert Tonyan and Muriel Fincher graduated from the same high school."

"What?" I asked, opening my eyes and staring across the office.

"Gilbert Tonyan, the man crushed by a flying cow, and Muriel Fincher, the woman crushed by a Taco Bell sign, graduated from the same school. Do you know what that means?"

"There's a connection," Alina said, dropping her phone in her lap and sitting up straighter.

"How did you find that information so quickly?" I asked.

"I typed both their names into Google at the same time. A couple yearbooks and school newspapers popped up in the results." Fred raised his head above the counter. "Investigative research really isn't too hard these days."

Alina leaped from the chair and marched across the room, spinning on her heel and pacing back, speaking her mind the entire time. "Two deaths in two days. They found a voodoo doll at the victims' homes in both cases. Each victim attended the same high school. That's about two more coincidences than I'm comfortable with."

The coffee beeped completion. I poured a cup into my favorite mug and returned to my desk, sitting. "Fred."

"Yup?"

"Did they graduate in the same class?"

"Nope. Muriel was a few years older."

"So, our connection is based on two people, two of thousands of people, who attended the same high school within three, four, five years of each other?"

"And the voodoo dolls," Alina said. "That's another important connection."

I sipped the steaming hot coffee.

"Do you drink that with the gum in your mouth?" Alina asked.

"He does," Fred said, "and it's absolutely revolting."

"Alright, let's entertain your theory," I said, allowing the coffee to melt away my discomfort. "One of you needs to make a list, including all those who might have known both Muriel and Gilbert. Did they share the same principal or teacher? Did they know the same students? Did they volunteer for the same organizations or spend their time in the same clubs? I need a list of everyone who would have known them both. From there, narrow the list down to those still alive. From there, narrow the list to those still living within a, I don't know, fifty-mile radius. Once you have completed the list, knock on doors and ask questions. Pay attention to their homes. Do they have anything related to the occult or voodoo on their shelves? Make notes of anything out of the ordinary that you notice."

"What are you going to do?" Alina asked.

I cracked my neck and massaged my shoulder. "I'm going to speak with Gilbert Tonyan's wife."

An Unwelcome Visit. Friday, April 22nd. 1102hrs.

I crossed the hallway to Sarah Herling's office, pausing before her door. My hand hovered around the doorknob as I contemplated barging into her space and apologizing again to Giovanni for Alina's earlier behavior.

As I stood there, the door opened inward, eliminating my ability to choose.

Sarah appeared in the doorway, hopping back a step and releasing a surprised yelp. Her stiletto slipped on the hardwood flooring, and her foot rolled, and she dropped to a knee. August Watson, always smooth with the ladies. She climbed back to her feet, shaking her head as she stood before me—tall, taut, and tawny hair, almost, but not quite orange.

"August," Sarah said, "what are you doing standing there?" She bent over and massaged her ankle.

"Sorry," I said, suddenly clammy from embarrassment. "Hi. How's it going?"

"Hi. And good. Is everything okay?"

"Yeah."

She straightened her posture, raising her eyes and tilting her head. "You're sure?"

The problem with having an attractive, intelligent, and interesting person working across the hall from me was having to avoid her at all costs, lest I embarrass myself. I looked better from a distance, when people only had the chance to look at me. God forbid a pretty girl comes close enough to incite a conversation, and I had to stutter my way through a sentence.

"I just… I wanted to apologize to Giovanni."

Sarah smirked, which quickly evolved into a light chuckle. "He told me about your spitfire intern. His words, not mine."

"Alina, that's her name, was supposed to start Monday, not today, and…" I cut myself off, realizing my admittance made me sound incompetent and unprepared. How did one prepare for Alina, though? How did I explain Alina to someone without it sounding like a complaint or an excuse? "She's young, and she's still practicing her professionalism."

"Well, maybe you shouldn't tell her that Giovanni threw his cigarettes in the trash."

"I won't," I said. "She doesn't need that knowledge as ammunition. Believe me, the girl has enough to say as it is."

"Well, if your intern ever bores of hunting the paranormal, send her my way. I could use someone with a little passion and grit."

"Yeah, well, um, I need to go, but I'm glad Giovanni… yeah." I smiled with only my lips and spun around, walking too fast toward the stairwell and jogging down the steps to the first floor. Without daring to look back to see if she had followed me out of the building, I hurried to my car and ducked inside, reaching for my cupholder and realizing I had forgotten my coffee. Not daring to run back upstairs and run back into Sarah, I started the car, deciding to swing by a cafe instead.

First, though, I had to speak with Maya again.

Her phone rang twice. "Hey."

"I'm in."

"Double date?"

"No. Definitely not that. The voodoo doll case. I'm in."

"Oh, yeah. Batman and Robin are at it again. You're Robin, of course."

"Of course? What's that mean?"

"It's your legs," Maya said. "You look amazing in short-shorts."

"Fred found a loose connection between the two victims," I said, rolling my eyes and pulling into the street.

"Same high school?"

I groaned, disappointed. "You already know?"

"Of course I know. You think I didn't type their names into Google? Come on, August."

"Did Eddie provide you with more information about the voodoo stuff?"

"Nothing. I mean, he didn't respond to the scene earlier, not like he did yesterday, so he only knows what was told to him, which I already shared with you."

"They're not investigating the voodoo dolls as a connection?"

"Doubtful. Even if they found someone who dabbled in voodoo and supposedly cursed both Muriel and Gilbert, the police would have to prove that a person committed a crime. How do you prove someone murdered another person through magical means? I don't think you do. So, they rule the deaths accidental, close the case, and move on."

I scratched my neck. "So you and I, we're not stepping on anyone's toes by investigating a paranormal possibility?"

"Nope," Maya said, popping her lips. "Eddie even told me to go for it, to secure my promotion into full-time journalism. Don't dare mention anything about sensationalist writing not equating to factual writing. You've dipped your toes into the supernatural, as well. If you can label yourself as an investigator, I can label myself as a journalist. Also, it's a stepping stone to something more legitimate."

"Hey, slow down," I said. "You always do that."

"Do what?"

"Try to convince me of the legitimacy of your job, when I'm already convinced. So, why do you keep doing it? To convince yourself?"

"Don't psychoanalyze me."

"Quit lecturing me, then." I pulled into the cafe's parking lot and killed the engine. "Can you get Gilbert's address?"

"Already have it," Maya said. "I'm always three steps ahead of you, Watson."

"Well, does Batman want to accompany Robin over to Gilbert's house to speak with his wife?"

"Did you just refer to me as Batman?"

"Short-shorts fit me well," I said.

Maya chuckled. "Well, I want to speak to his widowed wife more than anything. When?"

"Now."

"I'm on my way."

"Do you want some coffee?" I asked.

"You're going to give yourself a heart attack the way you drink coffee."

"Do you want any or not?"

"Yes, please."

Maya shared her coffee order and Gilbert's home address with me. Twenty minutes later, I met her in front of the residential home, parking along the curb behind her car.

She stepped out of the vehicle, wearing loose jeans, a tied-up baggy T-shirt with a classic rock band logo on the front and the past tour dates on the back. She had lightened her hair, and it stood off her head in an afro. Her cool blue eyes smiled along with her broad grin, and she beamed at me, illuminated by the sun—or my rose-colored glasses.

I had had a thing for Maya since first seeing her at our shared second job. Too nervous to make a move, my hesitation had allowed her plenty of space to find Eddie, her now boyfriend.

I stepped from my car, grabbing her coffee and shutting the door behind me. "Good morning," I said, handing her the hot drink.

Maya accepted it with both hands, palming the paper cup and holding it close to her face, sniffing. "I swear, the only reason I tolerate coffee is for the smell of it. Caffeine makes me feel weird—all shaky and sweaty, kind of like your constant state of existence—and it tastes too bitter. I'm a sweets girl. Candy. Cake. Pie. Cinnamon rolls. Holy Smokes, August. If you ever surprised me with a cinnamon roll, I'd birth your children for you. If you brought me two cinnamon rolls, I would raise said children. And I'm not a mom by nature, so promising to mother the children I pooched out for you... that's true love. For cinnamon rolls, of course. Not you."

"The relation between you and Alina is more and more obvious," I said.

"What's that mean?"

"You have a shared strange genetic trait which allows you to talk without having to breathe. It's fascinating."

"Oh yeah. That girl can talk, and she can talk a lot about nothing, too. It's quite impressive. Have you asked her about movies yet?"

"She brought them up."

"Well, if you're bored, needing to kill a lot of time, and not wanting to listen to the radio, tell her *The Godfather* was so boring, you didn't even bother to watch the second one."

"I haven't seen either of them."

"Oh, my God. Yes! Say that instead." Maya chuckled. "She will lose her little mind over that."

I noted that and faced Gilbert Tonyan's house, walking up the driveway.

He had an immaculate yard, with cross-pattern lines cutting across the grass. Hedged bushes lined the driveway, which sloped upward to a pair of steps leading to the front door. A welcome mat lay in the entryway, welcoming guests into the lovely home. By appearance alone, Gilbert went to great lengths to take care of his possessions.

"What's in the box?" Maya asked, altering her voice into a strange frenzy. We stood before the front door.

"What?" I asked, glancing at the white pinstriped box I held. It contained a half-dozen donuts and a few pastries for the widowed woman we intended to ambush.

"What?"

"Why did you ask like that—all... crazy?"

"You're serious?"

"You asked, like, you're afraid of what's in the box."

"What's in the box?" She asked again, raising her voice into near panic.

"Why do you keep doing that?"

"You've never seen the movie *Seven*? With Morgan Freeman and Brad Pitt."

"No."

Maya looked at me with severe disappointment, shaking her head back and forth and clicking her tongue. "I'm going to ask you a question, and depending on how you answer will determine if we ever speak again. Have you ever seen any *Star Wars* movie?"

"I don't watch movies."

"*Lord of the Rings*?"

"No."

"*Harry Potter*? No! Don't answer that. I can't bear to know the truth."

"I haven't."

Maya's eyes widened, and her jaw dropped. "What did you do during your childhood?"

"Well, I went outside and played."

"I knew you were older than me, but are you really... that old? So old you had to go outside to have fun? Oh, the horror!"

"I'm, what, five years older than you?"

"As if," Maya said. "Try six. Did you know that earlier today, Alina told me you were super lame? I argued with her, in your favor, too. But I don't know anymore, August. You not seeing any of those movies? Well, that's pretty lame."

"When did you speak with Alina?"

"There's this thing called texting, or have you never heard of that either since you're old enough to know what playing outside was like?"

I sighed. "Would you do the honors and knock on the door? I'm a little preoccupied." I glanced at my hands, which held my coffee cup and the box of pastries.

"We're doing date night—double date night—and we're watching a movie. It's embarrassing that you haven't seen a single movie ever."

"I've seen one or two of the *Twilight* movies."

Maya tore her eyes from me, not even bothering to respond, and she knocked on the front door. A few seconds passed, and Maya returned her attention to me. "I don't even know what to say. *Twilight*? Really?"

"What?"

"You're embarrassing."

"What?"

The deadbolt to the front door unlatched, and the door cracked open.

A woman about my mother's age stepped into view. Her eyes were red and swollen and heavy, as if she couldn't bear to keep them open any longer. "Who are you?"

"I'm August Watson, and this is my friend."

"Maya Adler. I'm a journalist for the *Here & Now*, and August is a paranormal investigator. We're extremely sorry to hear about the tragic loss of your husband, but his accident is also why we're here. It's come to our attention that you discovered a voodoo doll earlier this morning."

The woman licked her lips. "Who are you?"

I stepped an inch forward, placing myself before Maya. She might have an unnecessary amount of confidence about vomiting the first words that popped into her mind, but elegance often eluded her. I hoped to address Gilbert's widow with a little more tact.

"Ma'am, again, I apologize for your loss. I can't imagine the pain you're attempting to process right now. I know this means little, but I brought you a box of pastries—well, donuts." I extended the box to her. "It's not much, but you'll need to eat, and it's easier eating something that is halfway tasty."

The woman reluctantly accepted my gift. "Why are you here?"

"As my friend mentioned, we both work in… investigating paranormal occurrences. Yesterday, a woman died in a freak accident, and they discovered a voodoo doll in her home. This morning, your husband passed under extremely unlucky circumstances, and we heard you found a voodoo doll." I licked my lips after a second of silence. "I'm sorry. What was your name?"

"Greta," she whispered. "Do you think someone murdered my

husband through some kind of… magical curse?"

"It's unlikely," I said, "but the voodoo doll evidence connects your husband's death to that of the woman who died yesterday afternoon. We don't know how they're related beyond the voodoo dolls, but we would like to find out. We need your help to do that."

"A cow," she said, covering her mouth with her hand and trailing off.

"We want to help," I said. "And we want to make sure that there's not another potential target. May we come inside and ask a few questions?"

Greta said nothing for a stretch of time, staring off into her front yard at nothing in particular. Finally, she shook her head. "No. I don't think so. Two officers contacted me while I was at work. I ride my bike to work—I teach at the elementary school down the road. But I had come home to switch out my bike for my car so I could drive to the station. That's when I saw the doll for the first time. I thought little of it until I identified Gilbert's body. That was an hour ago. I just walked through the door a minute before you knocked. Our kids don't even know yet." She stopped to wipe tears from her eyes.

"Do you have it with you still?" Maya asked.

"The doll?"

"Yes."

"I do."

"Could we see it?"

"Why? It's just a… faceless doll. That's it. I told that to the officers, and they noted it, but they didn't seem too interested."

"The police are bound by certain rules and boundaries," I said. "Maya and I have more freedom in our investigations. We can, for example, follow paranormal trails where the police don't have that luxury. They noted it, but they can't really do much with that information."

"But you can?"

I shrugged, glancing at Maya.

"Maybe," Maya said. "Maybe not. We can at least explore this idea and provide you with an answer. An answer might provide closure to you. At most, though, we might save lives."

Greta stared, wide-eyed and unblinkingly beyond Maya and me. After a second, she said, "My husband died in a bizarre accident. Magic doesn't exist, and I will not allow you to exploit his death for money or fame or whatever it is you're after. No, you can't come inside my home. No, you can't see the voodoo doll. If you would kindly leave and allow me to process my husband's untimely death, I would appreciate that more than anything. Thank you for the donuts." The woman gently shut the door in our faces, securing the deadbolt.

Maya and I remained standing on the front porch.

"What now?" I asked.

Slow Afternoon at the Office. Friday, April 22nd. 1212hrs.

I drove back to the office from Greta Tonyan's house, and Maya followed me. As I drove, I dialed Fred's number to update him on the situation.

"Hey," he said. Surrounding traffic from his end of the line muffled his voice.

"You busy?"

"I'm at the taco truck."

"Where's Alina?"

"Right here. Don't worry. The girl is still alive and kicking—kicking hard. That girl doesn't stop."

"Grab a few extra tacos. Maya is coming to the office."

"What does she want?"

Another call cut into the conversation. I glanced at my phone. Lloyd Henderson called. "Anything. I don't care."

"Does she care?"

"I have to take this call. Get her anything." Before he could push back, I accepted Lloyd's call. "August here."

"Hey, it's Lloyd. I just finished speaking with Randall."

"How did it go?" I asked, running through a yellow light as I momentarily forgot Maya followed me.

I glanced in my rearview mirror. She waited at the red light, growing smaller as the distance between us grew. Oops. I couldn't remember another time she had swung by the office, so I wasn't entirely sure she knew how to get there without direction.

A stinging silence stretched through the car.

"August, did I lose you?" Lloyd asked.

My phone buzzed as another call came in. Maya showed on my screen, probably gearing to criticize my lack of awareness and consideration.

"I'm sorry," I said, speaking to Lloyd and ignoring Maya's call. "I missed what you said. How did it go?"

"Not great," Lloyd said, speaking somberly. "Randall had relied on his mother for every aspect of his life, for his entire life. He has no foundational skills to help him survive, let alone succeed. I'm afraid that if we leave him on his own, he will, sooner rather than later, hurt himself irreversibly, if not permanently."

I cracked my neck and massaged my shoulder, thinking to myself that Randall Fincher was not my responsibility. He had hired me to exorcise the curse he brought into the world, not to iron out the wrinkles of life.

Maya called again, pulling me from my thoughts.

I ignored her again. "What do we do?"

"I'm going to look into a supportive housing program for him, or assisted living—a place where staff can watch and help him, but also teach him to support himself."

"In the meantime?"

"The church has a volunteer outreach program where we serve the community. I'll make sure volunteers visit him daily, bringing him food and helping him clean the house and wash his clothes."

"Thank you," I said.

"There's no need," Lloyd said. "This is the responsibility of the church—to care for those who can't care for themselves. To love the unloved. To serve the unserved."

I flexed my wrist and wished what Lloyd said applied to all church people. "Does he still believe he summoned the curse and killed his mother?"

"He feels guilty about praying for his mother to die seconds before she died. Guilt does funny and dangerous things to a person's imagination and mind. He will suffer his guilt for a long time."

I thanked Lloyd for his time, ending our conversation and calling back Maya. She promptly cussed me out. Once she had released her steam, I shared the office address with her.

Ten minutes later, we pulled chairs around my desk and stuffed our faces. The silence was relaxing and energizing. For a moment, I could settle into my thoughts and allow the day to absorb, to marinate in my mind.

For the first time in years, I had awoken beside a beautiful woman—to any woman. My focus, despite the three ongoing and unsolved mysteries I poorly juggled, remained square on Glacia Vasquez. When I thought of her, though, I felt a remorseful excitement. My inner attention shifted to Maya, who sat across from me, stuffing a massive, messy burrito into her mouth and dropping the contents over her chin and onto my desk. Why did I feel shame thinking of Glacia when Maya sat beside me? Maya had Eddie, and she seemed happy with him. Why couldn't I have someone, too?

"What? You don't like the way I eat?" Maya asked, staring across the desk at me.

My face flushed with heat. She had caught me looking at her. "I cleaned my desk yesterday."

Maya glanced at Alina, who glanced at Fred. They all stared at each other for a second before simultaneously bursting into a coordinated flurry of laughter.

"What's so funny?" I asked.

"You're great," Fred said, laughing between words. He grabbed my shoulder with his bearish hand. "We love you, and we even respect you for many and multiple reasons. Cleanliness," he shook his head, "not one of those reasons."

"Your idea of cleaning is hiding the dirt beneath a rug," Maya said. "It's not cleaning, though... it's just redistributing the mess. Besides, there's no way you cleaned this desk yesterday. It's sticky." She pressed her palm to the surface and lifted it, proving her point while twisting her face in disgust.

"That stickiness is the cleaning product," I said, finishing my taco.

Alina pointed at me. "I got you, Mr. Abe. I thought you spoke honestly, always. It was your life's mission. Or was that nothing but a lie, too? How will I ever trust anything you say ever again?"

"Fine. I didn't clean it," I said. "But that doesn't mean I enjoy having food splatter all over my desk."

"Would you even notice it?" Maya asked. "I mean, if you hadn't watched it happen?"

"I don't know why I talk to any of you."

"Because you love us, with a capital L," Fred said, making kissing sounds.

"We should discuss the cases," I said, cleaning my hands with a napkin and leaning back in my chair. "First, there's the Bigfoot sighting. James Connors won't pay me unless I provide concrete evidence proving what he saw. Since Tempest Michaels' money hasn't come through yet, we need to further investigate Bigfoot and the legitimacy of Connors' sighting to collect our payment."

"Our?" Maya asked, tilting her head. "As in me?"

"Yes, as in you," I said. "Through association, you may earn some money. I've been thinking, and I meant to bring this up earlier, we should work together." I popped a knuckle. "I'm sure *Here & Now* receives plenty of paranormal leads to report. If you refer those clients this way, we can investigate their claims for a fee, and you can write the story. Of course, the street runs both ways. When we receive a case, we tip you off and provide you with content to report."

"I'm interested," Maya said, stroking her chin.

"So, if you want to work the Bigfoot sighting with us, we'd love to have your input and ideas."

"We starting there?" Fred asked.

"What do you mean?" I asked.

"We have three current cases, right? Well, there's no need to brainstorm all of them at once. Which one do we focus on first? Which one do we eliminate?"

I bit my lip, considering which of our three cases bore the most weight. Bigfoot promised us the most money, so we needed to come up with a way to conclude that investigation and collect our payment. The haunted house also boasted a paying client, but I had less confusion with that case. The evidence seemed obvious to me, and I had a sound idea of Glacia's ghost. The voodoo doll murders dropped to the bottom of my importance list, mainly because they offered no compensation. However, they meant a great deal to Maya, and I couldn't overlook that fact, especially if she and I were to help each other succeed in this paranormal field.

"Obviously there's the voodoo doll investigation," Maya said, dispelling my thoughts. "You mentioned the Bigfoot sighting. What else do we have?"

"A sexual foray with August and his client and the haunting night," Fred said, lowering his voice and attempting to sound spooky.

"Oh, please, tell," Maya said.

"Gross. I would rather not hear about that," Alina said.

"I'd rather not discuss anything like that," I said. "Besides, I think I've about wrapped up that case. There are a few loose ends, but I should tie them together tomorrow morning."

"Bigfoot or voodoo doll then?" Maya asked. "You know my vote."

"I vote voodoo doll," Alina said. "Fred?"

The big man sucked on his lip. "Honestly, I don't really need the cash from Bigfoot, and the voodoo doll sounds way more interesting and less likely to have a random bear encounter. So, let's go with the voodoo doll murders."

Everyone looked at me.

"Seems like I'm the odd man out," I said.

"You should be familiar with that feeling," Alina said.

"Ouch," I said, grabbing my chest.

"Yesterday afternoon," Maya said, "a middle-aged woman named Muriel Fincher died in a terrible, freak accident—crushed by a falling Taco Bell sign. Her living son reported finding a voodoo doll at their house. This morning, a middle-aged man named Gilbert Tonyan died in another terrible and freak accident—crushed by a flying cow. His wife reported finding a voodoo doll. Connection between the two victims... they attended the same high school."

"Fred, Alina," I said, glancing at each of them, "did you come up with a list of suspects?"

"We did, and we narrowed it down." Alina stood and waltzed to Fred's desk, swiped a piece of paper from the counter, and placed it before me. "Muriel was five years older than Gilbert, so they never stepped foot on campus together. Most of the teachers who had taught both of them have passed away from getting too old. The youngest of those still alive are in their late-seventies. We won't rule them out, but they're probably not our primary suspects, either. From there, we listed students with younger or older siblings who might have known both Muriel and Gilbert."

"A kid who attended the same year as Muriel and had a younger sibling who attended the same years as Gilbert," Fred said.

"Find anyone?" I asked.

"About three-hundred people," Alina said.

"That number includes both siblings, and sometimes, three or four siblings," Fred said.

"We narrowed those three-hundred down to a little over fifty, based on whether they still have a pulse, live within the fifty-mile radius you suggested, have landed themselves in prison, along with other eliminating factors."

"All this in the couple of hours I was gone?"

"I'm good on computers," Fred said.

"Same," Alina said. They fist-bumped each other, like two old pals achieving some kind of unspoken victory. "How did your home visit go?"

"Terrible," Maya said. "Greta told us nothing we didn't already know, and she refused to invite us into her home or entertain the idea of a curse having caused her husband's death."

"Randall's home wasn't that productive, either," I said, mentally falling into his backyard, over the casket with his father's remains. "At least not to our investigation."

"Unless we believe the curse is real," Alina said. "There was some strange, creepy religious stuff happening at Randall's house. If we want to consider the possibility of an actual voodoo curse, we have some building blocks to work with based on what we found there."

Maya looked at me. "What do you think? Are we entertaining the idea of the full-fledged curse?"

"Maybe Randall, after allowing a demon into his heart—his words, not mine," Alina said, "summoned the darkness into this world. It not only fulfilled Randall's wish for his mother to die, but now that it's here, it's fulfilling everyone's dark desires. Do you think Greta may have secretly wished for Gilbert to die? Were they in financial trouble? Was he secretly seeing someone, or maybe she saw another man? Had their relationship grown cold and stale? I mean, anything could have happened, right?"

I narrowed my eyes, impressed with the young girl. "Keep going."

"I think we should investigate their marriage and see if we can't find proof she wanted him gone. If so, maybe the connection isn't a classmate, but an actual demonic entity."

"I don't like the sound of that," Fred said, still eating. "I much prefer dealing in the mundane, easily explainable, avoiding bears and demons alike."

I chewed on Alina's idea for a few seconds. If I followed her path of questioning, we walked a supernatural trail I believed would lead us nowhere. The connection lived elsewhere, either with common classmates or somewhere we hadn't thought of yet.

"It wouldn't hurt," Maya said.

"What wouldn't?" I asked.

"Exploring the idea of an actual curse haunting Sacramento. Randall confessed to wishing his mother dead, right? If we can uncover some kind of similar truth about Greta and Gilbert, the information might not lead to a demon... but maybe it will lead to a more concrete connection."

I squinted at Fred. "I want you and Alina narrowing this list to ten people, fifteen at the most. Maya," I shifted my attention to her, "I don't know how you plan on revealing Greta's darkest secrets about wanting her husband gone, especially now that he is, but you can work on that angle."

"What are you going to do?" Alina asked.

"We have three cases. Someone needs to work the other two."

Before the Birthday Party. Friday, April 22nd. 1637hrs.

I trudged into my apartment, exhausted—wrung out like a wet towel.

Maya, Alina, and Fred had spent the rest of the afternoon in the office, narrowing down our suspect list, brainstorming ideas and leads, and planning our next steps.

I had scoured through local college staff directories, noting anyone with a background in cryptozoology. To my surprise, I had identified seven different professors, all with varying degrees of experience on the subject. I had sent each of them an email introducing myself, detailing the Bigfoot case, and providing them with the pictures I had taken from the forest.

Glacia hadn't texted or called me, and her avoidance further sapped my energy and spirits. Then again, I hadn't texted or called her either.

As I left the office, Maya reminded me of our double-date Sunday evening, claiming she had already told Eddie, made the menu, and I couldn't back out. So, I reluctantly agreed, book ending my Sunday with church in the morning and a double date with Maya's new boyfriend in the evening—two activities I rather would have avoided at all costs.

Tomorrow, or Saturday, I had a real estate appointment to walk through Glacia's inherited home, hopefully solve that case, collect some money, and then retire to my second job at the bookstore with Maya.

Tonight, though, before my jam-packed weekend, I would attend my grandmother's eightieth birthday party at my parents' house, where I would have to see and speak to my extended family for the first time in five years. Yay!

Usually, my weekend entailed working, investigating, researching, and reading—all mostly solitary activities that provided me with the amazing opportunity to avoid speaking with other people. It was safe to say I did not look forward to a single minute of this upcoming weekend.

I padded across my apartment, crashing onto my bed and staring at the ceiling.

Bam's party wouldn't begin until 1800hrs, and I needed thirty minutes to commute to my parents' house. So, I had an hour to relax and tempt a sliver of energy back into my body to prepare for the evening.

As my eyes grew heavy and the world filled with a sleep-induced haze, a quick, staccato knocking ripped me from the waves of slumber. I jerked awake, sitting up on my bed and rubbing my eyes. The knocking continued incessantly and without pause.

I planted my feet and shuffled to the door, neglecting in my state of confused exhaustion to use the peephole.

Alina stood in the hallway, her fist raised in the air. "Hi."

"No," I said, shutting the door in her face.

Before the door could latch, her foot wedged into the frame.

"Alina," I said. "This is my home. You can't be here."

"Can I come in?"

"Not a chance."

"Please?"

"No. Move your foot in the other direction and walk on home."

"That's why I'm here."

I ran my fingers through my hair and pinched the bridge of my nose.

My earlier headache threatened to return in full. "Alina, you coming into my apartment is inappropriate on more levels than I can count."

"It's here... or it's nowhere," Alina said, dropping her shoulders in a show of vulnerability she hadn't portrayed before.

"What about your home?"

Alina shook her head, staring at the floor. "Maya doesn't know any of this because I don't want to distract her from her opportunity with the tabloid, but... well, there's just a lot going on."

"Is this a sob story?"

"I'm serious, August. I'll leave, if you want me to. I will. But I really don't have anywhere to go. Nowhere to sleep." She shrugged. "And I won't go to Maya. Not until she's submitted her article on Tuesday."

I filled my cheeks with air and slowly allowed them to decompress as I glanced off to the side. "Why can't you go home?"

"I don't have a home. My dad left my mom and me a few months back. My mom doesn't have any work experience on account of her felony record and addictive history. She can't find a job, and it doesn't help that she doesn't have a high school diploma. Incapable of paying the rent, our landlord evicted us."

"Where's your mom now?" I asked.

Alina frowned. "I don't know. I really don't. She does this, which is why she can't find a job. She just disappears. Sometimes for days, sometimes for weeks. I couldn't go to Maya's and distract her from her work. I'm sorry, but I followed you here. I almost walked away." The girl pawed at her eyes. "But I had nowhere else to go."

I said nothing, unsure of what to say or how to proceed. If I called the cops, they would contact CPS. Until they located her mother, who knows where Alina would end up. Still, the system was in place for a reason, right? I couldn't skirt around it. Didn't I have a responsible obligation to report Alina's parents to CPS?

My silence allowed the girl a chance to continue speaking. "That's the main reason I skipped school today. The attendance system will notify my mother. I thought maybe if she learned of my absence, she might come back to look for me." Alina scowled and shrugged. "Didn't work."

I stretched my hands and twisted my wrists, reaching for any excuse to turn her away. I exhaled, buzzing my lips and stepping away from the door. "Come in."

Alina smirked at me, but her spunk and confidence from earlier had drained away. "Thank you." The girl entered my apartment, freezing in place. "What is this?"

"What?"

She turned her head toward me and coughed a brittle laugh. She extended her arm and swept it to present my apartment to me. "This."

"This is where I live."

"Oh, I didn't know you supervised a dump."

"You don't have to be here."

Alina navigated to the kitchen sink, peering at the tower of crusted dishes. "August, this is disgusting. It's, like, revolting. There's mold growing in the grout on your countertop."

I checked the time. 1713hrs. I had fifteen minutes to ready myself for the birthday party.

Ignoring Alina's complaints, I collected my outfit for the night—shirt and towel included, as I didn't care to repeat last night's situation with a teenage girl. I moseyed to the bathroom. "Make yourself at home, I guess."

"Impossible, unless I lived in a porta-potty at a concert."

"Well, do what makes you comfortable, then." I licked my teeth. "I'm heading out tonight, but I should be back before ten. Will you still be here?"

"Can I be here?"

I nodded. "You can sleep in my bed. I'll take the floor."

"August."

"Yeah?"

"Thank you."

I showered and dressed, tidying my hair and brushing my teeth before stepping out of the humid bathroom.

Alina stood before the kitchen sink, the faucet running and steaming as she put some elbow grease into scrubbing the accumulation of dirtied dishes.

"That's unnecessary," I said.

Alina turned off the faucet and dried her hands, looking back to me. "You're a good man. Do you know that?"

"I'm not."

"Can I say something silly?"

"Sure, but make it quick. I'm suddenly running late."

"A person's external world—their appearance and home and car and office—directly mirrors their internal world, or their thoughts and feelings. I don't know what pain makes you feel so... messy." Alina shifted her eyes to scan my apartment. "I don't know why you think you're not worth cleaning up, and I don't need to know either. But you're a good person and you have a good heart, and you can do a lot of good for the world. Before you can help others, though—like truly help others—you have to help yourself." She smiled. "Cleaning up your apartment might be a good place to help yourself. I mean, think of Randall and his home and his appearance and his inability to help himself. Do you want to end up like Randall?"

"Alina," I said, flirting with the thought of insulting her brief lecture by pointing out that the young lacked experience, thus they lacked knowledge, thus they lacked any credibility to deliver advice to anyone. But I bit my tongue, remembering why she stood in my apartment. The girl had experienced a lot in her young life.

"What?" she asked after I remained quiet for a few seconds.

"There's a laundry room downstairs. It takes quarters. You'll find some in that jar." I pointed to a mason jar filled with change atop the refrigerator. "You'll want to wash my sheets before sleeping in the bed." I turned and walked toward the door, opening it but pausing in the doorframe.

I wanted to say something encouraging or kind, something that validated her words and hinted that I not only heard her, but that what she said held weight. My love language wasn't words of affirmation, though, and coming up with the right words had always eluded me.

So, instead of sharing any parting positives, I grabbed the door, shutting it as I left her alone in my apartment.

In the hallway, I fished my cellphone from my pocket and scrolled to Maya's number. My thumb hovered over her name as I debated whether I should call her and inform her of this latest development. As I stared at the phone, going back and forth with my decision, Fred's name flashed across the screen.

"Hello," I answered.

"Just calling to remind you not to forget about Bam's birthday party. Starts in twenty minutes."

I sighed, rolling my eyes and continuing down the hallway. "I said you're not invited."

"Bam specifically invited me. Kim said so."

"Not Kim. You can't call my mom Kim."

"What do you want me to call her? Mrs. Watson? That's too weird."

"All of this is too weird."

"I'll see you there?" Fred asked.

"No."

"I'm already on the way over. Daphne is with me."

"Hi, August," Daphne said. "We love your family, and we're so honored to celebrate Bam's birthday."

"Also," Fred said, "there's a surprise waiting for you there."

"I hate surprises, and I've had enough surprises for one day."

"You'll like this one. See you there." Fred ended the call.

Birthday Party Surprises. Friday, April 22nd. 1808hrs.

My parents had found incredible success through their lives and careers, which further emphasized my disappointing status—no wife, no children, no income, no house that I owned. To avoid their constant questioning and glowering, I visited as little as possible.

An electronic gate opened up to their quarter-mile long driveway hugged by a canopy of trees from either side. Beyond the trees, a mature walnut orchard operated as a tax shelter, producing little income but providing a lot of expenses. I pulled into a gravel parking lot fifty yards from their manor. A two-acre yard surrounded their five-thousand square-foot home. What the two of them did with so much space always baffled me. They didn't have any grandchildren to busy the space, and their three children had all left home.

I strolled across the stamped cement, around the side yard, and into the backyard, where everyone congregated. When I say everyone, I mean my entire extended family. We seldom spoke, but for a family event to celebrate Bam or Poppa, everyone dropped everything to make an appearance.

My mom had four sisters and a brother, and they all had at least three children, who were mostly all married and with children. So, an event like Bam's eightieth birthday party drew close to a hundred people whom I barely knew or didn't know, and I really had no intentions of making small talk with. Still, there I was, entering the backyard party with a tight grin that pulled on the edges of my face.

My sister, Rachel, saw me first. She ran to me, nearly bulldozing me to the ground with her excitement. We hadn't spoken in over six months, and I hadn't seen her for over a year.

"Gussy," she said, pulling away from the hug and punching my arm.

"Thanks to you, I owe Jake money." Jake was her husband of almost six years.

"It's good to see you," I said, rubbing my arm. "Why do you owe him money?"

"He said you would show up, and I said no way. We bet ten dollars. Since you showed up, fork over the cash so I can pay my stupid husband his golf money. That's what he said he was using his winnings for. Whenever we bet and he wins, he stuffs the money in a mason jar until he has enough to buy a round on me. It's the worst feeling in the world, knowing I support that degenerate's golfing addiction. He's not even good at it."

"You really didn't think I would show up today?" I asked. "You have such little faith in me."

"Do I? Do I really have such little faith in you, big brother? Where were you at Christmas or Thanksgiving this past year? Or where were you on Poppa's eightieth birthday last year?"

Rachel was short. I peered over her head and saw Fred and Daphne standing with my mom and dad, all of them laughing and carrying on. Fred hadn't reminded me last year of my grandpa's eightieth birthday. That's why I hadn't attended the party—I had forgotten, not caring enough to remind myself.

"What's up with that?" I asked, nodding at the happy foursome behind my sister.

Rachel turned and chuckled. "Jealous much?"

"Mostly weirded out by the entire thing. Why do they hang out? Mom and dad are twenty-five years older than Fred and Daphne. I can't imagine they have much in common."

"Really?"

"What?"

"You've always been dumb, Gussy, but never stupid."

"They have me in common with each other."

"All of us. You're so cut off from everyone, though, that our only chance at catching a whiff of you is through them. Besides, they're a fun couple—at least until Fred eats everything in the house. I swear, I've never spent so much money on food in my life than when I started hanging out with them."

"I feel your pain."

"Speaking of spending money on food, though." Rachel splashed a grin across her face.

"What?" I asked.

"Well, let's just say that I'm going to have an additional mouth to feed in about six months."

My eyes widened, and I couldn't help but laugh. I grabbed my sister, hugging her again. "What? You're serious? I'm going to be an uncle?"

"You are!"

"I'm so excited! Congratulations!" I pulled away from the hug. "Do you mind if I ask... did it happen naturally?"

Rachel and Jake had tried to conceive since their wedding night. After months of negative test results, they had scheduled a fertility appointment. The tests showed Jake had slow swimmers—slow enough to plummet their chances of natural conceptions to a fraction.

Rachel nodded, her head moving up and down in an exaggerated, excited motion. "Yup! A freaking miracle, too. I had an in-vitro appointment scheduled the day after I found out. I canceled that faster than you'll get your awkward booty out of this party."

"I'm so happy for you."

"That makes you an uncle, though."

"I know."

"Do you? An uncle doesn't come in name only. You're going to have to visit us. You'll have to make time and a little effort to see your niece or nephew. There's no such thing as constantly making excuses and bailing on us."

"I won't," I said.

"You better not. Otherwise, we're trading you for Fred. Do you want Fred to be your niece or nephew's uncle?"

"I'll be around more." I scanned the partygoers, searching for Jake amongst the crowd. "Where's your husband? I want to congratulate him."

"He's around here somewhere. Go find Bam, though. I'm curious who will surprise her more... you or Adam."

"Adam?"

Rachel covered her mouth. "Oops. I'm so bad at keeping secrets."

"Is he in town?"

Adam was our little brother. He attended a university in San Diego and only visited on calendar holidays—not that it mattered when or how often he came up to Sacramento. I hadn't seen him since he graduated high school two years ago.

"I ruined the surprise," Rachel said. "But yeah, he's coming. Apparently, his professors allowed him to take his finals early so he could make Bam's eightieth. Pretty cool, huh?"

"Where is he?"

"Well, not here yet, but soon. That's where Jake went, actually. To pick Adam up from the airport." Rachel sniffed the air, snuffly. Her allergies had always hit her hard in the spring. "You doing okay?" she asked after a second of silence.

"Yeah, I'm alright."

"You would tell me otherwise?"

"I would."

"I hope so. I'm not Mom. I won't pry and interfere in your personal life, but don't think that means I don't care. If you need me, I'm waiting here for you, ready to help in any way possible."

"I know."

Rachel smirked. "Go find Bam."

"Have you told her yet, about…" I nodded at my sister's stomach.

"Say nothing to no one, not even mom and dad. I only told you because, well, who knows when I'll see you again after tonight? And that's if I see you again tonight, considering your record of sneaking away without a goodbye."

"It's a skill."

"It's annoying."

I patted her arm and slipped past her, steering myself through the backyard and trying to remain invisible to my cousins, aunts, and uncles—head down and not making eye contact with anyone. If I didn't see them, they wouldn't see me. Of course, my infallible logic crumbled like a frail house of sticks standing on a sandy beach in the middle of a hurricane.

"Rusty!"

My old nickname, in respects to my rusted hair color. Clever, I know. I lifted my chin toward Uncle Bobby's unmistakable, drunkenly jovial greeting. He stood a head taller than anyone else and was a shoulder broader. Kingly living—good food and too much drink—had swollen his stomach and neck and reddened his face. He stumbled toward me, holding a beer can in each hand.

"Shoot any more vermin recently?" he asked, wrapping his meaty arm around my body and pulling me in for a tight embrace. He stank of booze and body odor.

I didn't respond. I couldn't have responded if I had wanted to. What did I say to something like that? I cracked my knuckles.

"Seriously, though. How the hell have you been doing? I hear you're a ghost hunter now. How's that going?"

"Fine," I said.

"Pay good?"

"Good enough."

"You ever find one?"

"A ghost? No."

"They exist, though... you think?"

"Doubtful." I didn't care to expand on my desire to find proof of the paranormal. Even sober, Uncle Bobby couldn't grasp the complexity of why I needed to know something more than this material world existed. "Have you seen Bam anywhere?"

Bobby swiveled his head, glancing back and forth across the yard. "Over there, with the black people." He said the last as if he had bitten into something rotten.

I cringed, physically offended by his insensitivity. He meant Fred and Daphne, of course. Without bothering to excuse myself from his company, I pushed forward, heading toward my assistant, his wife, and my grandmother.

Fred noticed me first, waving his hand above his head. When I came within a few feet, the big man lunged forward and lifted me up in a massive bear hug. My feet dangled off the ground like a kid, and he squeezed my breath from my lungs.

"I'm so happy you made it. I honestly didn't think you would show." He dropped me to the ground and touched Bam's arm, gently guiding her around to face me. "Carol," he said, "this is my boss, the man I was gushing to you about. August Watson."

My grandmother sweetly smiled, reaching out her liver-spotted hand and grabbing mine. "I've heard so much about you, August."

"It's all lies. Whatever he's told you, it's all lies."

I leaned in and kissed her cheek. Bam had aged since I had last seen her. Her dark-gray hair had lightened, her wrinkles had deepened, and she leaned against a cane as she stood.

"Are you okay?" she asked, whispering as we embraced. "Truly, are you doing okay?"

"I'm hanging in there."

Bam pulled away, looking up at me. She stood all of five feet. "That's why I keep Fred around. Unlike you, he keeps in touch." That stung coming from her, more than it would have from anyone else. "Also, he doesn't hold the truth from me. I hear you're hunting Bigfoot."

"Apparently, Fred embellishes his truth," I said. "We're investigating a Bigfoot sighting. It's more sad than scary, really, and there's never any actual danger."

"What about the murderer?" Bam asked.

I glared at Fred, who failed miserably at making himself small. "There's no murderer. I'm looking into a few accidental deaths, connected by mysterious circumstances. There's not a murderer running around, threatening to kill me or any of my family." I faced Daphne—a strikingly beautiful and tall woman, though short beside Fred. "Hi."

"Hi, yourself." She closed the short distance between us and threw her arms around me. "Why do I see your family more than you?"

"That's not a bad thing, is it? They're much nicer, more sociable, and they drink."

"But you're August Watson, the lovable recluse." Daphne smiled at me, melting me from the inside out. She possessed an undeniable charm and warmth. How Fred had tricked such an incredible woman into marrying him was beyond my measly comprehension. "I hear you're replacing my husband with a teenage girl."

"What's the difference between the two?"

Daphne bit the tip of her tongue and smiled, looking up at Fred with pure admiration. "You are a big sissy sometimes, aren't you?"

"I'm cautious," Fred said.

"He's terrified of horror movies," Daphne said.

"I don't like the jump-scares. I can never predict them."

"You should have seen him yesterday in the forest. Did he tell you about that?" I asked. "He saved us from a bear attack."

"A bear attack!" Bam gasped. "You said your job presented no danger." She frowned, glancing at Fred. "Though I guess with him at your side, a bear would probably think twice before attacking."

"Gussy!" shouted a voice from behind me.

My mom hurried toward me. She wasn't much taller than her mother, but she moved with the determination of a lioness stalking her prey. Her slight body smashed into me with a massive hug. When she pushed away, she frowned. "Have you been eating? You feel skinny."

"Fred eats everything, and he refuses to share," I said.

"I'm a growing boy," Fred said.

"Gussy, you're taking care of yourself, right? You're eating and sleeping and exercising?"

"I'm doing most of those things."

My mom sighed. My dad, who enjoyed life at a more leisurely pace, caught up to my mom and stood beside her, extending his hand. I shook it, and we exchanged our greeting in silence. Men of few words.

Beside him stood my twenty-year-old brother, Adam. He had grown three inches since I last saw him and was nearly as tall as me, at a little over six feet.

"Hey," he said, his voice deep and reserved.

I stepped forward and hugged him. He wasn't the skinny, pimply kid from high school anymore, but a full-grown man. His arms dangled at his sides, not hugging me in return.

"How's it going?" I asked, stepping back.

Adam glanced beyond me, and his face broke into a wide grin. "Bam! Happy birthday," he said, moving around me to our grandma. They fell into conversation.

My mom grabbed my shoulder. "I'm so excited you're here." She was oblivious to what had happened, or choosing to pretend it hadn't happened. I would have to guess the latter. "Both you and your brother." She turned to Fred and Daphne. "All four of you. My heart is so full. And, the best part, I get to see you all at church on Sunday, too."

The birthday party continued in relative normalcy for a Menard family function—my mother's maiden name. A few of my aunts and cousins approached me, but only to ask how I have been, not where I have been. That was nice, as I didn't much care to explain myself to anyone, let alone them.

We ate a catered dinner. I sat between Jake and Fred, whose wives sat beside them. My mom and dad sat across from us. Adam found an empty chair next to our cousins on the opposite side of the yard, far away from us. Or more accurately, far away from me. The family sang happy birthday and divvied out slices of cake and opened a few presents, though Bam seemed to care the least for presents.

Fred and Daphne dipped out around 2030hrs. Their departure popped the dismissal bubble. Shortly after, everyone else said their goodbyes, trickling back to their respective homes. Only my immediate family remained.

I debated staying a little longer and forcing my brother into a conversation. In all honesty, though, neither of us would have wanted that, though we may have needed it.

Instead, I found my sister doing dishes with Jake. I grabbed a dish towel, drying the dishes she had already washed. Jake put them back in the cupboards and drawers.

"He hates me now?" I asked.

"No," Rachel said. "He's mad at you. I mean, we're all mad at you. You never call us. You don't text. You never show up to anything. Adam was home... how long ago, Jake?"

"Four or five months ago."

"Where were you?" Rachel asked. "You didn't even have the excuse of your new business yet. You just... weren't around. You didn't show up."

I nodded, ashamed.

"Growing up," Rachel said, "you were my hero. Keep this in perspective, too, we were close in age and of the opposite sex. I should have viewed you as a role model, not a hero. Gussy, you were intelligent and funny, athletic and caring. Everyone loved you. So, for you to be my brother made me so proud. Now, frame that example for Adam. You're twelve years older and of the same sex. He can see himself in you. To Adam, you weren't his hero, but his idol. He wanted to be you. And you... you didn't even notice him."

I slowed my drying and swallowed.

"Now that he's older and able to comprehend or recognize your absence, he's angry. He's mad he wasted so much time walking in your footsteps, because he thinks they led him nowhere."

I cleared my throat. "I guess you're staying busy with work."

Jake barked sharp laughter. "That's nothing," he said. "Don't get her going on parental problems."

Rachel frowned. She had worked as a family therapist, which made too much sense considering the family she came from.

"August asked, so I answered," Rachel said. "What's wrong with that? I refuse to sugarcoat my opinions so he feels better about himself. However, speaking of therapy, are you still seeing a therapist for… you know?"

Shooting and killing another human is how she meant to finish that sentence, but I guess everyone—even the most abrasive of us—sugarcoats a little.

"No."

"No? Why?"

"It's been five years. She helped me sober up and get on my feet and find a career I'm happy with."

"You, August Allan Watson… you're happy?" Rachel laughed, mocking me.

"Isn't that unprofessional?"

"I'm your sister. There's nothing professional going on here. You are the least optimistic person I've ever met. You know why?"

"Do I want to know?"

"Because you feel guilty about being happy. You don't think you deserve happiness."

"Do I?" I asked.

"We all do."

I thought of Aaron Brooks' parents. They deserved happiness. They deserved to have their son. Why should I live and feel joy when I had taken everything joyful from them?

"Anyway," Rachel said, "you should make more of an effort, at least with Adam." She bit her lip, as if debating whether to speak her thoughts.

"Say it," I said.

"Say what?"

"I thought you wouldn't sugarcoat things with me."

"You won't like it," Rachel said, setting the last pan before me and turning off the faucet.

"I can handle it."

Rachel sighed. "You feel guilty around your family because you think you destroyed another family."

"Think? I did. I know I did."

Rachel squeezed the sponge and wiped off the counter. "I mean, maybe I'm wrong, but—"

"She's always right," Jake said.

"But," Rachel said, "I'm usually right."

I snickered. "When did you become so smart? I remember you being a grumpy, mean, slightly stupid little girl."

"And I remember you being a happy-go-lucky, goofy, confident little boy. We all change, though. It's part of life."

I finished drying the dishes and leaned over the counter, staring across the kitchen into the living room. "Do you attend church with Mom?"

"God no. If I wanted to surround myself with rich, old white people, I would golf more, not go to mom and dad's church. Jake and I attend a church, though, but one aligned for the modern world. You know, one of those Satan-influenced churches where the preacher instructs the congregation how to love everyone, no matter their skin color or sexual orientation."

"You're going to Hell," I said.

"Don't I know it?"

The conversation sputtered again, which signaled to me my time there had run its course. I stood straight and cleared my throat. "Well, I should go. I have," I thought of Alina alone at my apartment, "something I need to address back at my place."

"A girl?"

"No," I said much too fast. My face flushed with heat.

"You have a girl waiting for you at your apartment?" Rachel asked. "Why didn't you bring her here? Never mind that question. I still feel uncomfortable having Jake come to these things, and we've been married for almost six years."

"It's complicated," I said.

"Well, tell Mom and Dad goodbye. Maybe sneak in a goodbye with Adam, too. He might say nothing back, but you acknowledging him will mean something."

"You're going to make an incredible mother," I said, hugging my sister.

After congratulating Jake one more time, I wandered through my parents' house, searching for them and my brother. I found all three of them in his room.

They had left the door cracked open an inch, enough for sound to slip through. I paused, not wanting to interrupt a serious conversation but overhearing their words.

"What were you thinking?" my mom asked, nearly hissing in a whisper. "Do you know what this will cost us?"

"I'll get a job," Adam said. "Pay for it myself."

"And what, go to community college? No. Not happening. You'll write a letter to the university, apologizing for what you did and begging them for a second chance."

"That's a waste of time."

"I don't care. You're going to give it a shot."

"I thought you were a lot smarter than this," my dad said.

"Are you a drug addict now?" my mom asked, unable to keep her tongue still for longer than a handful of seconds. "Do we need to put you in rehab before we try college again?"

"No, I'm not a drug addict. It was marijuana. That's it. Marijuana. It's legal."

"Drugs!" My mom gasped. "They are drugs!"

I silently backed away a few feet, then stomped toward the door, making as much noise as possible to announce my presence. I knocked, pushing the cracked door open and stepping into Adam's room.

"Hey. What's everyone doing in here? Avoiding me?" I faked a light chuckle and grinned.

My mom sighed. My dad scratched his opposite arm. My brother rolled his eyes and stared at the ceiling.

"I'm leaving," I said. "I need to head back home. I have to work late tonight and early tomorrow. You know how it goes."

"See you in a few years," Adam said.

"You'll see him Sunday morning," my mom said. "You're all going to church together. You all need it."

I swiped my tongue across the back of my teeth. "The party was fun. Thanks for hosting. I'll see you all on Sunday."

My parents returned to berating Adam, too distracted with him to send me off properly, which was fine with me. I didn't need the pounds of food my mom would most likely force upon me, or the hundreds of goodbyes and dozens of kisses. Sneaking away with no accosting worked fine for me.

I slipped back into the long hallway, avoiding the kitchen and living room where Rachel and Jake lounged on a couch and stared at their phones, and I snuck out through the garage. Once in my car, I exhaled for the first time since arriving at their house.

One More Surprise. Friday, April 22nd. 2159hrs.

I keyed my apartment door open and stepped inside, freezing in place. My jaw dropped nearly to the immaculate, spotless-clean floor. Alina had scrubbed the entire kitchen so that it sparkled.

I toed off my shoes, a habit which I had never practiced but felt obligated to perform, leaving them by the door, and I crossed through to my bed.

Alina lay on it, staring at her phone. "I didn't get into the carpeted area, though I carved out some extremely necessary time to wash your sheets. But the kitchen and the bathroom received a much-needed facelift. By the way, your bathroom had a swamp monster living in it. That's how disgusting it was. How you haven't died yet from mold poisoning is beyond me."

I stood at the foot of the bed, nearly speechless. "Thank you."

"How do you not have a TV in here?"

"I don't watch TV." I sat on the edge of the bed and stared across the room. "I watched the first *Godfather* and found it so boring that I gave my television away for free."

Alina dropped her phone into her lap and stared at me with utter confusion and disgust. Maybe a little hate. "Tell me you're joking."

"I'm joking," I said, grinning. "I haven't seen *The Godfather*, either of them."

"Either of them?"

"Yeah. I haven't watched part one or two."

"It's a trilogy."

"Oh."

"Oh? Oh? That's what you have to say? Oh? Oh my god." She looked back and forth, as if searching for something. "Do you have a computer?"

"In my bag."

"Grab your computer. We're watching *The Godfather*."

"Now?"

"Now." Alina jumped from the bed and scurried to the small dining table in the kitchen. With little effort, she dragged it beside my bed, returning to the kitchen to grab a chair and set it beside the table.

As she busied herself, I fetched my laptop and the charging cable from my bag.

"You'll sit in the chair." Alina said, typing on the computer and navigating to the movie. "Do you have popcorn or candy or anything that hasn't expired two years ago?"

"Doubtful."

"I thought you would say that. It doesn't matter. We don't need it. You ready? Sit down."

I obeyed, folding into the chair and leaning my head against the wall.

Alina pressed the spacebar, playing the movie. As the film rolled, I struggled to remember the last time I had experienced pure contentment. Sitting across from Alina in my clean apartment and listening to the opening monologue of the classic film, a subtle sense of happiness shined on me, warming me. I glanced at the girl, wanting to thank her for this moment, but I didn't want to interrupt the movie. So, I reverted my attention back to the screen and lost myself in Francis Ford Coppola's beautiful world.

The Cinnamon Challenge. Saturday, April 23rd. 0534hrs.

Peter Seed flirted with fifty-years-old, but he could have passed for sixty. The man didn't care, though. In fact, he didn't care about much—not his weight or diet, not his declining physical and mental health, and definitely not his hygiene. Peter did care, however, for young women. He cared for them so much that he only hired attractive females between the ages of seventeen and twenty to waitress at the failing diner he owned.

Though he never enforced a dress code, Peter often suggested ways in which his female waitresses could increase their tips. One such tactic included showing a lot of legs and chest—also, a little exposed belly hurt no one.

That morning, Vanessa and Presley arrived for their shifts. Vanessa had long legs, a tight, ample behind, and a flat chest, but her smile and pretty eyes helped with that. Presley, shorter and slightly heavier than Vanessa, had curves—hips and tits. The two girls wore daisy dukes in response to the warm spring morning, and button-down shirts tied at the bottom and unbuttoned at the top.

Peter greeted each of them with a morning hug and quick kiss to their cheeks, pressing their bodies tightly against his. They squirmed in his arms, but he enjoyed the fight—the revulsion they displayed. It reminded him of how his mother always treated him. Slightly revolted, but reluctantly accepting, as if no choice existed in the matter. That's exactly how he wanted them to feel, as if they didn't have a choice in anything—as if he owned them.

After his uncomfortable greeting, both women looked anywhere and everywhere but at him. They knew to wait until he had finished instructing them on the day's tasks. Peter took his time, too, looking them up and down, inspecting them with a detailed eye.

He stepped near Vanessa, leaning into her neck and smelling her. "You look pretty this morning, and you smell delightful. New perfume?"

She closed her eyes and nodded.

"What is it?"

"Brazilian Crush."

"I like that. Keep wearing it." Peter shuffled to Presley, staring directly at her chest without attempting to hide his gaze. He backed away, tilting his head and narrowing his eyes, carefully inspecting her body. "You're putting on weight," he said. "Not in a good way, either. Remember, if we see growth, we want to see it in your breasts or tushy, not in your stomach." He stepped up to Presley, reaching out and unbuttoning her shirt a notch, revealing her bra and most of her breasts. "If a customer sees your flabby stomach, they won't tip you. So, keep their eyes above it, on your tits. Also, your employee discount for food doesn't apply for the rest of the month, and you're losing your lunch break privileges. Let's eliminate the muffins from your diet, and hopefully, let's eliminate the muffin top from your waist."

The diner was currently empty, void of any customer. Peter and the two girls congregated in the kitchen. He wasted time by staring at his phone.

Vanessa and Presley prepared batter for pancakes. The industrial grade mixer powered through the large batches. Not only did they waitress, but they performed the duties of chefs, bussers, and dishwashers. Peter refused to hire more employees, preferring the two girls he had trained and mostly now controlled.

Peter exploded into laughter. "I forgot all about this," he said, hiccuping in his excitement. "Come here. Hurry."

The two girls ventured towards him, leaning in to see what he had on his phone. They saw a YouTube video of a teenage kid attempting to swallow a spoonful of cinnamon, but failing, coughing and spitting it out instead.

"We have to try this," Peter said. "Presley, I'll make you a deal. If you can complete the cinnamon challenge, I'll offer you all the free food you want for the rest of the month, and you can take as many breaks as you wish to eat as much as your fat stomach desires. If you fail… well, you get to go on a date with me." He grinned, showing his crooked, yellowed teeth.

"It's impossible to do," Presley said.

"So, you're saying you don't want to go on a date with me?"

"I'm saying it's not a real bet if we're betting on the impossible."

"Do you enjoy having this job? Do you enjoy having a job? Listen, I know many people in the restaurant industry—people who respect me and owe me favors. I'll tell you this much, if you find yourself out of work, they won't want to hire a lazy, incompetent, disobedient, fat, ugly employee." Peter flashed another smile. "So, Presley, Presley, Presley, what do you say? Try the cinnamon challenge. It'll be fun."

"I don't want to."

"It's no longer a question," Peter said. "Do it. That's an order. It's also an order that if you fail, you and I go on a date. At my house. So, Presley, I'm hoping you fail."

Presley glanced at Vanessa, who stared at the dirty floor. "If I do it, like if I succeed in the challenge, can I get an advance on my paycheck?" Presley had asked the same question before, a few times actually, but Peter had always denied her the request.

"To help pay for your mother's medical bills?"

"Yes. We're short on rent this month, and I would..." Presley trailed off.

"You would rather not whore around to earn the cash?" Peter asked, chuckling as if he found her situation amusing. "I get it. You probably couldn't find a client right now, anyway." He patted his stomach, then he placed his hand over his chest. "Out of the goodness in my heart, though, I will accept your condition. If you win, I'll write you an advance. If you lose, you go on a date with me. Deal?"

"Deal," Presley said, her voice small and quiet.

Peter slapped his meaty hands together in applause. "Deal!"

He hustled to find cinnamon and a spoon, pouring the powder onto the silverware and handing it to Presley.

Behind him, Vanessa continued to tend to the pancake mix—just in case a straggler found themselves lost and walked into the diner.

Presley closed her eyes tight and scrunched her face, readying herself for what happened next. Like taking a heaping bite of oatmeal, she shoved the spoon into her mouth. Her face contorted. She coughed from deep in her throat, spewing forth a cinnamon mist. As she forced herself to swallow the powder, she choked and dry-heaved, hacking plumes of cinnamon dust into the air. The byproduct shot into Peter's face, the minuscule grains catching his eyes.

Peter yelped, grabbing his face and stepping back, turning away from

Presley. "You stupid bi—"

The black and red checkered tie he always wore to work snagged and twisted in the running dough mixer, shortening its lead. His head pulled downward into the machine. The blades sliced at his skin, scraped against bone, fractured his skull. Blood and chunky fragments and dough splashed against the walls and across the kitchen. Peter's body went rigid and tense as he struggled against the power of the industrial-grade machine. Then it fell limp, and he sagged forward. Blood spilled over the lip of the bowl.

The entry door chimed, signaling a customer had entered the establishment.

Presley looked at Vanessa, and Vanessa stared back at Presley. They were both drenched in red-colored goopy dough. After a moment of silence, they both fell into a hysterical fit of laughter.

Sit and Wait. Saturday, April 23rd. 0803hrs.

Alina and I parked on the street before Glacia's house, arriving two hours before my scheduled meeting at 1000hrs. She fiddled with her cell phone and my car's dashboard, attempting to connect to the bluetooth so she could play her music.

I glanced at the girl. "Do you remember the plan?"

"I'm not an idiot." She hissed. "This won't connect because your car is so old. Why don't you buy a new one?"

"Repeat it," I said.

"Repeat what? That you're about ten years beyond needing a new car? Buy a new car. How's that?"

"Repeat the plan."

Alina grunted. "I hide on the property, watching for the real estate chick to arrive. Once she pulls into the driveway, I remain hidden and record everything I see." She spoke with a sarcastic tone. "It's not some master plan."

I twisted the steering wheel's grip in my hand. My neck ached from sleeping awkwardly in the chair. I hadn't slept long, though. My dreams had haunted me, replaying Aaron Brooks' fatal moment repeatedly.

To combat my chronic fatigue, I had exercised early that morning, about 0500hrs. After an hour of breaking down my body, I stopped at a cafe and picked out some pastries and coffee, delivering them to Alina.

My coffee—my lifeline, that is—rested in the cupholder, needing a refill. "Do not engage anyone for any reason," I said.

"I'm not a moron."

"Are you sure you're up for this?"

Without another word, Alina hopped out of the car, climbed the chain-link fence, and hustled onto the property. After she found a relatively inconspicuous location to hide, I called her.

"Hello," she answered.

"That's a perfect spot. I watched you hide, and I can barely see you."

"I know. I'm the world's greatest hide-and-seek player."

"Last chance," I said.

"Shut up with that nonsense. You allowed me to skip school and hang out yesterday, and you gave me a place to stay last night. I owe you this much—sitting here and waiting. What better way to experience the full investigator's job than to sit and wait?"

"Shoot me a text when Susan arrives." I ended the call, scrolling to Glacia's number and calling her as I drove away.

"Good morning, handsome," she said.

"I'll be at the house later this morning, around ten. Did Susan tell you?"

"Yup. She sure did."

"Will you be there?"

"I will. You think I would miss out on seeing you?" A quick moment of silence passed. "I'm sorry for wasting your time the other night. I swear, something was in the house the first night I stayed there, and Susan and her clients have all reported some kind of haunting. Maybe Nana's ghosts knew not to mess with you and remained quiet."

"Maybe, but not likely," I said.

"Not likely? What's that mean? Did you break the case wide open?"

"I have a strong hunch, based on a few circumstantial clues."

"Well, Sherlock, I'm excited to see you later this morning, and I can't wait for you to detail all the plot points we missed in a long, verbose monologue."

I cleared my throat, considering the idea of asking her on the double date then, but I withheld, knowing I should wait until after she paid me for the investigation.

"See you then," I said.

"Adios, amigo."

The Showing. Saturday, April 23rd. 1011hrs.

I purposefully arrived a little late to the appointment, hoping Susan could guarantee all her haunting affairs were in order, and that Alina could document evidence of the crime.

The girl hadn't sent me any videos or photographs, and that made me slightly nervous. What if Susan had noticed Alina hiding in the bushes? What if she had captured and harmed the girl? What if Alina had revealed our plan to guarantee her safety, and I now walked into a trap? I shoved the paranoid thoughts aside, chalking Alina's radio silence to recording Susan without stopping.

I parked my car off to the side of the gravel driveway, behind Susan's BMW. I cut the engine and enjoyed the morning sun for a second. At that moment, I glanced around the property for Alina, failing to find her even though I knew where she hid.

A new knot formed in my stomach—a flash of worry and dread. No matter how I convinced myself otherwise, I couldn't shake the sinking feeling.

I dialed Glacia's number. She didn't answer. I dialed again. Again, no answer.

Should I call Alina, risk her phone sounding and giving away her position, if she still hid and hadn't been located?

Squeezing my eyes shut, I weighed the pros and cons. In the end, I couldn't walk into a potential trap and blindly face whatever danger possibly awaited me. Besides, I believed Alina was intelligent enough to silence her phone during a stakeout.

As I scrolled through my recent calls, searching for Alina's contact, my phone buzzed in my hand. Glacia called me back.

I breathed a sigh of relief and answered. "Hey. I just pulled up. You here?"

"I'm inside talking with Susan. So far, no ghosts." She chuckled, though to me, she sounded more nervous than amused.

Reaching across the seat, I dug through my handy-dandy paranormal bag, grabbing my law enforcement canister of pepper spray. I still had contacts within the Galt Police Department, and they treated me well with a few off-market supplies. I also pocketed a pair of handcuffs before stepping out of my car and stretching, reaching for the sunshine.

I stole one more glance around the yard, searching for Alina and failing to locate her. Another thought crept into my mind. What if Glacia was in on everything?

"That makes zero sense," I muttered. Why would she hire me to investigate the hauntings? "Occam's Razor." The rule stating that when faced with two explanations, the simpler of the two is the one most likely to be true. Put more simply, overcomplicating matters usually proved detrimental to solving problems. Glacia hired me to investigate the haunting, meaning, simply, she had nothing to do with it.

I stepped onto the porch, gently knocked on the front door to alert those inside of my presence, and entered the house.

Glacia and Susan stood in the entryway. Glacia smiled, though she appeared nervous—fidgeting with her fingers, playing with her hair, moving back and forth on her restless feet.

Susan was physically average in every sense of the word. Her age was elusive, masked by the modifications to her face and the augmentations to her body. If I had to guess a number, I would say somewhere between mid-forties to early sixties.

A smile stretched across her frozen face. "Hello. I'm glad you could make it."

"I'm glad you could fit me in this morning. Thank you." I reached out to shake each of their hands. "The front yard is gorgeous. Immaculate."

"We have taken great measures to insure it's well taken of," Susan said. "Please, though, follow me, and I'll show you the home."

We entered the kitchen first. Glacia had disposed of any evidence proving we had stayed the night there. I circled the island, resting my palms on the countertop and staring across the room at Susan.

"I love the finishes," I said.

Susan educated me about the original construction of the home and the multiple custom remodels the house had undergone. "The Luna family, that's Maria Luna's family."

"Nana," Glacia said. "My mother's maiden name is Luna."

"Her family built and rebuilt this house with their own hands," Susan said. "They constructed it over the years to match what they saw in their dreams. They paid for everything you see with their hard work, their sweat and blood." The realtor glanced around, swiveling her head on her shoulders. She suddenly trembled, as if racked by chills. "Anyway, shall we continue forward?"

As we abandoned the kitchen, a cacophonous crash issued from a back room. Glacia yelped, covering her mouth and retreating into the kitchen. Susan froze, her physical demeanor matching the injected paralysis over her face.

"Not again," the realtor said, finding the courage to pedal her feet backwards, following Glacia into the kitchen. "Not again."

I have to give credit where credit is due. Susan could act. In a different life, she may have found a decent career in Hollywood.

I turned to her, frowning. "What was that?"

"I don't know. A spirit, perhaps. The one that haunts this house."

"Nonsense. Spirits don't exist. Neither do haunted houses."

Another distant rattling, followed by stomping footsteps and exaggerated moans, like someone trying too hard to mimic the wails of a ghost. Overacting. They should have left the perceivable performances to Susan.

"How do you explain that?" Susan asked, glancing down the hallway toward the front door. "We should leave. Now. Before someone gets hurt... or worse."

"Wait a second," I said, raising a single finger. "If a spirit really haunts this house, does that mean you can sell it to me at a bargain deal? I mean, I'm a willing and ready... I'm an eager and motivated buyer. Ghosts don't scare me either. In fact, I'm intrigued by them. So, what do you say? Shall we finish the tour?"

Susan's hand trembled as she raised it to her face and covered her mouth. With her other hand, also quivering, she pointed down the hallway beyond me.

I turned in time to see a crumpled sheet fly across the hallway, crash into the wall, and settle on the ground in a puddle of laundry. I blew a rush of air through my lips and shook my head, growing bored with the performance. I padded down the hallway, picked up the sheet, and entered the bedroom from where it had flown.

A man and a woman stood in the back room. They resembled each other, with their dark hair, long limbs, and sharp facial features. The woman was a striking image of Glacia in twenty years.

"Good morning, Mr. Luna. Mrs. Vasquez. You two must be the terrifying ghosts I've heard so much about."

"Who are you?" The man asked, anger fueling his tone, as if my presence in the house actually infuriated him.

"I'm August Watson, private investigator of all things paranormal. You, I'm guessing, are Miguel Luna. That's your sister, Janet Vasquez."

"Mom?" Glacia asked, stepping beside me. Her face was flat, though her eyes bounced around the room, as if looking for the cameras that signaled this was all one elaborate joke. "What are you doing here?"

"Glacia," I said, "meet the ghosts. I'm sure you already know your mother. I'm also quite certain you're familiar with your uncle."

"What? Why?"

"Simple," her uncle said. "You weren't her child. The property and this house didn't belong to you. It belonged to us."

"As did the fortune you would get after selling the house," Glacia's mother added.

Muriel, Janet, and Alina's mom must have all belonged to a terrible mom's club.

"Enough!" Susan shouted from the hallway. She held a small gun in her hand and pointed it at me. The firearm explained her sudden ability to overcome her fear of ghosts. "Get your back against the wall. Now!" Susan pointed the weapon at Glacia. "You, too."

I slowly crossed the room and leaned my back against the wall. "Easy,

Susan. No one needs to get hurt."

"Hands up. Place them high over your head. Sit on the ground, knees to your chest. Now!"

"We can work this out," I said, hesitating to comply. I turned to Janet. "That woman has a gun pointed at your daughter. Why won't you stop this craziness?"

"Do as Susan says," Miguel said, grabbing Janet's arm and guiding her behind him. He reached into his pocket and produced a folding knife. He pried it open and directed the blade in my direction. "Knees to your chest. Now! Hands over your head."

"Okay. Okay." I slid down the wall, sitting on the carpet. My hands settled on the top of my head, and I walked my knees into my chest.

Glacia followed my lead, staring at her mother the entire time.

"Okay," I said. "What's the plan here? You going to shoot me? Are you going to shoot her?"

Miguel glanced at Susan, desperation in his eyes. "What do we do?"

"We agreed not to kill her," Janet said, moving between the realtor and her brother. "We all agreed not to kill Glacia." Mother turned to daughter. "Baby, why don't you join us?"

Glacia openly gasped, sobbing. "Join you in what?"

"We'll sell the home and split the money four ways."

"What? That's what this is about? The money?"

"You inherited a fortune when Nana gave you this house. Unfairly, I should add. You're not one of her children. You don't deserve this. She wasn't in her right mind when she penned the will."

Glacia choked on cries of heartbreak, having nothing to say in response.

My phone buzzed in my pocket, but there was no chance I could answer it. Instead, I cleared my throat, drawing everyone's attention to me. "Janet, you became upset that Glacia, your daughter, inherited this property? So, what? You two geniuses wanted it as your own to sell and profit from. Then what? You brought Susan in, cut her a deal, and she agreed to the terms. Who was the mastermind, though? You?" I looked at the realtor. "Was it your idea to escort these two bozos along to scheduled showings, arrive early to the appointments, stow them in the attic, and stage them as ghosts to scare away the buyers?"

No one said a word. Only Glacia made a noise, snuffling and slowly exhaling to calm herself.

"Am I close to the mark?" I asked.

Miguel, Janet, and Susan all glared at me, proving my assessment and my hunch correct.

"Awesome, possum. Well, if you're willing, seeing that we have the time now, could you answer a few questions that truly baffle me. Such as, why didn't you just... I don't know, speak to your daughter about how you felt? I've only known her for a day or two, but she seems like a genuine, empathetic person, and I'm willing to bet she would have split any potential profits with you had you only asked."

Glacia nodded. "I never planned to keep all the money. I didn't even want to sell the house without your permission. But I couldn't ever get ahold of you."

"Haunting is very demanding of a person's time," I said. "I mean, you spent the night here on multiple occasions. I found a bed in the attic, food in the refrigerator. Who gets credit for that, by the way? Susan? Did she feed you?" I waved away the questions. "It doesn't matter. But my second question really perplexed me. You broke the attic window from the outside inward. Why? You arrived early, before any clients showed. Why not climb through the hatch?"

"You have no leverage to questions us," Susan said, emphasizing her point by centering the gun at my chest.

"My knee," Miguel said at the same time as Susan spoke. "And shoulder. I couldn't get through the hatch door without a ladder. We discovered, though, that we could climb the steel lattice easily. It also made it simpler to sneak in and out and get to different locations around the property without having to be inside the house."

"So, you figured you'd haunt the house and scare potential buyers away until Glacia became annoyed at managing the property from a state away. You thought she would sell it to you for cheap, and you would reap the full rewards? That the gist?"

"Enough!" Susan demanded.

"Do you really plan on shooting us?" I asked. "Is that your end game? Shoot me to shut me up on your little arrangement? Then what? Will you bury me in the garden? Susan, people know I'm here, meeting with you to buy this house. I set up this meeting, in case you didn't know, because I had you pegged. I knew your scheme. You think I have told no one what you planned?" I had told no one. Oops. "What will you do when the police ask questions? Not only about my missing body, but your ridiculous operation to steal the house and profit off of Glacia. Speaking of Glacia, what will you do with her? Shoot and kill her like you will with me? Bury her in the garden? You think her mom will allow that?"

"We agreed to not kill my daughter," Janet said.

"Over a million dollars split three ways!" Susan said, glancing at Janet. "That's what we'll get for this."

Janet, surprisingly, or maybe unsurprisingly given the circumstances, said nothing, as if Susan's financial argument penciled out to equal the life of her daughter.

Miguel butted into the conversation with a much more convincing nail-in-the-coffin argument. "Janet, we can't allow either of them to leave. They know everything. If they walk from here, they'll report us. I'll die before I go back to jail, I swear. I'll do next to anything not to go back to jail. I'm leaving here with a worry-free mind, with or without you. Without you, Susan and I split the money fifty-fifty, and that sounds nice, too."

"Wow," I said. "Not only is murdering a stranger and a niece-slash-daughter on the table, but now we're murdering a sister. I thought I had complicated family dynamics."

"Enough from you!" Miguel shouted. "If you say another word, I'll carve off your face. Don't think I won't either."

I saw frenetic bloodlust in the man's eyes—desperation to achieve a goal at any wild cost. I believed he would cut off my face if given the chance. Too bad he wouldn't have the chance.

"Susan, behind you," I said.

Stalking through the bedroom door from the hallway, Alina appeared, holding a wooden stake used to support young trees with underdeveloped roots. She cocked it over her shoulder and hammered downward, slamming the stake into Susan's shoulder and neck area.

Susan gasped, staggering away from Alina and into Miguel and dropping the gun.

I didn't waste a second, leaping to my feet and prying the pepper spray from my pocket, holding the familiar canister in the correct direction and not hesitating to deploy the chemical agent.

Pepper spray is an incredible tool to subdue violent and dangerous offenders in a nonlethal manner. However, it is incredibly painful, especially when the spray cuts directly across the target's eye line.

A direct shot sprayed into Miguel's face, and he dropped, wailing and rubbing at his eyes. Snot and drool poured from his features as he crawled and rolled around the room. After only a second or two, he paused, turned his head, and vomited onto Susan, who hadn't evaded the effects of the pepper spray and suffered the burning pain herself. Though she experienced indirect exposure, the realtor still rubbed at her face as it leaked and burned.

Unfortunately, no one in the room was immune to the effects. Janet, who stood near Susan and Miguel, also received searing discomfort. She sprinted out of the bedroom and into the hallway. The chemical agent spread throughout the room, catching Glacia, Alina, and myself in its mist, though not to such dramatic effect.

I experienced a slight leakage of my sinuses and a subtle burn, like spending too much time in the sun without proper protection.

Glacia stood and stumbled from the room, chasing after her mother.

Alina, who seemed less affected by the spray than anyone else, dashed forward and picked up the fallen gun.

I darted forward, toward Miguel and Susan.

While in the police academy, we had completed an assignment where our commanding officer sprayed us with pepper spray. As we suffered from a direct hit on the brow line, he instructed us to perform a series of tasks, which included handcuffing an unwilling subject. If we ever deployed the pepper spray on the job, we would suffer milder, but similar pain as the target we had sprayed. If we could handcuff someone after a direct shot, we could arrest someone after minimal exposure.

So, I knew I could power through the pain and discomfort to employ the handcuffs to Miguel and Susan.

In a fluid motion, I snapped one side around Miguel's wrist. I grabbed Susan's hand, bringing it toward me, and snapped the other cuff around her wrist. They were now shackled together, slathered in each other's drool, snot, and vomit, crying and begging for me to relieve them of the pain.

"Don't take a shower tonight," I said, blinking my eyes to combat the pain. "That's my word of helpful advice. The water reactivates the burn. I don't actually know how it works, but when they sprayed me, it hurt more during my shower that night. So, don't shower."

Glacia returned to the bedroom. She had her mother with her, and they argued. What they had to argue about in a situation like this was beyond me.

I peeked over my shoulder to greet them. Alina stood in the center of us all, holding the gun. She had it pointed downward, at the floor.

Glacia and her mother stopped arguing and fell silent when they noticed what I saw.

Alina must have recognized the shift in the room. She looked at me, a wry smile splashed across her face. "I don't want it, but I didn't think they should pick it up either." The girl extended the weapon, handing it to me. "Take it."

The room, the property, the world crashed around me. I hadn't held a gun since I last fired one into another human. What would happen if I accepted the weapon from her? I knew it wouldn't transform me into a murdering machine, but I didn't know how I would handle touching the steel. Considering the idea of accepting the weapon stunned me. If I grabbed it, would I faint? Would I drop it? Would I snap into an uncontrollable, emotional wreck?

I swallowed and breathed. "Give it to Glacia. I have to deal with them." I turned away from Alina.

A second later, Glacia forced her mother beside her uncle and realtor. She now held the gun, though she aimed it at the floor and not at any of our prisoners. All three conspirators now sat in a line, awaiting our judgment.

Judgement. Saturday, April 23rd. 1017hrs.

We all gathered around like participants in a game of cops and robbers. The cops, of course, the good guys and victors—Glacia, Alina and me. In front of us, handcuffed, gagging on whatever concentrated ingredient made up pepper spray, crying from the chemical compound, pathetically I might add, sat the robbers—Susan, Miguel, and Janet.

"What do we do now?" Glacia asked. She appeared older, more fractured. Where before she had hidden whatever scars her past had placed upon her, she now carried the heavy pain with obvious effort.

"What would you like to do?" I asked.

I was a private paranormal investigator with no authority, beyond a citizen's arrest, to detain anyone. Also, I wasn't a lawyer or anywhere close to knowing the laws broken during this offense. If we called the cops, what would we charge these three desperate individuals with? Trespassing? Susan would surely have her real estate license revoked. Beyond that, what consequences would the three stooges face?

"What can we do?" Glacia asked.

I shook my head. "Call the cops and have them handle it from here."

"Will they get arrested?"

"Honestly, I don't know. They might get arrested for a few hours, but I don't think any judge will hold them, especially if we don't press charges. Not only did they trespass on your property, but they vandalized it. More incriminating, Susan had a gun. I'm sure she's smart enough to have a concealed weapon permit, so she's not carrying it illegally, but they all discussed the idea of murdering us. I'm not sure if discussion is a crime or not, but I think they could face fines, possibly community service, at the least."

Glacia glared at her mother. "What if we let them go?"

"All of them?"

She thought about it for a few seconds and nodded. "All of them."

"It's your house. You're paying me to investigate a haunting. You can do as you please with what we discovered. There's evidence supporting the trespassing." I nodded at Alina. "She recorded everything that happened." I glanced at the girl. "Right?"

"Of course," Alina said.

"If you wanted to press charges," I said to Glacia, "you have all the ammunition available. If not, I will see that Susan never sells another house to anyone ever again, but that's as far as I'll go."

"They're junkies," Glacia said, nearly spitting the word from her lips. "That's all they are. Junkies."

"That's not true," Janet said, crying—though I'm sure the tears sprouted because of the pepper spray rather than regret for her actions as a terrible mother. "I quit, remember?"

Glacia struggled to keep her face held together. "Why did you go behind my back, then?"

"You would've assumed I wanted the money for drugs. You would've said no."

"Can you blame her?" Alina asked, fire in her voice. This situation played close to home for the young woman. Anger clouded her face, clenched her hands into tight fists.

"You don't know what I would have assumed," Glacia said.

"No?" Janet asked. "You're always throwing my addiction in my face, refusing to loan me any money at all, refusing to help me. You think that just because you found a semblance of success, you're better than the rest of this family? You're not. You're my daughter. I know who you are and where you came from, and you won't ever run far enough away to hide from that. You're a junkie and a whore."

"I'm not your daughter! Nana raised me. Nana was my mother. Never you. Never!" Glacia fled from the room, leaving Alina and me in charge of the prisoners.

I turned to Alina. "What do you think?"

"What is Glacia paying you for?"

"She asked me to figure out what's haunting the house and, I don't know, exorcise it of any spirits."

"Well, these idiots are obviously the spirits. So exorcise them?"

"That's what I'm thinking... but Glacia doesn't want that."

Alina scratched her forehead, holding her tongue for a couple of seconds. "My mom, when she disappears, she relapses into hard drugs." The girl sighed, staring directly at Janet. "She always says that she quit, that the last time was the last time. But she's a liar. When she has a little extra money at the end of the month, she always celebrates her fortune the same way. Occasionally, during an especially hard time, like now, she'll return to drugs with no money at all. She'll do anything to earn a high. She'll be gone for days or weeks on end. She has no contact with me. No assurances that she's alive and well." Alina licked her lips, glaring at Glacia's mother. "Do you know what the craziest thing of all is?"

Janet shook her head slowly back and forth.

"No matter what she does, no matter how long she abandons me for, no matter what... I forgive her. Do you know why?"

"Why?" Janet asked.

"Because she's my mom. I love her more than anything. Because I believe, no matter how many times she has lied to me and let me down... I believe she will change. So, I allow her to continually, repeatedly, hurt me. To disappoint me. I forgive her because she's my mother. Do you understand what I'm saying?"

There was no question why Janet shed tears then. She dropped her head into the crook of her arm, and her shoulders trembled as she cried.

"What would you do, then?" I asked Alina. "What would you do with these three?"

Alina stared at our detainees. "There's not a right answer."

"There never is," I said. "Just the best answer."

"If I had this opportunity—my mom at my feet, waiting for me to decide her fate—I would..." Alina trailed off, her face twisting and contorting as she fought against tears of her own. She stepped forward and kneeled beside Janet, reaching out a hand and touching the woman's chin, lifting her face. "Do you know what kind of pain your selfishness creates?" Alina asked.

"No," Janet said.

"Glacia just wants a mom to love and to love her back. That's the hardest part. Glacia knows you don't care about her, that you only care for yourself. She wants to hate you so badly. She wants to see you suffer and feel what you have put her through. But then, when that opportunity arrives, and it all comes down to making the dreamed-of decision—when she has this opportunity, she just wants to hug you and tell you she still loves you. That you're her hero and her mom and she's going to get you the help you need." Alina looked over her shoulder at me, tears streaking down her face. "That's what I would do. If she were my mom, I would want to get her help."

I nodded. "The other two?"

"I called the police," Glacia said from behind me. She glided forward, brushing past me and approaching her mother.

Alina scooted away and stood.

Glacia kneeled before her mother. "Alina is still young. She still has faith in her mother, but only because her mother hasn't had the extra fifteen years that you had to shatter any faith I once had in you."

Janet coughed a wet sob. "Please, baby. Please."

"The girl was right. Mom, I only wanted to forgive and love you, always, no matter what you did. Not anymore, though. You not only disrespected me by conducting this utter, complete Scooby-Doo nonsense, but you disrespected Nana and her legacy. I will press any and every charge my lawyer can come up with. I will see that you, Miguel, and Susan receive the maximum punishment for this crime. Maybe you will finally learn. Maybe you will find the help you need." Glacia stood and backed away, settling beside me. "Either way, I notified the police."

What Next? Saturday, April 23rd. 1148hrs.

A little over an hour later, the police arrived, noted our statements, legally arrested the perpetrators, and drove them to jail, where they would await sentencing.

Glacia, Alina, and I stood around the island in the kitchen, staring at our planted palms on the countertop. I'm not sure how much time slipped away, but it moved unknowingly as we lost ourselves in thought.

Then, with a jolt of remembrance, I fished out my phone. It had rung during the earlier events, and I had ignored the call. Checking my notifications, I saw it had rung more than the one time I noticed it. I must have missed the vibrations in the commotion.

Maya had called four times, texted about twenty.

James Connors, the Bigfoot nut, had called once and left a voicemail.

Fred had also called, though he failed to leave a voicemail or a text message.

My last missed call and voicemail came from an unrecognized number with a Sacramento area code—maybe a potential client?

Looking at Alina and Glacia, I asked, "Could you two excuse me for a few minutes? I have to step outside and return some calls."

"Careful of ghosts around here," Alina said.

"Too soon," I said.

The sound of laughter chased me from the house. I stepped off the front patio and onto the gravel, pacing back and forth and despising the late-morning sunshine. The warmth triggered the residual pepper spray lingering on my skin, and it burned twice as much as before. At least it had mostly drained from my sinuses.

My first callback belonged to Fred. The big man treated his weekends like holy days, always turning off his cell phone and putting it away to spend unadulterated time with Daphne. I had never asked him what exactly that meant.

"How did the showing go?" Fred answered.

"I can't believe you're worried about work on a weekend. Who are you?"

"Hey, I'm worried about you, little man. You doing okay?"

"We caught ourselves three ghosts and sent them off to prison. Glacia's mom, uncle, and realtor. Apparently, in their thick skulls, they believed that if they created a haunted house, no right-minded client would purchase it. Glacia would have to sell the property to them, if not handing it over willingly to absolve herself of the headache."

"Not a bad idea," Fred said.

"Nope, not bad at all. It was a terrible idea. They thought nothing through, hoping more than planning it would all work out."

"You know what they say about hoping, right?"

"Was that why you called?" I asked. "To ask about the job?"

"I called about your brother."

I closed my eyes, steeling myself for what came next—Fred had heard, probably not through eavesdropping either, that the university had expelled my brother for drugs. "What about him?"

"He's home."

"I saw him last night. Our reunion went well."

"For good."

I cracked my neck, popping the stress bubbles. "I know."

"You do?"

"Don't sound shocked. I'm his brother. His actual family. How do you know?"

"Kim called me and asked for advice."

"My mom called you for advice? She's losing her mind, isn't she?"

"Apparently, he listens to some podcast, and the host always hypes up these hallucinogenic drugs. He says the drugs—LSD, DMT, mushrooms, whatever—open our minds, or they juice the brain so it uses more than the rumored ten percent. I guess time becomes irrelevant while high, and, I don't know, people have, like, world-altering experiences. They see angels and proof of life after death… and…" Fred trailed off, having pussyfooted around his point enough to circle it. If I wanted proof of the supernatural, I should experiment with psychedelic drugs.

"Is my brother okay?" I asked.

"I don't know. But you should call him and ask."

"Maybe I should."

"See you tomorrow?" Fred asked.

"Tomorrow?"

"Church. There are three services, and your parents go to the nine-thirty service. Don't be late. When I say that, get there at nine-fifteen. Your mom will want to take pictures and introduce you to a few people—

unless, of course, you want to stay after the service to do all that. If that's the case, you'll most likely get dragged into lunch."

"I'll be there early."

"My man."

We ended the conversation, leaving me to stare at my phone and decide who to contact next. Adam, Maya, James, or the unknown number. Two of those callbacks involved work cases, as Maya was surely blowing up my phone with new information regarding the voodoo doll murders and James probably had an update about Bigfoot. One potential case being the unknown number. Or I could call my brother, who's trouble with drugs expanded from marijuana into hallucinogens.

Was that my mother's worry and gift of exaggeration speaking, or had he downplayed his initial trouble?

I listened to the unknown caller's voicemail, which stated her name, how she had heard of me, and that she wished to hire me to look into a problem. So, figuring that would take the least amount of time, I called her.

"Hello," she answered after not even one full ring. Her voice sounded fragile, as if she might shatter at any moment.

"This is August Watson. I'm calling to speak with Claire Balzan."

"Yeah, that's me."

"You called me earlier and left a voicemail. I'm returning that call."

"Hi."

"How can I help you?"

A beat of silence. "Not over the phone. We can't have this conversation over the phone." She whispered, as if she feared being overheard. "Yesterday, I went to your office and waited on the sidewalk for you."

I scratched my head, not having noticed anyone waiting for me.

Before I could ask any clarifying questions, though, Claire continued. "It was in the morning. You showed up, and then you immediately left. I followed you to where you went."

"To grab—"

"Don't say it!"

I hushed myself, unsure of how to proceed. Yesterday morning, I had arrived at the office before leaving again to grab donuts. Had Claire followed me to the donut shop?

"Meet me there," she said.

"Where?"

"To the place I followed you to."

I considered my weekend plans—work at my second job in about three hours, church tomorrow morning, a double date tomorrow night. "I can't meet you until Monday morning at the earliest."

Silence for a few unnerving seconds. "Okay." Claire sputtered on the response, as if my timeline was anything but okay.

I was concerned about her wellbeing. "Are you safe?"

"I don't know."

"Can you tell me what's wrong?"

"What time Monday morning?"

"Can you make 0700hrs?"

"I hope so," she said.

We ended the call, but I felt extremely unsettled by the conversation. Should I have tried harder to meet with her? What could have possibly shaken her up so much? If she had contacted me, though, it most likely regarded the paranormal. The worst that could happen between now and Monday was an ever-growing sense of fear and dread.

Hopefully.

I crossed my fingers before dialing Maya.

"Where the bleep have you been?" She actually said the word bleep, as if she had to edit her real-life verbiage like she edited her tabloid writing.

"Working a case. What's up?"

"Did you read the text messages I sent you? Listen to my voicemails?"

"No. You left about a hundred notifications. I figured it would go quicker if I called you back."

"Why do I even waste my time leaving them, then?"

"I don't know why you do what you do. What's going on?"

"So freaking much! I'm thinking of skipping work later today to sort everything out, but I need the money. I hate money so much. The necessity of it impedes on everything good in life."

"Maya," I said, "slow down. What happened?"

"First, Gilbert Tonyan was having an affair."

"Wait. Hold on. What?"

"Gilbert, the guy crushed by a cow, was having an affair with another man. Greta contacted me a few hours ago as soon as she learned of it. Apparently, after our conversation with her, she wanted to clear her name from our suspect list. She claims she did not know of the affair until after his death."

"Who was the other man?" I asked.

Maya mumbled a few incoherent words, most likely skimming through her notes. "Here he is. Christopher Steele. He's local to Sacramento and owns a chain of hardware stores exclusive to Sacramento County."

"Have the police talked to him?"

"About what?"

"Gilbert?"

"Why?" Maya asked. "No one committed a crime. A flying cow killed Gilbert. Case closed."

"We need to talk to him, then."

"Duh. Of course we do. But that's not all." Maya took a second to breathe, preparing her breath to carry her through a storm of words. "Check this out. This morning, at some rundown, nearly out-of-business diner, this pervert of a greaseball died in an industrial-sized dough mixer."

"What's a dough mixer?"

"Like a KitchenAid, only a hundred times the size. Anyway, apparently, after sexually harassing his two employees, he convinced one of them to attempt the cinnamon challenge. You remember that challenge?"

"No."

"You're so culturally deaf and blind." Maya dove back into the story. "Well, the employee agreed to the challenge, but she choked and coughed, as everyone else in the world does. The girl coughed in... what's his name?" A second of silence as pages flipped. "Ah, Peter Seed. She coughed in Peter's face. He turned around to escape the cinnamon dust cloud, and his tie caught in the dough mixer, and he was pulled into the machine. The blades shredded his face and fractured his skull. He died from extreme blood loss. Of course, the slime ball lives alone, and he has no friends or family who really care about his passing. But, but, but... I stumbled upon his address. Also, I'm here, in his neighborhood, and I may have peeked through his windows."

"Maya, what?"

"Get your panties out of a wad and check this out. Guess what I saw lying on his counter? Ding, ding, ding. Winner, winner, chicken dinner, baby. A voodoo doll! And Petey had plenty of haters and people to wish him dead." Maya finally stopped long enough to breathe.

"Three deaths in three days," I said.

"Bingo. Bango. Bongo."

"Did Peter Seed attend the same high school as the other victims?" I asked because I knew Maya would have looked that up the first chance she had.

"Nope," she said. "He moved to Sacramento from Southern California about ten years ago. No past connections with the other victims. We're back to square one."

"Does anyone else know about the voodoo doll you found in his house?"

"I don't think so."

"Eddie?"

"He told me about Pete's gruesome demise, but he didn't mention the voodoo doll. I found that out on my own. If I had to guess, not even the police know about the doll yet. Why would they, you know? Accidental death, not a homicide. They don't have a reason to search his home."

I clicked my tongue and popped my knuckles. "I can't believe I'm suggesting this. Do you want to break a few laws before we go to work?"

"Are you talking dirty to me, Mr. Watson? Please share all the rated-R details. What did you have in mind?"

"I want that doll for investigative purposes. We need to know if they're being bought or created. That's our only connection right now, and we don't have one in our possession. So, we're breaking into and entering a dead man's house."

Maya giggled. "You continually surprise me, and in a good way. Let's break some laws for the betterment of the world."

I hate to admit this, but in my excitement, I forgot to call my brother. James Connors had left a voicemail, though, so I had a big, notifying reminder to call him back. No such reminder existed, nudging me to get in touch with Adam. Deciding I would conduct my business with James in the car on my way to Peter Seed's house—which Maya had texted me the address to—I returned to Glacia's house.

"So, you're leaving me with a stranger?" Alina asked, glancing at Glacia after I informed them of my plan.

"If you're both okay with it," I said. "If not, I'll take you back to my apartment. Either way, you're not tagging along during this part of the voodoo doll investigation."

"Why not? Maya's my aunt. Doesn't it make sense for me to join her rather than stay alone at your place, or here with her?" Alina nodded at Glacia.

"Sure, tag along with Maya and me. If she asks why you're working with me on a Saturday, what do we tell her? That your mom jumped ship, leaving you homeless?"

"We can lie."

"I won't lie to her," I said.

"Why? Because you love her?" Alina asked like a teenager ridiculing a friend about a crush.

And like a teenager, my face flushed with embarrassment. "No, because I respect her enough not to lie to her. Now, what will it be?"

"I can take her to lunch," Glacia said. "We have a lot in common, or so it seems—absent, drug-addicted moms. Maybe we will even have some fun conversation about that."

Alina frowned and shook her head. "I'd rather pluck my hair from my head, one strand at a time."

"I think lunch is a great idea," I said, removing my wallet and scrounging together enough cash for Alina to afford a soda. "Here's some money. Knock yourself out."

The girl scrunched her face. "Four dollars? What can I buy with four dollars? A bean and cheese burrito from Taco Bell?"

"If you're going there," I said, "please watch out for falling Taco Bell signs."

"I still owe you money," Glacia said. "I'll pay for Alina, and we'll eat somewhere decent. Afterward, if you're not back yet, we'll find something to do. Go shopping maybe."

"I hate shopping," Alina said. "Almost as much as I hate Barbies." She winked at me.

"Should we see a movie?" Glacia asked.

"That's more like it."

"There we have it." Glacia smirked at me. "We'll see a movie after lunch. She'll be fine."

"Thank you," I said. "Oh, when do you leave for Oregon?"

"Tomorrow."

"That's a bummer."

"Why?"

"Well, I'm busy tonight, but I was hoping you would stick around long enough for me… you know… I thought maybe, if you were up for it—"

"Holy smokes," Alina said. "He's asking you out, I think. Possibly for dinner tomorrow night."

I pointed at the kid. "Exactly."

"Well," Glacia said, biting her lower lip and staring at me with a hungry look, "I'll see what I can do."

"It's a double date, if that makes your decision easier. With Maya and her boyfriend."

"Will that be awkward?" Alina asked.

"Why would it be awkward?"

"Considering you're in love with my aunt, and you're asking Glacia to join you. The situation seems a little awkward, and you're not the smoothest or most charming person I know."

"I have to go now," I said. "Think about it and let me know. You have my number." I faced Alina, glaring at her. "You."

"Me."

"Don't do anything crazy."

"Never."

"I'm trusting you. Lunch and a movie. That's all."

"I cross my heart," Alina said.

I pointed at Glacia, then at Alina, but I had nothing more to add, so I slowly exited the house once more.

Breaking and Entering. Saturday, April 23rd. 1223hrs.

Peter Seed had lived in one of the seedier areas of Sacramento, pun intended. He had caged his windows with steel bars, and the front entrance had a metallic security door in front of it.

His property was the polar opposite of Nana's property—dead, forgotten, littered with junk and trash. It differed from Randall's home, though. The Fincher's house was dirty, a byproduct, or so it seemed, of neglect. On reflection, it had reminded me of an old ranch house, always in disarray. Too much dust to even try beyond sweeping it under a rug, or too busy to properly sanitize, or too tired to tackle the yard, or too many odds and ends to sort through and purge. Peter's house, though, was grimy. There's a difference, I think. It was an eyesore in a neighborhood not filled with much to look at. I hesitated to step out of my car and breathe the noxious air most likely permeating from his rotting foundation.

Maya sat in her car, parked along the curb beside Peter's driveway. I parked on the opposite side of the street, in the shade. We stepped out of our vehicles in perfect sync, shutting the doors at exactly the same time. We even chorused an identical greeting.

"What's up?"

"Jinx," Maya said, cutting in before I had the chance to think of a response. "You owe me a Coke. But I don't drink soda, so I'll settle for a beer. How about tomorrow night, during our double date? Speaking of, Eddie can't wait. He's stoked to meet the man I talk nonstop about—his words. Don't worry, I only say mostly good things."

"Why do you talk about me with your boyfriend?"

"I have to make him jealous and want to stick around, you know? Guys love competition. If he doesn't think there's competition, he'll grow complacent and bored with me."

"That's ridiculous."

"Did you find a date?"

"Possibly."

"I honestly thought you would show up with Fred," Maya said, giggling.

"You don't think I could snag a date?"

"August, you're smoking hot and all that jazz, but in the met-at-church way."

I scrunched my face. "What's that mean?"

"You're not great with the... you don't have game. Unless someone takes the time to get to know you, you're awkward."

"You're a great confidence booster. It's why I enjoy hanging out with you so much."

"It's just that... you're hard to talk to at first. For example, pretend we're at a bar. I look you up and down—obvious enough for even you to notice—and I say, 'Hey.' Just like that, slow and syrupy, batting my eyes. What would you say?"

I shrugged. "I don't know. Probably something like, 'How's it going?'"

Maya stuck out her tongue and made a disgusted sound. "Gross. No. Never say that. No one really cares how it's going, so don't ask."

I glanced across the street at the house. "I'm not picking girls up at the bar, anyway. Let's focus on what matters here."

"You're not picking girls up at all. That's the problem. You're stiff as a three-day corpse because you don't have a pretty lady to loosen those buttons."

She and I stepped onto the cracked and uneven drive leading up to the rusted garage door. Weeds grew from the moss-covered cement.

"I just told you I possibly had a date for tomorrow night," I said.

"You paying her?"

"She's paying me."

"Ew. Really?"

"What?"

"She's a client?" Maya asked, turning up her nose.

"Past client. I solved her case earlier this morning."

Maya took the lead on the narrow walkway, moving around the garage to the side gate. "You really have zero skills with the ladies." Without a string dangling from the gate, we had no access to pop the latch from the outside. Maya stepped aside, allowing me to advance forward. "You might suck with words, Mr. Watson, but at least you're tall and muscular. Put those blessed genetics to use."

"That's all I am to you? A piece of meat for you to use as you please."

"Mm. Yes! Always as I please."

I rolled my eyes and hoisted myself over the gate, landing in the side yard. I spared a second studying the vicinity—spider webs stretched from the exterior wall to the gutters. Dried, papery wasp nests nestled into eaves. Wet garbage spattered in mud lay strewn across the mucky ground.

"Hopefully you didn't wear your nice shoes," I said, unlatching the gate.

Maya joined me, shutting it behind her. "See," she said, punching my arm, "you're not completely useless. Just talk less. You're sexier that way." She walked into the backyard—a further separation from cleanliness than even the front yard.

Bars didn't cover the back windows, nor did a security door protect the sliding glass door leading into what appeared to be the kitchen. The Fincher's had old junk tossed into their overgrown yard—sheet metal, lumber, and some loose trash. Peter, though, had a hoarder's collection of junk and trash heaped in his backyard. It stank like something from a nightmare, rancid beyond the imagination.

I raised my shirt above my face to stifle the rotten stench. "How do we get in?"

Maya tiptoed toward the sliding glass door, careful not to step on the littering of garbage. She tried the handle, pulling, but the door didn't budge.

"It was worth a try," I said.

"Most people have hiding spots for their spare keys." Maya bent over and lifted a rock from the flower bed. "Maybe look around, see what you can find."

I moved toward the welcome mat lying before the sliding glass door—one of the more oxymoronic sightings I've ever witnessed. Who had Peter tried to fool with the mat? Was he wiping his feet before entering his home?

As I leaned over to peel the mat off the cement, an explosive shattering spun me around, saving me from having to touch something.

Maya had taken the rock from the overgrown flowerbed and thrown it through a window. In a quick, effortless motion, she removed her shirt. Maya wore nothing but a lacy bra beneath it—black and sheer.

My stomach twisted in tight little circles. Other parts of my anatomy also responded to her bare body.

Maya wrapped her shirt around her hand and forearm, clearing away the jagged glass from the frame. When she finished, she turned to me and smiled. "Do I have something stuck in my teeth?"

"What?" I asked, or maybe thought. Time and reality operated differently at that moment. Everything seemed to move so fast that it stopped moving altogether.

"You're staring at me like something is wrong?" Maya unraveled the shirt and shook out the broken glass.

"Nothing is wrong."

"Why are you staring at me?"

"Uh, um… I'm surprised."

"Surprised?"

"I'm shocked that you're so adept at… breaking into houses."

Maya tilted her head, still grinning. "You have no game." She pulled the shirt back over her head and climbed through the open window. A second later, she appeared at the sliding glass door, unlocked it, and slid it open. "Welcome to my humble abode. Ignore the mess. I'm a bit of a slob."

I entered Peter Seed's home and paused in the kitchen, flabbergasted at the condition in which he lived. No. It was more than that. I was beyond disgusted and shocked, but not entirely with Peter. With me. For the past five years, I hadn't lived too far off in the cleanliness category. My apartment, at least before Alina had sanitized it last night, was only a few steps from devolving into the utter madness and rancidity that Peter had lived in. How had I allowed myself to digress so far, to care so little, to avoid so much? The mess had overtaken everything in my life, too—my cleanliness, my relationships, my work. I had no healthy boundaries. For me, it was all or nothing. Work, I gave it my all. Exercise, I gave it everything I had. Relationships, who cared? Cleanliness, why bother?

"Yo! You okay?" Maya asked. "It looks like you saw a ghost, or someone walked over your grave... whatever that means."

"I'm fine," I said, flexing my wrists.

"There's the doll." Maya gestured to the dining room table. Unopened mail, food crumbs, greasy paper bags, soda cans, cigarette ash, and one voodoo doll lay scattered atop it.

The doll appeared as I had imagined it—formed from burlap and stuffed with straw to form limbs, a torso, and a head. No face. No details. Only the vague impression of a humanoid. A single pin stuck out from its head.

"There's not a tag on it," I said, picking the doll off the table. "It's homemade. Virtually untraceable."

"So, we broke into a house, committing who knows how many crimes, for no reason at all. Great. Hopefully, Jonah doesn't learn about this extracurricular activity. He'll never hire me full time." Jonah, of course, being her boss at *Here & Now*.

"We should go." I glanced around the kitchen, not caring to explore Peter's house and discover whatever other unknown horrors he hid. "I'm taking the doll, though."

"Add it to your collection. You seem like a guy who would collect dolls."

"They're called action figures, not dolls."

Maya snickered. "Whatever you say."

We shut and locked the sliding glass door, climbed out the broken window, and circled to the front of the house, reconvening near Maya's vehicle.

I looked up and down the street for any obvious witnesses who may have watched us enter and leave Peter's house, but I doubted anyone would say anything to the police. That's if the police came out here to ask questions about Peter's death—an idea less likely to happen than winning the lottery three times in a row.

"Three murders. Three days. Three voodoo dolls," I said. "Zero connections beyond the untraceable dolls and the victims' incredibly unlucky deaths. What now? Where do we go? What lead do we follow?"

Maya sighed. "As much as it pains me to suggest this, I think we have to rip a page from law enforcement's handbook on how to catch serial killers."

"Which is?"

"We need another death. Another victim creates more clues, and more clues point to more suspects or answers."

"Our job is to prevent another death, not wait for one."

"Well, it's that, or we accept Randall never lied. He summoned a demon that grants people their wish to kill someone." Maya shrugged. "Wilder things have happened. Apparently, you might have a date for tomorrow night."

I rolled my eyes. "Nothing as wild as a summoned demon has ever happened. We have to do something, though. What will waiting achieve? We'll have a fourth victim and a fourth doll and no connections."

"You don't know that."

"They're all random. Every death has been random."

"It's a demon," Maya said, throwing up her hands. "What else? Either coincidence exists or it doesn't. Unless a serial killer is dabbling in voodoo and murdering through curses… I don't know. How do you explain it beyond the paranormal?"

"There's an explanation," I said. "We just don't have it yet."

"Well, I'm starving. It's past lunchtime. So, what do you say? Want to grab lunch, or do you have better things to do?"

I cracked my knuckles, one at a time. "I have a couple of things to take care of before our shift. I'll see you at the store, though."

Maya sucked on her lips and shook her head. "No game at all."

The Rest of the Day. Saturday, April 23rd. 1306hrs.

As I drove to my apartment, I called James Connors.

"James here," the old man answered.

"It's August."

"Oh, yeah. Hey, I'm sorry to call on a Saturday, but I saw her again."

"Sasquatch."

"I saw her last night in the same spot I showed you."

"Where we encountered the bear."

"This wasn't no bear. I know a Sasquatch from a black bear. She was thrashing at trees again, howling and roaring. I hid before she could see me and funnel her anger at me. Once I felt safe, I fumbled with my phone to turn on the camera."

"Did you snap a picture?"

"She was gone. Disappeared into the night. I kept the video rolling, just in case she returned. She never did. I didn't even hear her hollering again. I know we saw a bear that day you came out, and I know what you think about that. But I also know what I saw. I know the difference between a black bear and a Sasquatch. And this Sasquatch is rabid. Don't take any other sightings from anyone else seriously, that's fine. But you have to consider this one. She's rabid and dangerous."

"Won't the rabies virus kill her naturally?" I asked.

"Dogs die within seven days of infection. Humans usually can last up to ten days. Who knows how much longer Sasquatch can terrorize anyone she comes across? Two weeks. Who knows how long she's already had it? Maybe three days. Maybe seven. It doesn't matter, though, now does it?

We have to stop her."

I clicked my tongue for a second. "You saw her in the same spot as before?"

"Yes."

"Where you brought Fred and me?"

"Yup."

"Was it at night, same as when you spotted her last time?"

"I saw her at night."

I scratched at my eye. "You last showed us that location during the day. Maybe Sasquatch prefers to come out after sundown. I don't know. To thoroughly investigate, though, I'll visit the site again. This time, we're staying overnight."

"When?" James asked, a hint of excitement creeping into his tone.

Fred wouldn't get caught dead camping, unless forced to do so or paid extremely well. I had no power to force him into anything on his hallowed weekend, nor did I have the money to offer him.

"I work tonight, and tomorrow I'm busy, as well." I thought of church and the double date—the weekend from Hell. "How's Monday night work?"

"It has to be earlier," James said.

"I can't make it happen earlier. I'm sorry. Monday is the earliest I can do. There are dozens of other paranormal investigators around the area. Hire one of them if you need something sooner." I didn't say it with malice or pettiness, but with concern. I truly cared about his troubles and wanted to help him, but I couldn't meet his timeframe.

"You're the only one who takes this job seriously. The others," James spat, "they do what they do for a story and a moment of fame. If I hired a Bigfoot hunter or another paranormal investigator, they would doctor some evidence and footage to boost whatever rating they're looking for. I don't care about fame, Mr. Watson. I don't want this rabid Sasquatch hurting anyone. You're the only one I think can help with that."

"I appreciate your confidence in me, but I can't make it out there any earlier than Monday. I'm sorry."

"I'll keep an eye out for her, then. If I see her, though, I'm shooting her."

I thought of pranksters wearing ape costumes and venturing out at night to scare gullible folk living in one of the world's Bigfoot capitals.

"Don't shoot her," I said. "Maybe monitor her. Don't worry about the camera, just watch her. Follow her from a distance to see where she goes. Okay? From a distance, though. Don't get yourself in trouble and do not shoot her."

"If you're not around to help, I'll do what I need to do to protect myself and the citizens of this community." James disconnected the line.

I rubbed my temples and headed into my apartment, lost in thoughts of Sasquatch and voodoo dolls, completely forgetting about Glacia, Alina, and Adam. Not until I stepped into my immaculate kitchen did I remember the girls.

"Crap!" I fished out my phone and called Glacia.

She ignored the call, but sent a quick text message advising me not to worry. They were in a movie. I responded, telling her I had to head into work at 1500hrs and to drop Alina off at my place, or hang out with her until I returned at 2230hrs. She liked the message.

I showered and dressed for work, jumped in my car and drove to a nearby sandwich shop, where I consumed my lunch and continued to ponder the two cases left in my lap. Nothing made any sense about either of them, so my thoughts pretty much worked in circles.

After lunch, I drove to the used bookstore. It wasn't Powell's City of Books in Portland, Oregon, taking up an entire block and multiple stories, but the shop was fairly popular and well-known. Maya worked three days a week, from 1500hrs to 2100hrs. I only worked on Saturdays. The Dragon's Hoard was open to the public until 2100hrs, but the owner scheduled Maya and me to stay late to clean the store and reorganize the books before locking up and setting the alarm.

Maya worked the floor, assisting people with whatever they needed. I manned the register. When we weren't with customers, Maya usually leaned on the front counter and chatted with me about all things supernatural. Our mutual interest in all things bizarre helped us grow close together and form our friendship.

The shift went without a hiccup, per usual. Glacia called me when the movie ended. No one other than Maya and me occupied the bookstore, so I stepped in the backroom and answered Glacia's call.

"Hey," I said. "How was the movie?"

"Amazing," Glacia said. "Um, don't worry about picking up Alina. She said you're creepy, and she would rather not stay another night in your apartment. So I'm going to keep her at my place."

"Wait, what? She said what? Listen, I slept on the chair." I ran my hand through my hair. What had I done to make Alina uncomfortable? I panicked. My mind rifled through memories.

Glacia burst into amused laughter. Somewhere near her, I heard Alina laughing, speaking through her cacophonous chortles. "August, you're so sensitive. It's great. Don't worry, you're only as perverted as every other normal man. Which, honestly, is obscenely too much perversion. Like, why does everything have to boil down to sex with you guys? It's disgusting. You're disgusting."

As I stuttered to respond, Glacia saved me from the hassle, saying, "Alina and I wanted to ask you, temporary dad, if we could turn our girl's night into a sleepover?"

"Sure," I said. "I'm okay with that."

"We're going to sleep at Nana's house," Glacia said. "Now that it's free of ghosts."

"And watch haunted house movies," Alina said.

"Seems a little... masochistic, but sure. Knock yourselves out."

"Okay. Bye."

"Wait!" I shouted into the receiver.

"What?" Glacia asked.

I cleared my throat. "How are you two doing? I mean, a lot happened with your family. Susan pointed a gun at us. By the way, what happened to that?"

"I have it," Glacia said. "And..." she trailed, falling into a quick quiet. "I'm okay. I'm better when I'm distracting myself with movies. I don't know. I keep thinking about my mom. Did I do the right thing?"

"I think so," I said. "She has to account for her actions, eventually."

"I'm afraid she'll grow more bitter and angry, rather than learning anything from this." Another second of silence. "Anyway! We're good."

"Alina is good?" I asked.

"I'm surviving one second at a time."

Neither of the women sounded great, at least through the phone, but I couldn't do anything to help them while at work. Hopefully, they could lean on each other, though.

"If you need anything—"

"We know, Dad" Glacia said.

"We'll call you to save the damsels in distress," Alina said. "Don't worry. We never thought for a second we could take care of ourselves. I mean, how could two helpless, dependent, pathetic women possibly do anything for themselves, right?"

I rolled my eyes and told them to have fun, hanging up the phone and returning to work.

At exactly 2100hrs, I moseyed to the front doors and locked them, flipping the sign to signal our closing for the night.

"Another day, another dollar," Maya said, scooping up a stack of books.

She navigated from shelf to shelf, placing them where they belonged, speaking loudly so I could hear her from across the building. I counted and recounted the money. Maya had a terrible habit of never allowing me to concentrate while I counted.

"We had that hour where no one showed up," she said.

"We did," I said.

"I bet you missed me not spending that free time ogling at your muscular body and pretty blue eyes."

"I didn't."

"Don't be rude. Anyway, I didn't join you at your little station because I was researching voodoo dolls. Apparently, we have an entire occult section, which includes many books containing information about ancient forms of magic, summoning demons, invoking curses, and practicing voodoo. You name it."

"Find anything useful?"

"People misunderstand voodoo dolls. Check this out." Maya approached the counter and set down a book. "Voodoo practitioners use the dolls for completely different purposes than revenge. They're used to help people heal or to communicate with their loved ones who have passed. Western culture and Hollywood have attached curses to voodoo dolls, but their interpretation can't be further from the truth."

I chewed on what she said, having completely abandoned counting the money for the moment. "If that's correct," I said, speaking slowly, "a curse wouldn't be possible, right?"

"Explain yourself."

"If the dolls were historically used to heal or communicate with the dead, but western culture has perverted our perception of them so we think curses come from the doll," I held up a finger and inhaled, catching my breath, "then only someone with general, common knowledge of the voodoo doll would use them as a curse."

Maya narrowed her eyes and scrunched her face. "I don't know what you're saying."

My thoughts were still fuzzy with the information, so I found it difficult to articulate what I meant to say. "If someone used the voodoo dolls to curse their victims, they would have failed, right? Because voodoo dolls, as you said, were used to promote healing, not hurting."

Maya scratched the side of her head. "Maybe healing in their lives was removing the infection—Muriel with Randall, Gilbert with Greta, and Peter with all of humankind."

I massaged a kink in my shoulder. "We're missing something important here, and I feel like it's right in front of our faces. Can I have that book?"

"Yeah." Maya handed it to me.

"Thankfully, I have yet to count the register, since you don't know how to sit in silence." I rang up the book and paid with my business card, calling the purchase a business expense. "I'll leaf through this when I get to the office."

"You're going to your office after this?"

"What else would I do?"

"I don't know. Go to bed."

"If only sleep were that simple."

"Dude, just take an edible. It'll knock your socks off and put you to sleep like a baby full on his momma's teat." Maya walked away from the counter, returning to work and cleaning up the store.

I counted the money within the register. Maya and I finished our tasks around the same time. We still had fifteen minutes until our shifts officially ended, but Raymond—our boss—didn't mind if we left a little early, as long as we properly prepared the store for the next day.

"Mission complete," Maya said, opening the front door.

After I stepped outside, she punched in the code, setting the alarm. She closed the door, locking it.

"If you had to make a final guess right now, what would you conclude about this voodoo thing?" I asked.

"What do you mean?"

"Is there a certain person behind everything? Is there a demon or a curse? What's your verdict?"

"Honestly, I don't know. Do I believe in the supernatural? Yes. Do I think this case connects to the supernatural?" Maya cocked her head back and forth, weighing her answer. "No. From what little I read in that book you have, voodoo doesn't work like what we're experiencing. Maybe along the way it became distorted, used for evil, but originally, the practice was for something positive." Maya bit her lip and tapped her chin. "I don't know how to answer your question. Sorry."

I cracked my knuckles and stared down the street. "I'm going to grab some coffee and head to the office. If you're not doing anything tonight, you're welcome to join me. I'll be reading and researching until I can't keep my eyes open."

"Thanks, but unlike you, I need sleep to function. I'm going to go home, take a bath, drink a bottle of wine, and pass out."

"Okay. Well..." I trailed off, debating whether I wanted to explore another path of conversation with Maya—one far more personal. For Alina's sake, I did. "Have you heard from your sister?"

Maya side eyed me. "What do you mean?"

"Have you heard from her? What do you mean by what do I mean?"

"Why would you care if I've heard from her?"

"Because Alina skipped school and worked her first day yesterday. I was curious if you heard from your sister to see what she or Alina thought of it."

"Oh."

"Have you?"

"No." An abrupt no. "We don't really talk like that, though. Alina and I are close, but Wanda and me… not so much. We had our beef, and we did our own things, and we've never really come back, you know?"

I thought of my brother, Adam. Shoot. I had forgotten to call him and check on him, as Fred had suggested. "I have to go," I said.

"See you tomorrow night."

"See you then."

I hurried to my car, climbing in and slapping the steering wheel. How had I forgotten to contact my brother? It was nearly 2300hrs. He was twenty, though, and more than likely just now getting ready for the night.

I dialed his number. It, predictably, went straight to voicemail.

I hung up and stared at the city street, clicking my tongue and wondering what to do next. After a second of indecision, I called Adam again. Again, he sent me to voicemail. I left a message.

"Hey, it's me. Um, yeah, I know. I'm a terrible person and a worse brother, but I'm working on it. I'd like a chance, you know?" I popped my knuckles, not sure what to say next. "Anyway, call me when you can." Acting on pure impulse and reaction, I added, "I'm doing this case involving a Sasquatch sighting on Monday night. If you're free, want to camp with me and look for a Bigfoot? I'd love to have you join."

I hung up the phone and drove to my office.

Four Real. Sunday, April 24th. 0011hrs.

Stacey never went to bed before 0200hrs. Even if she turned off her cell phone and television, eliminating unnatural lights, and cooled the house and drank a soothing tea, as soon as she plopped into her bed, her thoughts exploded. They sprinted, moving from event to event, from problem to problem, from stress to stress. She relived and rethought everything.

To combat her riddling mind, Stacey practiced two proven sleep techniques. One, she drank, drinking until she drowned her mind in alcohol. Two, she stayed up late and watched YouTube or read or cleaned the house, something and anything, until she could no longer keep her eyes open.

The next morning, Stacey had a brunch date with her girlfriends—mimosas paired with waffles topped with whipped cream and strawberries.

She wanted to sleep, which meant she desperately needed to get drunk, but she hadn't seen most of these girls since college—nearly a decade. Everyone had returned to attend a wedding from whatever new city or state they had migrated to. Stacey didn't want to nurse a debilitating hangover while catching up with her long-lost friends.

So, she curled onto the couch with a bowl of popcorn and watched the first thirty minutes of about ten different movies, growing bored with each one. She had never really enjoyed cinema—film or television, which was why it was usually so effective at helping her sleep.

As she dozed on the couch, slipping away from reality for a few minutes, an aggressive rapping sound ripped her from the shallows of sleep.

Stacey startled awake, glancing around the dark room. It was lit only by the glowing television screen. The scene from the movie playing showed two people at a restaurant, happy in conversation. The knocking hadn't occurred in the movie, but from her house.

Slowly standing, Stacey dropped her blanket on the ground and tiptoed toward the kitchen. She pulled a knife from the rack and backed into a dark corner, waiting in the dark for something to happen.

Had she dreamed the sound? Had it happened in the previous scene of the movie?

Fists hammered against the door leading into her backyard. Someone had knocked, and they continued to knock. Stacey gasped, covering her mouth to muffle a yelp. She held the knife close to her chest.

"Stacey! It's me!" The voice whisper-shouted, disguising who it belonged to, but it sounded oddly familiar. "Let me in!"

Keeping out of sight from the glass door, Stacey crept toward the wall and flipped a light switch, illuminating her back patio. She immediately recognized the man standing at her door, and she sighed with relief. Tension poured from her body as she relaxed. She placed the kitchen knife on the nook table and opened the door.

"What are you doing?" Stacey asked, stepping aside and allowing the visitor into her home.

The man stepped into her house and glanced around, fidgety and on edge. "Is someone here?"

"No one is here. Why would someone be here?" She crossed her arms and rolled her eyes, hoping he would catch her obvious annoyance. "Why does it matter, anyway? We broke up."

"You broke up with me!" The man stepped toward her, posturing.

Stacey had faced enough of his mental and physical abuse to know he would strike her. He would hurt her if pushed far enough. She didn't back away from him, but she lowered her voice, losing confidence. "Sorry." Why had she opened the door for him? "I think you should go."

"I'm not going anywhere." He trudged past her and into the living room, his head on a swivel. "Hello!"

"No one is here. It's just me."

"Why're you up so late by yourself?"

"You know I can't sleep."

The man disappeared down the hallway, flipping on lights in the back bedrooms. Stacey could no longer see him, but she had experienced this same night many times before with him. He would barge into her home and check every room for a man she might have over.

Tears welled in her eyes, and she wiped them away, refusing to cry in front of him.

They had dated for five years, going back to college. On their fifth anniversary, he had asked Stacey to marry him, and she had agreed. That was before he had shown obvious signs of abuse. Maybe he had flashed subtle signs, though. Signs that love had blinded her to. Once engaged, everything changed. The mental abuse came first—body shaming, criticizing her intelligence and skills. After that, when she stood up to the abuse, defending herself, he grew physically and sexually abusive. Calling the cops wouldn't have worked, either. He was a cop, and they looked out for each other. She had thought of running away and leaving him, but she knew he would find and kill her.

Stacey had become his property. Unless he willingly gave her up, threw her away from growing tired of her, Stacey wouldn't have escaped. Instead of seeking help or running, she bided her time and endured his abuse, waiting for him to make a mistake, to stumble.

He not only stumbled, but he fell, and he fell hard.

Stacey had followed him to work one day, followed him as he patrolled Sacramento. She discovered rather quickly that he didn't serve and protect the community during his shift.

His first stop was arresting a sex worker, who he drove into an abandoned lot. With the handcuffs still on the woman, Stacey watched as her fiancé dragged the sex worker from the backseat of the police vehicle and threw her against the hood. Not only did Stacey watch, she recorded the entire ordeal. He never paid the woman, either, and Stacey could only imagine what excuses he gave her for not forking out the cash.

"Be thankful I'm not taking you to prison, you filthy whore. That's your payment."

He left her in the lot and drove away.

Torn between continuing her reconnaissance and helping the woman, Stacey went to the sex worker. She could always follow her fiancé again, on another night. And she did, multiple times. Enough to build quite a dossier of incriminating evidence against him. Soliciting sex workers while on duty. Accepting bribes from criminals. Confiscating drugs, indulging in those drugs while wearing the badge. Targeting. Profiling. Inciting fights just to punch someone. Dangling sexual acts in front of women to keep them out of jail.

Stacey had confronted him about everything, presenting him with the accumulated proof of his perverted abuse of power. Approaching him with the evidence terrified her beyond belief. She did not know how he would respond. Would he beat her? Would he kill her?

Her fiancé stared at the videos and pictures, speechless, which was more frightening than if he had exploded into a fiery rage.

"What's this?" he asked casually, as if reading a book on a beach.

"I don't want to marry you," Stacey said, barely breathing. "I want to break up with you."

He had remained calm, most likely calculating the situation. "What do you mean?"

The moment of truth had arrived. Stacey swallowed back her nerves. "If anything happens to me, I scheduled an email that will release to your chief and to every news media outlet within the area. If I don't log into my email account and cancel the draft, it will send."

He laughed, amused by her threat. "You don't think I know your password?"

"I created a new account on a library computer. You wouldn't know my username or password, and you would have no way of accessing it from our history. We're going to break up. You're going to allow me to leave, and no one will ever have to know about any of this."

Stacey's ex-fiancé returned to the kitchen, rubbing his palms together. "Alright. Let's do this."

"Do what? Why are you here?" Stacey asked, backing away from him.

"To celebrate and drink." He proceeded to the cupboard above her refrigerator, where she stored the alcohol. He removed a bottle of tequila. Popping the cork, he walked to where Stacey stored her glasses.

He poured the tequila into two cups, handing one to her. "To me."

She reluctantly accepted. "To you. Why?"

The man ran his tongue over his lower lip and grinned. "I'm in love, completely over you." He chuckled. "Do you not want to celebrate my happiness?" He raised his glass of tequila.

Stacey raised her glass, clinking her cup to his. "Cheers."

They both shot the liquor.

He smacked an open palm on the counter. "That's good stuff. Another round?"

"I'd rather not."

"Nonsense. We're celebrating by getting drunk tonight."

"Does your new girlfriend know you're here with me, planning to get drunk?"

"Stacey, Stacey, Stacey. That's none of your business. Your business is getting blackout drunk with me. Well, your business is getting blackout drunk while I supervise." He reached behind him and drew a pistol, pointing it directly at her face.

Her heart shriveled and ceased to beat. Her breath grew heavy. "What—what are you doing?"

"I'm extremely happy in my new relationship. I would hate for anything, or anyone, to ruin that happiness. Now, you possess certain videos and photographs I would prefer deleted from existence. That's it." He spread out his arms and painted a grin across his face. "I figured if you're drunk, you would be in a more accommodating mood. I mean, that's how it worked when we dated." He snickered. "Stacey, you have nothing to worry about. Over the past couple of years, I have grown and matured to realize you're nothing but a stupid, selfish slut. I want nothing to do with you. Now, drink." He poured another glass of tequila for Stacey, this time the alcohol filled half the cup.

She reluctantly accepted and sniffed the contents. It smelled terrible. She gagged.

"In one gulp," he said, strolling over to the kitchen table and picking up the knife Stacey had placed there. "If you refuse, I'll cut you."

Stacey couldn't fight her tears anymore. They leaked down her trembling face. "I don't want to."

"Drink it!"

She put the glass to her lips and tipped it upward, consuming the generous pouring of tequila, coughing and sputtering when she had finished her gulp.

The man fitted his gun behind his back again, holding the knife and lifting the bottle of alcohol, pouring the cup to the brim. He cleared his throat, carefully lifting the glass off the counter to not spill a single drop. He handed it to Stacey. "One minute."

"What?"

"You have one minute to finish that serving, otherwise... well, I'm not sure what I'll do. But it will involve this knife and parts of your body."

"I'll delete the video. I swear. I'll do it right now, in front of you."

He crossed his arms. His watch faced upward. "Drink the drink." He glanced at the time and counted her minute. "One. Two."

Stacey finished the glass of tequila before he hit fifty seconds. She dry heaved, but didn't vomit. Her head felt light and dizzy, and her lips tingled. The alcohol had already taken effect.

The man poured another full glass, emptying the bottle of tequila. He threw it across the kitchen, and it shattered on the floor.

He smiled at her, handing her the glass. "I apparently underestimated your ability to drink. Fifty seconds this time."

"I don't want to. I don't want to. Please. I'll delete the pictures and the videos. Please."

"Shut up! Shut up! Shut up! You really think this is only about the videos? You ruined my life. You stole everything from me. I lost sleep, living in fear that at any point in time you would release everything to the public. How do you think that made me feel? I was terrified. Have you ever lived every second of your life so scared you couldn't breathe?"

Stacey's face contorted into a mess of sobs.

"Drink the tequila in the next fifty seconds, otherwise I'll slowly plunge this knife through your arm. I wouldn't want to kill you, of course. I would only want to make it hurt." He smirked. "I would only want to make you afraid of every second remaining in your life. At first, that is. Now, drink. One."

Stacey guzzled, gulping the tequila, finishing the glass within the parameters of the allotted time. Her entire body caught fire, flushed with heat, and she sweated. Her mouth pooled with saliva, threatening to vomit the copious amount of alcohol he had forced her to consume. She feared how he might respond if she heaved. So she swallowed the sour bile. Her vision blurred, and she stood wobbly on her feet.

Stacey reached out to the wall for support, but she misjudged the distance, leaning too far and falling, crashing to the floor.

"You stupid drunk," he said. "You still can't contain your alcohol."

His hands wriggled beneath her body and lifted her off the ground—he was a big man, two-hundred pounds and over six-feet tall. She was small, barely over five-feet and just over a hundred pounds.

He carried her through the hallway and laid her in bed, on her back, wedging her head between two pillows so her face remained upright.

"That was three-quarters of the bottle you drank in less than five minutes. Impressive. Based on your size and weight, I would guess alcohol poisoning will take effect soon. Don't worry, though. I'll wait by your side and make sure nothing bad happens."

Stacey wanted to tell him she would delete the pictures and the videos, that she would cancel the scheduled releases of them, which reset every week just in case he showed up to hurt her.

When she spoke, though, her words slurred, and she couldn't even understand herself.

"Shh, shh," he said, touching her lips with the knife's blade. "Don't talk. Sleep. Close your eyes and sleep."

He was right. Stacey felt tired. She should steal some rest before her mind clicked on and kept her awake.

As the room twirled around her, faster and faster and faster, and she grew warmer and warmer and warmer, she noticed something odd. The man had a doll—one made of burlap. He placed it on her nightstand.

"What is that?" she asked, or maybe she only thought it. Her lips were numb, her tongue heavy and stuck in her mouth.

The tight spiral of the spinning room closed completely. Only darkness, forever darkness, remained.

Sunday Best. Sunday, April 24th. 0821hrs.

If I'm being generous with myself, I maybe slept two hours. Rather than catching up on much-needed sleep, I spent my night flipping through the book on voodoo, paying close attention to the section on voodoo dolls.

As history goes, the voodoo doll's origins aren't completely clear, though it's believed to have originated in Benin. I had to look that place up on a map. It's a French-speaking, West African nation, and the birthplace of the vodun, or voodoo, religion. I guess it makes sense the voodoo doll would originate from there.

Voodoo dolls grew in popularity, mostly from Louisiana and the queen of voodoo, Marie Laveau. There's a lot of conflicting information about different religious practices and beliefs of the voodoo doll, so I had to paint in broad strokes to make logical conclusions. The voodoo doll is the material incarnation of a person. People often employ voodoo dolls for personal needs, whether those needs be health, success, or revenge.

As interesting as I find this information, I don't want to turn this into a history lecture. I'll try to keep it short.

In Louisiana, it's thought that slaves used the voodoo doll to stand up to their masters. They could release their negative emotions—fear and anger—into the inanimate object, aiming to hurt those who harmed them. As a result, slave owners shunned the dolls, and they banned them.

Now, this is where things grow murky and complicated. Customarily, only a Voodoo Queen or Doctor could invoke spirits to harm another human through the doll. To do so, they must complete a ritual, which includes making the doll physically similar to the target—such as adding the victim's blood or hair. Also, the pins are not usually used to inflict harm.

Now, contrarily, the Nkondi—a type of Minkisi, or a wooden figurine—translates to the hunter, and is used to hunt evil people down. I won't go too far down that rabbit hole, other than to say that most people might mistake a voodoo doll for a Nkondi.

The mythology behind voodoo remains inconsistent from region to region, as does the mythology in most religions, which makes it difficult to deduce hard, factual conclusions.

However, I came up with a few thoughts that might assist our case.

Based on my research, I highly doubted someone worked from the shadows and cursed the victims with voodoo dolls. First off, the doll would have to remain with the Voodoo Doctor or Queen in order to inflict harm on someone else. Sending the doll away or planting at a crime scene wouldn't do anything. So, that led me to believe the dolls were nothing more than a distraction. The other thing I noted was that if someone really wished to hunt down 'evil' people, and they really knew and understood how to use vodun, they would have implemented the use of a Nkondi, not a voodoo doll. That thought forced me to focus on why someone would use the voodoo doll in these murders. Who would use the doll, especially so incorrectly?

I made a profile detailing that person.

"What's your sketch look like, Mr. FBI?" Maya asked that morning.

I had my phone on the bathroom counter as I readied myself for church.

"The person is planting the dolls. They hope the dolls create a distraction, such as making it appear that someone cursed the victims.

They're creating a pattern. Does that make sense?"

Maya clicked her tongue. "Why would they need to create a distraction? Why use voodoo dolls? Why insert themselves into obviously random deaths?"

"For the illusion of voodoo. They want to create a pattern, and in their mind, that pattern will distract us from them."

"I don't know if I can buy that. What else do you have?"

"The person knows little to nothing about actual voodoo culture, meaning they didn't curse anyone. There's no curse. It's as simple as that."

Maya sighed. "So, the perpetrator, for whatever reason, learns of the crazy deaths, finds out the addresses of the victims, and plants voodoo dolls in their homes? That's what you're going with."

I chewed on my cheeks. "Yeah."

"Why?"

"To get away with murder."

"What?" Maya asked.

"They created a pattern, a precedent, right? Voodoo dolls were found in the homes of people who died in completely impossible scenarios."

"Correct," Maya said.

"The perpetrator plans to commit an actual murder. He will stage an accident and plant another voodoo doll, making his murder appear like the other situations. Accidental. The perfect murder."

"That's the craziest thing I've ever heard. How does a person even do that? How do they get that idea in their head and learn of all the correct addresses and... it's impossible. You need to sleep. You need to reset your mind."

"Other than this actually being voodoo, which I know it's not based on my research, there's no other explanation. None that I could think of, at least. If you have something to add, though, I'm all ears."

"How about this?" Maya asked. "I'll relay your theory to Eddie. I'll have him think about it for the day. I'll think about it. You continue to think about it. We'll share our thoughts later tonight and see what we come up with."

"Deal. By the way, what are we doing tonight? Where are we meeting?"

"Eddie's house. He lives on some land—a few acres. He also has a fire pit. So, I thought s'mores under stars sounded fun."

I agreed with her, and we hung up. I finished with my tie and moseyed into the kitchen. The voodoo doll I had stolen from Peter's house lay on the table. I had cut it open. Burlap skin stuffed with hay. A simple pushpin with a red tip shoved into the head.

I left it there and drove to church, calling Glacia on the way.

"Good morning," she answered.

"How's everyone doing?"

"We're good. Alina is still sleeping. We had a late night binge-watching horror movies."

"I promised my mom I would attend church with her this morning. You okay with Alina until about noon?"

"Yeah. We're good."

"Thanks," I said, falling silent as I debated whether to bring up the date tonight. Luckily, I didn't have to.

"We are still on for later?" Glacia asked. "Double date, right?"

"I'll pick you up at seven."

"What should I wear?"

"We're going to sit around a campfire and roast marshmallows. So, campfire clothes."

"I like the sound of that."

At church, I found my mother and father standing with my sister, Jake, Adam, Fred, and Daphne. Before they noticed me, I glanced over my shoulder at my car, strongly considering slipping away, driving into a tree, and claiming I lost control of my vehicle. Instead, I plastered a smile across my face and stepped into formation.

"Gussy," my mom squealed, throwing her arms around me.

"Hey, Mom."

I went around the circle, hugging the women, shaking hands with the men.

When I greeted my brother, he left my hand suspended for a second before accepting it. "I got your message," he said, scratching his neck. "I'd like that."

"Gus," my mom said, tapping on my shoulder.

I turned around and saw a woman standing beside my mother. She had straight, blonde hair cut short, a dazzling smile, and big brown eyes.

"This is Cambria."

"Hi," I said. "It's a pleasure to meet you." I took her hand, which was like accepting a dead fish—floppy, cold, and oddly damp.

"I've heard a lot about you," Cambria said. "You have your own business. A private detective?"

"A paranormal investigator."

"What's that mean?"

"Would you look at the time?" My mother said, chuckling. "We should head inside before we're late."

We went into the service, sang the songs, listened to the message, which centered on love.

I sat between Fred and Cambria, though I continually inched toward Fred to keep my distance from the woman. She scooted toward me, brushing my legs with fingers, pinching the side of my butt, and whenever we stood, brushing her hands across my crotch in a nonchalant motion. It was clear she liked me, or at least liked the appearance of me.

After the pastor closed with prayer and excused us for the day, Cambria pulled me aside into an empty hallway. My parents and siblings, along with Fred and Daphne, continued outside into the courtyard.

"I want you," Cambria whispered into my ear, wrapping her arms around my waist. "I want you now."

I scratched at my ear and glanced into the foyer. A crowd of people streamed past us. Only a quick glance in our direction, and they would find two people strangely intertwined with each other.

I pushed myself away, separating from her grasp. "We're at church... in the church, actually."

"I get so hot being bad." Cambria leaned forward, brushing her lips over my neck as she spoke, breathing hot air on my skin. One of her hands slipped off my waist and found my groin. "I'll let you punish me for behaving so sinfully. Seventy-seven lashes. Is that what scripture says?"

I cleared my throat as her hand slipped from my groin to massaging... well, massaging me. My breath caught. When was the last time a woman had touched me? Five years ago, before the shooting. Why had I waited so long? I grunted, feeling my anatomy rebel against my thoughts.

"I say we head to your place," I said.

"You think I should sit in timeout?" The woman continued to work out my stress.

"Yes," I said, barely capable of forming the words. "You need timeout."

"Will you spank me?"

"I will."

"And if I talk back to you, will you gag me?"

I coughed. "Only if you talk back, so watch your tongue."

"Oh, I think you'll have to watch my tongue."

My phone vibrated in my pocket, startling me. I instinctively pushed away from Cambria and removed my cell, answering it and escaping into the hallway as I adjusted my pants.

"Maya, what's up?"

"Four bodies," she said.

"What?" I asked, glancing around for a quiet place to hide. I had to choose between the empty hallway or the sanctuary. I walked back into the sanctuary. "There's another one?"

"A young woman. Stacey Stokes. I know that name, too. She's our age, and I've seen her somewhere before."

"What happened?"

"She had breakfast planned for this morning with some old friends from college. She never showed. When she didn't answer her phone, they ran by her house to see if she was okay. They found her in bed, having choked on her own vomit. A voodoo doll was on her nightstand."

I propped the phone between my ear and shoulder and cracked my knuckles. "It doesn't fit."

"What do you mean, it doesn't fit?"

"It's not…" I snapped my fingers, searching for the right explanation. "It's not a sign or cow falling on someone, or a blender grinding their face off. It's not an absurd, unbelievable accident."

"Stacey drank an entire bottle of tequila and suffocated on her vomit."

"What's the coroner say?"

"Eddie doesn't know. He's off work today, but a buddy called him and told him about the murder. I'll get ahold of you as soon as I know more—or if I figure out why I know her name."

"This one's different," I said. "It happened at her home. None of the others died at home. They found the doll with her body. The deaths, before this one, occurred outside of the house, but someone always found the dolls inside. This incident breaks the pattern. This is…

accidental, but not freakish." My theory seemed more and more likely now.

"Do you think someone murdered her?"

I nodded, though Maya couldn't see my head gesture.

"Why?" Maya asked, most likely assuming my stance. "If you're right, why plant the other voodoo dolls only to murder this girl?"

I shook my head, back and forth, keeping silent.

"I'm going to head over to Eddie's around four," Maya said. "You can swing by whenever after that. I think he's barbecuing burgers around seven, though. But anyway, when I get there, I'll talk to him and see what he thinks about all this."

I walked to the courtyard after ending the call. Cambria stood near my mom. She winked at me as I joined their huddle.

"We're all going to lunch," my mom said. "Want to join us?"

"I can't." My voice was distant as I remained present with my thoughts. "I have work today—a potential break in a case. Raincheck, though?"

Cambria frowned, appearing disappointed. "Could I get your number? I'll call you later."

"No," I said. "That's okay." I faced Adam. "Want to meet at my apartment tomorrow, about three?"

Adam agreed with a grin.

I shuffled back to my car, lost in thought. Even if I had figured the case correctly, I was too late. The murder had occurred, and the murderer remained unknown.

Getting Ready for the Date. Sunday, April 24th. 1301hrs.

After church, I picked up Alina from Glacia's house. We drove back to my apartment. As we maneuvered through the city, the kid couldn't stop talking.

"Glacia is incredible. Like, honestly, Dude, marrying material. You're an idiot if you don't take this opportunity seriously."

"What opportunity?" I asked, edging in a couple of words.

"She hasn't only seen all the important movies from cinematic history, but she likes all the same ones I do. That's a massive deal. I have impeccable taste. She loves, like loves, horror movies. That's another plus. Yes, I know what you're thinking."

"Not possible."

"A lot of horror films are thin in plot, acting, and character development. They're also predictable. True. However, you're watching the wrong horror movies. I mean, she's into what I call literary horror, or elevated horror. That's where they really play with complex emotional themes, like grief or anger. And Glacia loves that stuff. Anyway, I know you're going on this double-date." She put double-date in air quotes. "But Eddie is nothing, man. You'll have to decide between Glacia and Maya, because even my aunt will see, eventually, that Eddie is a loser. She will crawl to you. Since you're in love with her, you'll welcome her with open arms. But it's a trap! Well, not a trap-trap, but like an emotional trap. Your feelings will blind you and you will discard Glacia and run directly to Maya. I'll say this now. You would be wrong to listen to those feelings. Glacia is the right woman. Not Maya. Come on, Dude. Open your eyes. She's smoking hot. She has an awesome career. She's independent. She's intelligent. She's funny. She loves great movies. Maya is my aunt, and she's fun, and, yes, most people find her physically sexy, but she's, like... she's like the girl next door and Glacia is a freaking knockout." Alina inhaled, finally taking a breath.

"You've put a lot of thought into my dating life."

"Well, you're lonely and depressed, and that's depressing for everyone. You have the potential to be a pretty cool dude. I think Glacia could spruce you up a bit, help you realize your potential. That's all."

"Did she talk about me?" I cringed at my question, feeling like a teenager discussing his crush.

"The better question would be, when did she not talk about you?" Alina glanced at me and smirked. "It was quite pathetic the way she went on and on about you. Gross, actually. She called you handsome, which sure, yeah... I can see that from certain shirtless angles. However, she also called you smart. Eh. That's debatable. Worst of all, she said you were witty. That's just plain wrong." Alina stuck out her tongue and fake coughed. "You're obsessive and compulsive and neurotic, but I'm not sure those are positive qualities. You're also a disgusting slob."

"She thought I was charming?"

"Handsome. Witty. Smart. Not charming. And believe me, I can speak for her on that point. You're about as charming as a horse lifting its tail to fart."

I sucked on my lower lip, forcing myself not to laugh and encourage the girl. "Have you heard from your mom?"

"Nope. I mean, it hasn't even been two full days. She'll be out of commission for at least another week." Alina sighed and looked at me. "You don't have to harbor me for that long, though. I understand it's inconvenient to look after me, pick me up, chauffeur me around."

"It's not the worst thing in the world."

"Maya said her article for promotion is due on Wednesday. I can come clean to her after she writes that. In the meantime, if you don't want me, I'll take my chances with Eddie. I already called him and mentioned I'm staying with you, and that I would probably need his couch soon."

"Eddie? Really?" I asked.

"He's a douchebag and all, but I don't know… I think he can keep a secret and not tell Maya he's housing her baby niece."

"You really don't like the guy?"

"You can form your own opinion tonight, I guess, but he's just… it's hard to explain. Have you stood on a high cliff and had this terrible sensation of just jumping off? Of course, you would never do it, you wouldn't even entertain it, but you still feel like jumping for a split second."

"It called the Call of the Void," I said. "It's a common impulse."

"Well, Eddie is like that, except instead of having the sensation to jump, I feel like I should run away as fast as possible."

"It's because he bought you a Barbie, huh?"

Alina snickered. "He bought me a Barbie for my sixteenth birthday. Who does that? Get me a gift card if you don't know what to get me." Alina stared out the passenger window.

"But Maya likes him," I said.

"Sure she does," Alina said, sighing. "Maya is gullible, and that's exacerbated by insecurities. She has a track record of choosing men who fall well below the standard of functional boyfriends. Eventually, she learns of their shortcomings, often when it's too late."

I had a few follow-up questions for that observation, but it wasn't my place to ask. I held my tongue.

Alina continued to speak anyway. "Even if you and Glacia can't figure out how to navigate the long-distance thing, Maya will eventually break things off with Eddie, and you can have a run at her. But I'll tell you right now, you're not her type."

"You said I was handsome."

"Handsome makes up like three points on a girl's one-to-ten scale."

"So, I'm a three?"

Alina turned to face me, frowning. "For Maya, you're like a six."

"A six?" My heart sank.

"You're just too nice. Nice, though nice... nice is secure. It's safe. And safe, though safe... well, safe is ultimately boring. There are no thrills in predictability. Maya needs a little. She craves adrenaline and drama. It's in the Adler blood. I'm a Moore through my dad's name, but my mom is an Adler. I know first hand we have terrible taste in men. However, at least we have fun during the rollercoaster ride. You know what Freud says?"

"Something incestuous," I said.

"Boys are always trying to recreate their mothers with love."

"Gross and wrong. Neither Maya nor Glacia remind me of my mother."

"So you love both Maya and Glacia?"

"What? No."

Alina snickered. "I'm kidding. Anyway, girls are always trying to recreate their fathers. Well, the women in my family have dads like a jet plane. Sleek, powerful, handsome, and never in one place for too long. We look for men who make us feel like we're flying." Alina patted my shoulder. "Sorry, champ, but you're ground control."

We stopped and had lunch before returning to my apartment, arriving back at my place a little after 1400hrs.

When I had picked up Alina from Glacia's house, I mentioned to Glacia that Maya would arrive at Eddie's around 1600hrs.

"We can show up after that," I had said.

"Why not show up early?" Glacia had asked, leaning against her doorjamb and tilting her head so her hair fell across her face. "If we show up around four-thirty, not 1630hrs. We're normal citizens, not military personal. Stop with the military time."

"It's a habit from my law enforcement days."

"Well, either way, we should arrive at four-thirty." Glacia emphasized the time, speaking it slowly. "If we arrive early, we have an excuse to leave early, if we're not having fun. If we have fun, showing up early allows us more time with them. Win-win."

I preferred not to go at all, so I enjoyed the idea of showing up early to leave early. We had agreed I would pick Glacia up from Nana's house around 1630hrs. I had two hours to rest and ready myself for the evening.

"What are you going to wear?" Alina asked, lying on my bed.

"What I'm wearing," I said, surveying my church outfit. It was the nicest I had dressed in years.

The girl cringed. "Really?"

"What's wrong with it?"

"Your shirt doesn't match your jeans, which are too baggy, and nothing matches your shoes. Honestly, you're dressed like a seventy-year-old widower who doesn't understand how to put himself together after fifty years of being told how to do so. Also, your beard is disgusting. Some men," Alina kissed her fingers and pointed at the ceiling, "know how to grow a beard. You? No. Yuck. It looks like you glued a handful of orange pubes to your face. It's disgusting, uneven, and... no." She grimaced, waving her hands before her face as if she had caught a whiff of something foul. "Shave it off. At the very least, trim it."

"I'm not sure I enjoy hanging out with you."

"Get over yourself. Also, do something with your hair. I mean, I understand the annoyance of having to style it every single day. Believe me. Have you seen my hair?" She pointed to extremely naturally curly hair. "Difficult to maintain, and annoying to do so. But I do it, because I'm a functioning member of society. You don't even splash water in your hair to give it a stylized, messy look. You wake up and you leave. I'd recommend cutting it short and really not worrying about it at all, or manipulating the texture a little. I mean, you're what, late-thirties?"

"Thirty-two."

Alina frowned. "Well, either way, you're not bald. You have hair, which, honestly, who cares? But you have it. Not only that, it's thick and wavy. Unruly to deal with. Doesn't matter, though. You're a grown man. Clean up after yourself. Do your dishes. Sweep the floor. Wipe your nasty toilet. Shave your face. And do your hair. It's not that difficult, and it's pretty important when you're going on a date."

"How did I ever survive without you?" I asked, forcing my sarcasm so it wouldn't go unnoticed.

"I honestly don't know," Alina said. "Glacia told me you brought her by. What were you thinking?" She widened her eyes, dropped her jaw, and shrugged. "I'm honestly embarrassed for you. She was concerned about my health after learning I stayed the night here. Were you trying to ruin any chance you had with her before even having a chance with her?"

"She's going on a date with me, isn't she? Didn't seem to matter."

"It mattered, Dummy. It all matters. Maybe she overlooks a few things now." Alina pouted her lip and shook her head back and forth. "But those things get harder and harder to overlook as time goes by. Pretty soon, she meets another man—a man who knows how to handle a broom, use a sponge, style his hair. I mean, Gussy—"

"Only my mom calls me Gussy."

"August, muscles only take you so far in life. If I can be brutally honest with you, it's not even that far unless you're looking for a modeling career. Believe me, no one wants to date a male model. They're insecure, self-centered, and needy."

I caved to the teenage girl and obeyed her command, shaving my face and styling my hair to her advice. I even allowed her to dress me for the evening. A simple pair of tight-fitting jeans and a T-shirt.

"Bring a hoodie," Alina said. "It's warm outside and you'll be sitting by a fire, so you probably won't need it, but Glacia might feel cold later. She'll appreciate the forethought."

Once I showered, shaved, and dressed, I stepped into the kitchen like a runway model, even providing Alina with a smooth spin.

"First," she said, scowling, "never do that again. Second, you look great. Tomorrow we'll work on your personality. Who knows, maybe by the end of the week, I'll have turned you into an actual catch."

"Ha. Ha. You're hilarious. I laughed so hard, I fell off my dinosaur." I stared at her with a stoic, straight face.

"What did you say?" Alina asked, nearly breathless.

"I said, I laughed so hard, I fell off my dinosaur."

Alina slowly shook her head back and forth, a smile creeping outward and curling upward across her face. "Did you quote *Step Brothers* just now?"

I chuckled. "I'm full of surprises, aren't I?"

"When did you watch *Step Brothers*?"

"Years and years ago. I don't know why, but that line popped into my head just now."

"Greatest moment of my life," Alina said. "You shaved and dressed and cleaned up, saying something worthwhile and funny. I'm so proud of you." The girl placed a hand over her heart and sighed. "Are you nervous? From what I understand, you don't excel in social situations."

"I'm okay."

"Yeah, I really taught you well."

"Hey," I said.

"Yeah?"

"You can stay as long as you want. It's not inconvenient for me. Honestly, it's nice having someone around. You know, a friend. Someone I can, well, not talk to, but listen to."

Alina laughed. "Thank you."

"If you're looking for something to do, look into Stacey Stokes for me. She's the latest voodoo doll victim, but her death doesn't quite fit with the others. At least, it feels different to me."

"In what way?"

I bit my lip and shook my head, unsure of how to explain myself to Alina without reciting the entire voodoo history to her. "Just a hunch, and one I don't want polluting your thoughts. Let me know what you think later tonight."

"I hope I don't see you tonight."

"What's that mean?" I asked.

"If I see you later? It means you blew your chance with Glacia. Hopefully, you're staying the night at her place." Alina winked at me.

"You're sixteen, Kid. Maybe you can coach me on how to be a functioning adult, but you should also practice acting like a kid every once in a while. It's healthy for your soul." I turned and opened the front door.

"August," Alina said.

"Yeah?"

"Thank you again. No one has ever—no one other than Maya has ever really, you know, done much for me. And she's family. You… you don't know me, but you trust me."

I thought of Aaron Brooks, and how I had failed to trust him, despite the situation. "No more scary movies. Watch something that will make you laugh."

"Maybe horror movies make me laugh." Alina burst into evil laughter.

I shook my head but chuckled, turning and leaving my apartment.

Date Ruined. Sunday, April 24th. 1602hrs.

Maya wore ripped jeans and a black T-shirt. The outfit was casual and comfortable, but she felt sexy enough in it, especially for the type of date—grilling, drinking cheap beers, and a fire. She stepped out of her car onto the dirt driveway.

Eddie lived in the country southeast of Sacramento. He owned three acres of land, which he had converted into a pasture for his two horses, Earl Thomas and Jameson Jack. Before him, they had belonged to his late father. Jameson and Jack Daniels were Eddie's dad's favorite whiskeys, and Earl Thomas was a hard-hitting safety for his father's favorite football team, the Seattle Seahawks. Eddie barely talked about his family, let alone his deceased father, so Maya enjoyed knowing the history of the horses names.

She strolled to the electric fence and clicked her tongue, beckoning the horses.

They ignored her.

Maya shuffled to the haystack and peeled off a flake, pausing and frowning.

A burlap sack lay on the bales of hay, folded in half.

Maya shoved the uneasy feeling from her mind and returned to the horses, tempting them over with a handful of treats. Earl Thomas, a palomino, trotted to her and accepted her peace offering. Maya scratched his face and cooed, "That's a good boy. Yeah. That's a good boy."

Growing up, Maya had never been in the presence of horses. In fact, she had never touched the beautiful animals until she began dating Eddie a couple of months ago. They were terrifying and majestic, though—like all the incredible things in life. Storms, the night sky, the depths of the ocean, love.

After Earl Thomas finished the hay, Maya headed toward Eddie's house, walking around the sidewalk to the front door. She knocked and waited.

Eddie appeared a few seconds later. He had short, blonde hair and a clean-shaven face, as most police officers had. Tattoos riddled every square inch of exposed skin on his body—his rather chiseled body. Maya rarely cared too much about a man's outward appearance. As with all people who say appearance doesn't matter, though, when someone is hot as Hades, hard and toned... well, it doesn't hurt. He wore jeans, flip-flops, and a tank top, exposing the sleeves of tattoos that drove Maya wild.

"Hey," Eddie said, looking her up and down with ravenous eyes.

Maya's stomach lurched, and she wanted to jump him, but she exhaled and resisted. "Hi. May I come in?"

Eddie snickered. He had a perverted, juvenile mind, which Maya actually enjoyed rather than despised. "I might use that line later."

"Not a chance that I'll ever say yes."

"Well, maybe I'll get you drunk." He winked at her. "No one knows what Maya Adler will do or say when she's drunk, not even herself."

Maya shoved her way into his house. It was a cozy country cottage with two bedrooms, one-and-a-half bathrooms, a small living room, and a cramped kitchen. The real allure of the home lived in the backyard, though. Eddie had improved it himself, pouring the cement to create a beautiful patio, constructing a gorgeous fire pit, and growing a luscious yard.

Maya leaned against his body and tiptoed up to him, kissing him long and passionately. "How's your day off been?" she asked, pulling away ever so slightly. She didn't want to separate herself too far. What if she needed another one of his kisses?

"Great," Eddie said. "I finally finished the fire pit. It's ready for S'mores tonight. I know how you love those hot, gooey marshmallows."

Maya smacked him on the chest before raising up and kissing him again. "What's for dinner?"

"The burger patties are prepared and in the refrigerator, just waiting for our company to arrive."

"Our company?" Maya asked. "I like the sound of that. It's almost like, I don't know, we enjoy the luxuries of this house together."

"We've enjoyed more than the luxuries of this house together." Eddie grabbed her, pulling her tighter against his body, kissing her. "So, how's your investigation with August going? You learn anything new?"

"Nothing beyond what you told me earlier about Stacey Stokes. Did you know her?"

Eddie's body went rigid. "What do you mean?" His voice was a tight whisper.

His response to the question threw Maya off for a beat, but she shook her head and ignored his reaction. "I feel like I recognize her name, but I can't figure out from where."

"It's a unique name. I mean, the alliteration aspect."

"Alliteration aspect?" Maya asked, biting her lower lip. "Look at you, Mr. Literary."

"In case you have forgotten, I graduated high school with honors.

English was my favorite class."

"I'm suddenly feeling," Maya waved a hand before her face, cooling herself off, "extremely hot."

Eddie smirked and backed away from her, venturing from the entryway into the kitchen. He opened the refrigerator and grabbed a beer, cracking the tab. "I have tequila for margaritas. There's beer. And whiskey. What's your poison?"

"Do you have to ask?" Maya asked, leaning on the kitchen wall and watching Eddie.

"My little whiskey girl. Straight or with soda?"

"Shots."

Eddie moved to a cabinet, reached for a couple of shot glasses, and set them on the counter. He moved to a liquor cabinet, removed a bottle of Jameson, and poured it, sliding one shot glass over to Maya.

Maya grabbed it and slowly twirled the contents, inspecting the liquor. Her mind jumped to Stacey Stokes, found dead in a puddle of her own vomit with a voodoo doll beside her nightstand. The voodoo doll shifted her thoughts to August.

"August doesn't drink," she said. "He's been sober for a while now. So, I don't know, don't offer him alcohol. Okay?"

"Yeah, of course." Eddie raised his shot glass. "Cheers."

"To what?"

"To your article. Four accidental deaths in four days, and four voodoo dolls. If that's not a story to get you promoted, I don't know what is."

Maya clinked her shot glass with Eddie's, bringing the glass to her lips before pausing. "Wait. What did you say?"

"About what?"

"Four voodoo dolls."

"Were there not four voodoo dolls found at the victims' houses?"

"Three voodoo dolls, right? Muriel Fincher. Gilbert Tonyan. Stacey Stokes." Maya and August had stolen Peter Seed's voodoo doll before the police had learned about it. Only Maya and August knew that four voodoo dolls existed.

"Four, I thought," Eddie said, shrugging. "I could be wrong, of course." Eddie glanced up at the ceiling. "I responded to Muriel Fincher. I found a doll at her house. One of my buddies told me about Gilbert Tonyan and that his wife called in, reporting a doll at their house. I also heard from another buddy that Peter Seed..." Eddie trailed off and licked his lips. "No one found a doll at Peter Seed's house, did they?"

"No," Maya whispered.

"Well, ain't that the pits?"

Maya thought of the haystack and the burlap sack sitting atop it. She thought of the voodoo doll at Peter Seed's house being made of hay and burlap.

"How did I overlook that?" Eddie asked, stepping toward Maya. She stood in the corner of the two counters. He clicked his tongue. "This puts us in a predicament, doesn't it?"

"Stacey Stokes." The name slammed into Maya like lightning striking. "What... what's his name? Mason! Your old buddy Mason. Yeah. He... he told me about your crazy ex-girlfriend. Stacey. Stacey Stokes. You killed her, didn't you?"

Eddie cleared his throat. "Here's the thing, Maya. Wanda, your sister, went AWOL, as she does. Apparently, Stephen jumped ship." Stephen was Alina's dad, Wanda's husband, Maya's brother-in-law. "He found someone younger and more attractive. I really can't blame him for leaving that crazy junkie. Anyway, that's not the point. Stephen went away. Wanda, in response, disappeared into the night. She left behind sweet, young Alina to fend for herself. Do you know where Alina found comfort and refuge?"

Maya knew none of that information, and it had come from left field. Why had Eddie told her all that after she had asked about him murdering his ex-girlfriend? "What?"

Eddie sighed. "One perk of being a cop is the ability to keep track of everyone, at all times. It's not that hard when you have access to the resources available to me. With Stephen in the wind and your sister smoking something again—pipe or, well, pipe—Alina had to find a place to stay. Enter the knight in shining armor. August Watson."

"I don't understand," Maya said, completely lost in the conversation's progression.

"Don't worry about it." Eddie looked backward, as if searching for something. Lightning fast and thunderously powerful, he struck Maya across the jaw.

Maya wavered, lost her balance, and collapsed to the ground.

Eddie flicked his wrist and cursed, but he leaned over Maya. "Well, I guess we have no choice left in the matter but to find your niece. The more hostages, the better for my survival and continued freedom."

Maya squeezed her hands into fists, readying herself to fight back. As she did, she felt something sturdy in her palm. Throughout everything, she had continued to hold onto the shot glass. Without thinking, acting only on impulse and instinct, Maya quick-tossed whatever whiskey—if any—remained in her shot glass. Her intentions weren't to soak him, but to surprise him. To buy herself a half-second.

It worked. Eddie flinched, allowing Maya the space to bolt upright and grasp the Jameson bottle.

Eddie drove upward from his crouch, smashing his shoulder into her stomach, lifting her off the ground, slamming her back into the upper cabinets. She folded over his shoulder like a survivor getting rescued by a firefighter. Oh, the irony. From her awkward position, Maya reached around Eddie's head and clobbered the Jameson bottle against the side of his face. With little power behind her strike, the bottle didn't break, as it often does in movies. However, Eddie dropped her, reaching for his face.

She fell, crashing into the edge of the counter before stumbling to the hardwood floor. Ignoring the pain, Maya climbed to her feet.

Eddie held his face where she had struck him, moaning in pain. Through the chaos, she noticed his facial structure had collapsed and cratered. She must have shattered his cheekbone.

That left her a vital choice.

Run while she had the chance, or take a cocked-back swing and hit him until he died.

Maya obsessed over true-crime everything. She knew that when a victim faces the opportunity to flee from or kill their captor, their abuser, their potential killer, they should always hit the offender until they were no longer moving. If the victim ran, they would get pursued and most likely caught.

Maya knew that in her head. Yet, she decided in a fraction of a split second—more from impulse and survival instinct than conscious thought.

Eddie stood nearly a foot taller and weighed about a hundred pounds more. She fared slim to zero chances of killing him. Despite the information she knew, Maya followed her gut and ran to the front door.

"You ungrateful slut!" Eddie roared. "I did everything for you!"

Maya reached the door and fumbled with the deadbolt. It was old, sticking unless manipulated just… it clicked open. Maya grabbed the door handle, pulling on the door to throw it wide open.

It crashed shut, breaking free of her grip, slamming so hard against the jamb that pictures on the wall rattled.

Eddie's strong, practiced hand viced around her biceps and wheeled her around to face him. She felt a sense of pride to see his broken, sunken, bleeding face.

Maya had endured a lot during her life, and her pain had scarred her, creating a chitinous armor around her heart. Despite her fear and confusion and pain, Maya would not cry or scream for Eddie. She would not show Eddie how much he terrified her. So, instead, she snaked out her free arm—the one he didn't have a hold of—and she slapped him across his broken cheekbone.

Eddie hissed and cussed. His grip tightened, and fingers pressed hard into her skin, digging against her bone. "That's enough," he hissed through the pain.

"You killed her," Maya said, recalling what August had said—it doesn't feel like the others. "You murdered Stacey Stokes."

Eddie rolled his eyes. "Christ," he said. He jerked on Maya's arm, yanking her toward him as his forehead charged toward her. He connected square with her nose.

Maya's world exploded into billions of tiny lights—intense lights that burned behind her eyes like someone had planted a searing-hot pan in her head.

Stood Up. Sunday, April 24th. 1611hrs.

The world slipped away from me—like my grasp on reality vanished.

I'm not an expert on women or the female psyche, but I know men can occasionally become single-minded. A tunnel forms in their vision, blinding them to all else but the light waiting so beautifully at the end. That's what happened to me when Glacia opened Nana's front door.

She wore white sneakers and a short, red sundress with patterned white flower petals. It was full-shouldered with sleeves, but had a string—untied—that would have held together the... I don't know fashion words. I'll put it this way. There was very little about Glacia's cleavage or legs left to the imagination.

"Did you have a stroke?" Glacia asked, giggling.

"I think so. You short-circuited my brain."

"Is that a compliment?"

"Yes."

Glacia stepped toward me, tiptoeing upward and kissing my cheek. "I'm flattered. You look nice, too. Did Alina help?"

"How did you know?"

Glacia giggled again, shaking her head. "Well, you shaved first off. You also styled your hair—though, don't tell Alina this—but I liked the unkempt look."

"I'm definitely telling her that. She needs to know she is wrong occasionally."

"A woman, especially one her age, is never wrong. Never say otherwise."

"I'll keep that in mind."

"Practice that creed like your life depended on it... because it very well might one day."

"Now you're threatening me?" I asked.

Glacia bit her lower lip and stared at me with wide eyes. "What will you do about it?"

The back-and-forth banter I was decent at. I could at least keep up. The overt flirting, especially about sexually charged topics with the woman I was potentially going to become sexually charged with... not so decent at.

I popped my lips and pointed to my car. "Should we head out? Earlier we're there, the earlier we can leave."

Eddie lived about ten minutes from Nana's house. We parked next to Maya's car, which was parked off to the side near the horse pasture. Two horses grazed in the back of the field.

Glacia rounded my vehicle and grabbed my hand. Together, we approached the front door. She carried a bottle of red wine. I had nothing to contribute, which reasserted my professional ability to sabotage relationships—I brought nothing to the table.

I rang the doorbell, turned and smiled at Glacia.

"What?" she asked.

"What?" I asked.

"Why did you look at me like that?"

"Like what?"

"You know."

"I think you're really pretty."

Glacia grinned. "I think you're very handsome."

After a few seconds, I rang the doorbell again. Again, no response.

"Strange," I said, feeling uneasy. I'm not sure why, but something didn't sit right.

"You think they're having sex?" Glacia asked, lifting her eyebrows. "I mean, maybe they wanted to punch out a quickie, and we showed up right in the middle of it."

I moved into the flowerbed and peered through the front window, where I could see straight into the kitchen through a dining room.

"Gross," Glacia said. "Are you trying to catch them in the act? I want to see." She shouldered beside me and cupped her hands over the screen to see through the window. "What's that?"

"What?"

"On the kitchen floor. You see it?"

I squinted, noticing the pooling liquid, as if someone had spilled something and neglected to clean it. The uneasy feeling intensified.

"They probably had a water fight and had to change clothes, and well... you know how that goes," Glacia said.

My phone vibrated in my pocket. I gasped, momentarily startled at the sudden sensation under the current circumstances. Once I realized it was only my phone, I hurriedly fished it out and checked the caller. Alina Moore showed on the screen. I ignored the call, scrolled through my contacts, and dialed Maya's phone. It rang five times and went to voicemail.

"Hey," Glacia said.

I glanced at her. She stepped away from the window, holding her phone to her ear. She nodded and stared at me, moving her cell from her face and handing it to me. "It's Alina. She needs to talk to you."

"Alina," I said.

"August, where are you?"

"I'm at Eddie's."

"Get out of there. Now."

"Slow down. What's going on?"

"Get on your phone and look at the news. Or Google Stacey Stokes. She dated Eddie."

"Wait, what?" I pulled the phone from my ear and turned it to speakerphone. With my free hand, I went to the browser and typed in Stacey Stokes, clicking on the most recent news article.

As I skimmed, Alina continued to talk. "Stacey released footage of Eddie in uniform doing all kinds of crazy things. The videos and the photographs went to every media outlet in the area. He... Eddie murdered her."

The article I had pulled up confirmed everything Alina said.

"Where is he now?" she asked. "Do you see him?"

I shook my head, staring at the dark window.

"Where's Maya?"

My heart hammered in my chest, my mouth went dry, and my jaw dropped.

"Where's Maya?" Alina repeated.

"I don't know."

"Are they there?"

"No."

"Where are they?"

I looked at Glacia, and she stood frozen, statuesque apart from the soft breeze manipulating her dress and hair.

"Alina," I said, forcing myself to remain calm. "Does he know where you are? When you asked him if you could stay with him, did you tell him where you were staying?"

In response to my question, a thunderous report sounded on the other line—like someone banging on a door with a baseball bat.

Alina's voice caught, and her breath trembled in the receiver like static.

"Don't answer the door! Do not open that door," I said, repeating it. "Alina, there's a fire escape out the back. Do you hear me?"

An explosive crash.

Alina screamed.

Grunting. Cussing. Begging.

Ragged breathing, distant at first, but growing clearer and louder. "August," said a male voice.

"Eddie," I said.

"From what I hear, you're an intelligent, reasonable man. So, let's practice those traits, shall we? Here's what will happen. If you want Maya and Alina to live, you won't call the police. Are we crystal clear on that condition?"

"Yes."

"If I so much as hear a siren in the distance, they will both die. If I so much as even think you considered calling the cops, they will die."

"No cops. I swear it."

"From what I hear, you're a pretty honest man. Are you an honest man?"

"I try my best."

"Well, you're going to have to try really, really hard right now. Do I have your word, August, that you will not call the cops? Like I said, if I can't trust you, if I even think that I can't trust your word, they're dead."

"You can trust me."

"Say it then."

"I swear, Eddie, on everything, I won't call anyone. No cops. No back up. No one."

The phone remained on speaker, and Glacia heard the entire conversation. She stared at me, terrified and chewing on her thumb.

"Now, here's how this will happen." Eddie cleared his throat. "You're going to meet us at Peter Seed's house in twenty minutes. Alone. Your date—hello, by the way. She's listening right now, yeah?"

I couldn't risk lying to him. "Yeah."

"Thank you for your honesty, but her presence complicates things, August. I can trust you, but I don't trust her. I know nothing about her, especially whether I can trust her."

"You can," Glacia said.

"What if she already called the cops during this conversation?" Eddie asked. "That would ruin everything, wouldn't it?"

"She didn't," I said. "Eddie, I swear to you, she has called no one."

"I hope you're telling the truth. I have my police scanner on, and I can hear everything happening. I will know. I will know."

"I know," I said.

"So, here's what's going to happen, August. You'll meet me at Peter's house in twenty minutes with a hundred thousand dollars."

"I don't have that kind of money."

"Figure it out then."

"Eddie, let's be realistic here."

"Here's what's realistic. I'm a cop. I have a gun, and I know how to use it. If you do not meet my demands, I'll kill Maya and Alina. Are you ready to listen to my terms?"

"Yes."

"I need your vehicle and one-hundred thousand dollars in cash. When you get to the house, call Alina... this number. If anyone attempts to enter the home without calling this number first, the girls die. No hesitation."

"I need to know they're alive," I said.

"No, you need to trust they're alive. You have no leverage in this matter. Either you show up with my demands met, and they live, or you don't follow through, and they die." The call ended, washing the area in utter, deafening silence.

"What do we do?" Glacia asked after a second.

I scrolled through my phone and called Daphne, knowing Fred would have his phone turned off on a Sunday. Hopefully, she didn't follow the same strict weekend rituals he did. Someone had to have a phone on them, in case of emergencies, right?

"Hello?" Daphne answered. I hadn't even noticed the ringing.

"Where's Fred?"

I must have sounded panicked, because her tone shifted. "August, is everything okay?"

"Where's Fred? I need to speak to him now."

"He's right here." A second passed.

Fred's voice sounded over the line. "Hey, buddy, you okay?"

"The voodoo doll case. We broke it wide open. It's Eddie, Maya's boyfriend."

"He knows voodoo?"

"Listen, Fred, he has Maya and Alina. He has them hostage, and he's threatening to kill them. Google Stacey Stokes, if you need to know more, but we don't have the time to go over it right now. Listen, buddy, I need a hundred-thousand dollars cash. Do you have that?"

"No."

"No? You're always bragging about how rich you are."

"Not on hand. Banks are closed this time on Sundays, too. There's ATMs, but, man, I don't think I can come close to withdrawing that much money."

I cursed under my breath, running out of ideas. Apart from Fred, my parents were the only other people who might have that much cash lying around. It would take thirty minutes to get to their house, though, thirty minutes to drive back—and that's if they had it.

"August?" Fred asked.

"How much cash do you have on hand?" I asked.

"We invest everything. I mean, there are penalties for moving it or taking it out, and there're waiting periods. We don't really mess with cold cash like that."

"How much cash do you have access to?"

"I don't know. Maybe five thousand dollars."

I looked at Glacia. "You?"

"Less than that."

I had about forty-two dollars in cash. Running my hands through my done-up hair, I sighed.

"Call the cops," Fred said.

"No cops. Eddie will kill them. He wants to meet us at Peter's place."

"Who?"

"Peter Seed." Fred wouldn't know that name. He blinded himself to work on weekends, and Peter's death had occurred the day before, on Saturday. "Yesterday's voodoo victim. He lives in a neighborhood that probably doesn't see too many strangers. I'm thinking Eddie chose that location for a reason. If he sees a cop or someone who's not me, well… you know."

Fred sighed into the receiver. "What's the plan?"

I cracked my knuckles and stared at Glacia. "Fred, if you don't hear from me in an hour, call the police. Eddie will have my car by then. Give them the make and model. I'll have Glacia send you a picture of the license plate. Give them that, too."

"What are you going to do?" Fred asked.

I disconnected the call, keeping my eyes on Glacia. I knew exactly what I had to do to save Alina and Maya. The question was, could I do it when the time came and it mattered most?

"Do you still have Susan's gun?"

Double Date. Sunday, April 24th. 1647hrs.

"Get down," I said, prompting Glacia to slink lower in the passenger seat to hide from plain view. We turned onto Peter Seed's street, and I didn't want to risk Eddie noticing Glacia through a window.

Eddie had parked his car in Peter's driveway. I parked at the curb a few dozen feet beyond the house. If Eddie was watching us from within the home, he wouldn't have the proper angle to locate Glacia.

Reaching into my backseat, I grabbed my bag filled with paranormal trinkets. With the time restraints Eddie had imposed, I couldn't do any better. However, the backpack had enough weight to initially—hopefully—convince Eddie that I had collected the cash. The illusion wouldn't last too long, dispelling as soon as Eddie unzipped it.

"You can do this?" I faced Glacia.

She remained slouched in the chair, peeking over the dashboard and through the windshield. In her hand, she held Susan's gun.

"Glacia?"

"Yes, I can," she said, facing me. Her lips twitched as she forced a ragged smile.

"You're sure?"

She took a big breath and chuckled. "Believe it or not, I've been on crazier first dates."

I echoed her laughter. The snapshot of bliss sapped some of the tension. "Crawl through the window," I said. "If you open the door, you'll have to close it, and that might alert Eddie to you being here. Once you're inside the house, aim for the body. It's the biggest target."

"What if he's wearing a bullet-proof vest?"

"Won't matter. It'll feel like a horse kicking him in the chest—short of breath, folded over, intense pain. We don't want to kill him, anyway. Aim for the chest." I exhaled and opened the car door. "Good luck."

I trudged up the driveway, walking along the sidewalk leading to the front entry. During my brief tenure with the Galt Police Department, I had knocked on plenty of doors, not knowing what I might find behind them. I had knocked on plenty of doors, knowing exactly what I would find behind them. My adrenaline would spike and my stomach would freefall, but beyond basic nerves, I never feared the door opening. Back then, though, I feared little, if anything at all.

That's the crux of youth, though. Lack of fear. Running into dangerous situations with your head down, like an angry bull charging. What the inexperienced don't understand, fear only weakens when it controls.

Eddie opened the door before I made it to the front mat. I had never met the man before, so I didn't know what to expect. We stood about the same height. Where I had lean muscle, he was broad and thick, probably having twenty to thirty pounds on me. A smudgy bruise covered half of his face. In his right hand, he held a standard-issue Glock 19. He waved me into the dingy house, closing the door behind me.

"You have the money?" he asked.

I turned slightly, showing him my backpack. "Where's Maya and Alina?"

"We're not playing this game. Hand me the money."

"Eddie, we had a deal," I said. "A hundred-thousand dollars and my car for Maya and Alina. My car is out front. I have your money." I grabbed a handful of my shirt, raising it to expose my waistline. "No weapons, either. Okay? You trusted me and I trusted you. Now, I need to see that you held up your end of the bargain. Where are they?"

Eddie licked his teeth and pawed at his collarbone.

I held my breath, knowing he could pull that trigger any time he wanted to. I had pulled that trigger before and I knew what it felt like. I bet my life, Maya's life, and Alina's life that Eddie preferred not to pull the trigger.

"They're down the hallway," he said. "First door to the right. In the bathtub. You go in first."

"Of course." I stepped in front of Eddie, moving slowly and carefully—both for my safety and to buy a little time.

I entered the flickering-light bathroom, taking in the grimy, moldy, and disgusting area. It sickened me to think someone could live in such filth, and it sickened me more to think I was one of those someones.

The bathroom curtain was closed, but I could hear soft whimpering and moaning from behind it. Grabbing the plastic sheet, I slid the rings across the bar.

Maya and Alina sat in the tub. Duct tape wrapped tightly around their head, into their mouths, cutting at the corners of their lips. Blood dribbled down their chin like tear trails. Twine, like that used to hold together bales of hay, held their wrists and ankles together. The skin around the rope had bruised and crusted with blood. They both looked at me with wide, terrified eyes.

Anger fueled my mind, nearly blinding me and forcing me to react. I swallowed the rage, knowing impulsive behavior—charging with my head down like an angry bull—would lead to all of our deaths.

As I calmed myself, something hard, cold, and metallic bit into the back of my skull. I glanced in the mirror. In the reflection, I saw Eddie had pressed the Glock to my head. As if he had a microphone pressed to his lips, I could hear his breathing on full blast.

"August, here's what will happen now. You'll slowly remove your backpack and place it on the counter. Once I confirm the right amount of money is in the bag, I'll sneak out the front door and drive into the sunset. You'll never have to see or hear from me again."

I returned my attention to Maya and Alina, subtly nodding at the two women and hoping to reassure them. I removed one strap from my shoulder, peeling off the second.

Eddie kept his gun pressed against my skull.

I held the backpack by the top handle with my right hand, extending it across my body toward the bathroom counter. Naturally, my shoulders shifted so my body angled to the left, toward Eddie's chest.

I had one chance at this. Hopefully, all those hours in the gym would pay off.

Through the mirror's reflection, I watched as Eddie's eyes followed the bag, no longer fixating on me. He never noticed me tense as my muscles flexed, preparing to launch.

I dropped the bag, simultaneously leaning my head forward, out of the way of the gun. I circled my left arm over Eddie's hand, pinning the gun against my body so it pointed downward.

He fired.

My calf exploded with pain, but I ignored it. In the same continuous motion from clasping Eddie's gun arm to my body, I wheeled and hooked across the face with a quick punch. With my body twisted to face him, I drew my right knee directly into his crotch.

All that in the space of a second.

Eddie folded, but regained his stance. He was a law enforcement officer, and he had fought many times before. He knew how to take and handle sudden, bursting pain from a strike.

In an effortless motion, he ripped his arm free of my restraint and shoved me away from him, back pedaling and purchasing a few feet of distance between us.

Before he could take aim and fire, I lowered my shoulder and charged, driving into his solar plexus, carrying him out the bathroom door, and slamming him against the hallway wall. My left shoulder popped and sagged from the impact.

Eddie's ribs cracked like dry branches. The gun flew from his hand, clattering to the ground somewhere behind me.

I pushed away from him, preparing to land a solid punch to his throat. As I stepped back, planting weight on my wounded leg, my calf gave out. I dropped, landing hard on my dislocated shoulder.

Eddie wavered, coughed and grunted, but remained standing. He loomed over me like a real-life monster ready to kill.

Glacia burst into the entryway. She had snuck around the house, entering through the broken window. She held Susan's gun in both of her trembling hands, pointing it at Eddie. Her face twisted with fear, and tears slipped down her cheeks.

"Freeze!"

Eddie coughed and growled, transferring his attention from me to her. He cocked his head when he saw Glacia and smirked. "You must be August's date. I'm so happy we all made it to the party, after all." He stepped toward her.

Glacia stepped back. "Don't move any closer."

"Are you going to shoot me?" he asked, breathing hard.

"Don't think I won't."

Eddie blurred. For a big man with broken ribs, he moved fast.

Glacia hadn't trained for this situation. She did not know how to compose herself during life or death combat. The inexperienced and the untrained respond to threats in one of three ways. Some fight. Some flee. Most of them freeze—at least for a split second as they process the danger.

Glacia froze, failing to pull the trigger. Eddie crashed into her like a linebacker blindsiding a quarterback. Her head lashed against the ground with a sickening thud. Her entire body went obviously and terrifyingly limp.

The universe pressed pause on my mind and my thoughts right then. I stopped consciously thinking. Instead, I devolved into pure instinct. My body acted of its own accord, and I was a passenger on the ride.

My hand reached back, locating the gun ejected from Eddie's hand when I had slammed him into the wall. I raised it, pointing it at Aaron—at Eddie. Their faces, the ghost of the kid who I had killed and that of Eddie's, blurred together into one misshapen visage.

One second I saw Aaron picking up Susan's gun and standing. The next second, Eddie stood like a demon in the entryway, holding the gun, pointing it at Glacia's unconscious body.

Was the gun he held real? Or was it only an air soft gun?

The thought crossed my mind, and I hesitated, falling back into the memory of the park, of the basketball court, of the asphalt. Blood surrounded Aaron's lifeless body, and an air soft gun lay a few inches from his limp hand.

An explosion ripped through the house as a weapon fired.

Aftermath. Sunday, April 24th. 1707hrs.

Maya and Alina hugged each other in the back of an ambulance. An EMT stood near them, taking notes after evaluating their condition. By all appearances, at least from what I could observe with my untrained eye, the two women appeared physically unharmed.

Glacia, however, lay on a stretcher inside another ambulance, hooked up to tubes and IVs. She was still unconscious from bouncing her head off the floor. An EMT pulled the backdoors shut, the sirens flicked on, and the emergency vehicle sped away.

I lived in the past, stuck somewhere between five years ago and fifteen minutes ago, holding a gun and shooting another human with it.

The bullet had slammed into the side of Eddie's body, and he folded into the impact. A second bullet caught him in the shoulder, which pushed him back a step and spun him around. That's when he dropped Susan's gun. A third bullet caught him square in the chest, shoving him to the ground, and sitting on him so he couldn't get back up.

Fortunately, none of the shots had killed Eddie—at least, not yet. An ambulance with sirens blaring and lights flashing had hurried him to the nearest hospital, escorted by two police vehicles.

Yet another EMT popped my dislocated shoulder back into socket and bandaged my leg.

She looked at me, shaking her head, when she finished. "Lucky."

"Me?"

"Bullet grazed your skin. Didn't even enter your leg. It's a nasty cut, but one that will heal without needing surgery."

A Sacramento Police Officer lingered nearby. The EMT must have gestured to him, because after she finished informing me of my condition, the man appeared. He was a large man—three inches taller than me, and fifty pounds heavier.

"August Watson. That your name?" the officer asked.

I rolled my eyes. Officer Ted Wilson and I had attended the police academy together. I went to Galt, and Sacramento hired him. We hadn't spoken since going our different ways after graduation. He had a reputation as a hothead, though, and from what I heard, he worked through his anger by punching bad guys whenever he could.

"What happened?" he asked.

"You'll have to get the full story from Eddie," I said, grimacing as a jolt of pain shot up my leg. "From what I pieced together, Eddie planted voodoo dolls in the homes of victims of accidental deaths." I shrugged. "I guess he wanted to create a pattern to distract from the finale—his actual act of murder. I don't know if there's evidence to support this, but I'm sure he killed Stacey Stokes, though he made it appear like an accident. He left the voodoo doll at her place to continue with the theme of these people dying through a curse. Maya must have figured it out before our date night, because he kidnapped her and then went for Alina, kidnapping the girl as well. That's when he contacted me." I recounted the events leading up to me shooting Eddie three times.

Ted removed a can of Copenhagen and packed a large dip into his mouth. He sighed and stared off into the distance. A collection of residents who lived on the street gathered in the distance, watching the scene unfold without getting too close to the police.

"Eddie would have shot those girls dead in a second," I said, knowing Ted would ask why I hadn't notified the police. "You know he would have. This was the best way."

"You're a private investigator, Watson, helping people talk to their dead aunts and all that. You're no longer a cop. You decided that. And you're not a vigilante. You don't get to make those calls, no matter how authentic they seem. You call us when something like this happens. We'll deal with it."

"What would you have done?" I asked.

"I don't deal in the business of 'what ifs' or hypotheticals. I'm in the business of 'what is.'" He picked at his nails. "Stacey Stokes scheduled a weekly email for those files to send out. She canceled the email and rescheduled it every week. If she died, she couldn't reschedule, and the documents would land in every local media's inbox, and in the Chief of Police's inbox." Ted chuckled, though with no humor—just a noise to avoid the quiet. "The evidence Stacey had would have exposed Eddie, and we could have arrested him years ago. Can you imagine living your life that terrified? She was too scared to report him, but she feared for her life so much that she kept the draft scheduled to send. Unbelievable." Ted exhaled and turned to me. "You should have shot him between the eyes." The officer turned away from me and joined his fellow brothers in blue a few yards away.

I stood, grunting. A current of tight pain pulsed through my leg, but I weathered it and hobbled over to Alina and Maya, sitting beside them in the ambulance.

"You okay?" I asked.

"I feel like I'm the protagonist at the end of a horror movie," Alina said. "Sitting here, waiting for the monster to re-emerge. You know they always do, right? Unless you kill them, like kill them-kill them, they always come back."

"This isn't a movie," I said. "Eddie's not coming back."

"You should have killed him," Alina said. "You should have shot him until he was dead. That's what I would have done to him. That psycho." The girl glanced at her aunt. "Maya, you sure know how to pick them, don't you? Remember Tony? Antonio." She said it with a smooth accent. "Yeah, he was almost as awesome as Eddie. Who are you going to date next? Ted Bundy? Marilyn Manson? The Unabomber?"

"Hey," I said, subtly shaking my head at Alina. "Now's not the time."

"She's not wrong," Maya said. "My track record speaks for itself. I think I'm going to remain single for a while. Maybe then I can avoid attracting serial killers into my personal bubble. I'll have to take notes from you, though, won't I? How to remain single?" She looked at her niece. "You're a professional at that."

"Guys, enough," I said.

"By the way," Maya said, narrowing her eyes and looking back and forth between Alina and me. "Why was my sixteen-year-old niece at your apartment? That seems odd, don't you think?"

"We're hooking up," Alina said. "How's that for professionally single?"

"What?" Maya said, shooting to her feet and facing me with the wrath of God and Lucifer and every other god and demon in existence.

"Nope. No. No. No. Nope," I said, waving my hands before my face. "Not hooking up. Nothing close to that. Nope."

"We're not hooking up, you pervert," Alina said, shaking her head. "Why would you think so little of me or him?"

"Why are you with him, then?" Maya asked.

Alina sighed.

"She has to know," I said.

"Know what?" Maya asked.

"I needed a place to stay," Alina said, staring at her dangling feet. "My dad left us two or three months back, and my mom spiraled. She lost her job. We lost the apartment. Then, recently, she went and disappeared again. I had nowhere to sleep, so I asked August if I could crash with him."

"First off, wildly inappropriate." Maya glared at me. "That's to you. She's sixteen. Are you insane? Are you, like, actually out of your mind? Second." Maya returned her attention to Alina. "Why didn't you ask to stay with me?"

"You have that important article to write. I didn't want to distract you from that."

Maya rubbed her earlobe for a second. "So you stayed with a strange man in his thirties?"

"I'm not a stranger," I said. "You know me well."

"You keep your pervert mouth shut. I'll deal with you in a minute."

"I would have stayed with Eddie," Alina said, "but he gave me major creeper vibes. Turns out, I wasn't wrong to suspect him of being a weirdo. I knew it when he gave me a Barbie for my birthday."

"Enough about the Barbie!" Maya said, throwing up her arms. "Get over it. Girls like Barbies."

Alina faced me, frustration pained red across her face. "How does this work?"

"How does what work?"

"This?" The girl gestured at all the emergency vehicles surrounding Peter's house. "Can we leave?"

"An officer will want to speak with you."

"One already did," Maya said. "EMTs bandaged us up when the officer interviewed us. I think we can head out if we want to."

"Do you want to?" I asked.

"I'm starving," Alina said.

"I was looking forward to burgers and s'mores," Maya said.

I popped a knuckle, pondering what to do next. "I'll drop you two off at Fred's house. Daphne is overwhelmingly talented in the kitchen."

"No," Maya said.

"No?"

"We're not barging in on Fred's weekend. We'll go with you to check on Glacia at the hospital. I'm sure the cafeteria can whip up something edible."

"Yeah, we're going with you," Alina said. "Besides, imagine if Glacia woke up to only see your goofy, creepy, perverted face. I would hate that. I mean, sure, it's sweet and all, but it's weird. You've known her for like two days, and you're waiting all by yourself for her to wake up. No. If we're there, it's just as sweet on your end, but far less creepy."

"Is that true?" I asked, looking at Maya.

Maya shook her head and shrugged. "I don't know. But Alina will say just about anything to get what she wants."

"Fine. We'll go to the hospital together."

Ghosted. Monday, April 25th. 0002hrs

Maya, Alina, and I spent the night in the hospital. The staff wouldn't allow us into Glacia's room, but they continually updated us on her condition—though they couldn't provide any direct medical information other than she was stable.

Glacia remained stable the entire night.

Much to my surprise, Janet—her mother—arrived around midnight. I'm not sure how she learned of her daughter's admittance. It didn't matter, though. She showed up, sitting alone on the other side of the waiting room from me.

I excused myself to Maya and Alina, shuffling across the room and sitting beside the woman, saying nothing at all, but hoping to provide a slight comfort with my familiar presence.

Janet held a silver cross in her hands, and she fiddled with it nonstop, moving it between her fingers and squeezing it between her palms, holding it near her lips and whispering, as if praying to the man nailed to it.

"I made bail," Janet said, her voice so quiet I barely heard her speak.

"What's that?"

"I made bail."

California law required that bail was available and affordable based on an individual's ability to pay, unless, of course, the court deemed them a danger to the community or as a flight risk. The judge must have set Janet's bail at pocket change, allowing her to walk free within hours of her arrest.

"What happened?" she asked.

"Glacia saved my life." I glanced over my shoulder at Maya and Alina. "And theirs."

"She won't want to see me, will she?"

"Probably not." I scrunched my face and popped a knuckle.

"I always do that... hurt her." Janet sighed and dropped her face into her palms, shaking her head back and forth. "Ever since she was little, I hurt her. I know when I'm doing it, but I still do it."

I watched Alina from across the waiting room. The girl leaned her head on Maya's lap and slept.

"I was a drunk," I said, lowering my voice and speaking slowly. "Alcohol controlled everything I did for three years. Every single choice I made. I lost three years of my life, like I can't remember most of that time. Worse, though, I lost family and friends. It was never the alcohol, though. It was me. It was my selfishness and fear. The alcohol was the crutch I gave myself to get through life, to help me escape." I stared forward at the white hospital wall.

"How did you get sober?"

My mouth watered, craving the taste of beer or wine or liquor—anything that might get me drunk. I reached into my pocket and unwrapped a piece of gum, sticking it into my mouth. I thought of my exercise regime, doing it religiously not for the benefits of physique or health, but to escape—to hurt and feel exhausted enough that I might sleep. I thought of the business I had formed and how I threw every waking second into it.

"I found new addictions."

Janet reached across the empty chair between us and grabbed my hand. "Will you… will you tell her I was here?"

I said nothing for a few seconds, shaking my head. "No. You're here when she wakes up or you're not. That's not on me, though. That's on you."

I stood and returned to Alina and Maya, slouching in the seat and closing my eyes. Sleep wouldn't come, though. It never did.

When I opened my eyes, Janet remained in the waiting room, chewing her nails. I considered that a minor victory.

Glacia woke early that morning—about 0400hrs. The doctor came into the waiting room and told us she was awake and that one of us could go into her room to see her.

Janet asked me to go in first, and I didn't argue.

Glacia's eyes sagged and her cheeks sunk into her face, and she appeared fatigued—as if she hadn't slept or eaten in days. The woman worked up the energy to spare me an affable grin when I entered her room, though.

We chatted for a few minutes before the nurse hurried me out, saying Glacia didn't have the energy for extended stays and other people wished to visit.

Alina went in next, exiting five minutes later, giving the nurse an earful all the way into the waiting room.

Janet went in last. She came back out only a minute or two after entering.

"How did it go?" I asked.

"She didn't talk to me. She wouldn't even look at me."

"Do you blame her?"

"No."

"Come back later," I said. "All you can do is try again and again… and again. But never give up."

Janet wiped a tear from the corner of her eye and sniffled. "I'm going to check myself into rehab when the facility opens this morning. I'm not sure if I'll be back here. I told Glacia as much, too, and I left her the number to the clinic I decided on."

"Word of advice?" I asked.

"Anything."

I looked at Maya, and I thought of Fred and Daphne and my parents. I had pushed many people away, but those five individuals had remained rooted in my life. They were always there, bugging me, waiting for me, hoping and praying for me.

"Find your people—the people who won't ever let you down. Find them and never lose them."

I left the hospital around 0530hrs to exercise. After I finished, I showered and arrived at my scheduled appointment with the mystery caller at the donut shop. I waited for thirty minutes, fueling up on coffee and sugar. I scrolled through my recent call log, finding her number, and tapping on it.

Her voicemail answered. I left a quick message, reminding her of our meeting.

When the clock flirted with 0745hrs, and I felt nervous about Fred beating me to the office, I called it quits.

The woman had ghosted the meeting she arranged. Recalling how nervous and frightened she had sounded on the phone, her absence made me uncomfortable.

When I arrived at the office, a small man with a receding hairline, a thin mustache, and expensive suit leaned on the hallway wall beside the door, staring at his cellphone. He looked up at me when I appeared from the stairs.

"August Watson?" he asked.

"I am he."

"I'm Vincent Dupree, and I believe I require your services."

I unlocked the office door and showed him inside, prompting him to sit in the chair placed before my desk. I nearly brewed myself a carafe of coffee before dealing with Mr. Dupree, but I sat behind my desk and grabbed my notepad.

"How can I help you?" I asked.

"It's my wife," he said.

"Your wife?"

He nodded, removing a black handkerchief from his jacket pocket and dabbing his forehead.

"What about her?" I asked.

"She died last year."

"I'm sorry for your loss." I jotted down his name and that his wife had died a year ago.

"She's come back."

I cocked my head. "What do you mean?"

"Her spirit has returned. She blames me for her death, and she says she will return the favor once she grows in strength."

The office door flew open then. Mr. Dupree lurched from his chair, standing and wheeling around to watch Fred barge into the space. The big man nodded at me, eating a breakfast burrito.

"Howdy," Fred said with a mouthful of food.

Mr. Dupree shakily returned to his seat—visibly startled by Fred's sudden and boisterous entrance. I leveled my eyes on the man, tapping the pen against the notepad.

"Your wife's spirit haunts you?" I asked.

"She threatens to kill me."

"When did she first appear to you after her death?"

"A few weeks ago," Mr. Dupree said, staring at his feet. "It, it happened late at night. I woke up from my sleep to relieve my bladder, and I saw her. I thought I dreamed of her. She didn't engage with me then, and I didn't see her again for another week." He cleared his throat. "Weird things happened around the house. She left me notes, sharing inside jokes and private information only we knew. She messed up the kitchen one night, shattering plates and throwing knives into the ceiling, and writing with condiments on the wall that she will kill me. It's become worse every night. And she follows me. I stayed in a hotel, and I looked out the window, and she stood in the parking lot, waving at me." Mr. Dupree was nearly in hysterics by the end of his story, panting and shaking.

I allowed him a few seconds to regain his composure. "How did she die?" I asked.

The man squeezed his eyes shut. "We went hiking on a whim. She suggested it, claiming she had grown bored with our routine, and her friends and their husbands always went out and did things. We worked, and we came home and watched television until we fell asleep."

"How did she die while hiking?"

Mr. Dupree wiped his lips with his sleeve. "I'm not in the best shape and needed a break. While I sat and rested, she wanted to check out the scenery, so she wandered off. Ten minutes passed. Twenty. I grew worried, so I followed in the direction she went. It was fall. The ground was moist. I had no trouble following her tracks. They led through the foliage, ending suddenly at a blind ledge. I nearly fell off. She had."

I noted his story as he spoke, raising my head and shaking out my cramping hand. "You saw her body?"

He nodded his head. "It was… it's unforgettable how horrible it looked. A rescue party extracted her remains, though, and I buried her in the ground."

"And now she has returned to haunt you?"

"Yes, and she blames me for what happened. She says she'll kill me."

"But she hasn't killed you yet, because her spirit doesn't have enough strength?"

Mr. Dupree licked his lips. "That's what she has communicated."

I set down my pen. "I hate this next part, but we have to discuss payment before I proceed with the investigation."

"Anything. I've had an extremely successful dental practice for almost forty years now. I can afford any expenses you require, as long as you can guide her spirit from this world."

I shared an expected price range with him, and the man agreed to my costs.

"I'll contact you tomorrow," I said, standing up. My head throbbed, and I needed coffee before doing any more work. "We'll schedule a time for me to walk through your home and investigate for any signs of a spiritual presence."

When Mr. Dupree left, Fred looked at me and whistled. "Nothing prettier on a girl than a paycheck—and you, my girl, are getting paid."

I vibrated with positive energy. Fred was right. Customers were coming, as was the money. Maybe I could make a legitimate business out of this after all.

Bigfoot Conundrum. Monday, April 25th. 1446hrs.

I spent the rest of the morning working on the Bigfoot investigation, preparing for the overnight stay in the forest and coming up with nothing useful. After lunch, I returned to my apartment to pack.

The front door stood splintered, wide open for the world to walk through. At first, a sense of dread overcame me. I remembered Eddie had broken into my apartment to kidnap Alina, and I had forgotten that in the aftermath of everything that had happened. Luckily, if someone ransacked and looted my belongings, I had nothing worthwhile inside the place.

I crossed through the broken door and into my kitchen. Alina must have fought against Eddie's attempts to take her. The dining table lay on its side, flipped over. The chairs rested on their backs, and dishes and silverware were thrown across the floor. I stood amongst the chaos, wishing that Eddie had destroyed the place beyond repair so I could finally have the excuse to leave and rebuild my life.

Adam arrived twenty minutes later. I met him downstairs, leaving for the night with my door unlocked and broken. We drove out to Stanislaus National Park.

He and I set up and shared a tent a mile from Cherry Lake. James Connors had hiked us back to the spot where he had sighted Sasquatch, walking us to the exact location where the creature had thrashed and howled. As before, there were signs consistent with James' claims—gashes through the tree trunk, large clumps of hair left in the bark, and disturbed dirt.

At my office that morning, conducting my research, I had Googled bears marking trees, and a whirlwind of results appeared. Bears marked trees by rubbing their scent on the tree, shedding their fur, clawing, or biting. Most of the pictures I saw on the internet were in line with the ones James showed us, the ones he adamantly insisted belonged to Bigfoot.

I absorbed everything James showed us, comparing it to my light research on bears, specifically black bears. I didn't say a word of rebuttal to the man. He seemed more unhinged than when we had last met a couple of days before. His eyes were swollen and red, his hair wild and unkempt, his beard a mane of untamed wires, and he stank of body odor, like he hadn't showered in weeks.

"What now?" Adam asked, standing by a marked tree, touching the scars.

"We wait," I said.

"For what?"

A bear, I thought. "Sasquatch."

"Really?"

"I saw her myself," James said. "We need to head back to camp."

We had constructed the camp a hundred yards from where we now stood.

"Once there, it's quiet time," James continued. "Low conversation. No fire. We don't want to scare her away. When the sun drops, no conversation at all. Bigfoot, she's a nocturnal creature."

Adam glanced at me and turned up his nose. "Really? No talking at all?"

"We can't scare the creature away," I said, hiking back toward the tent.

James kept pace with me, his short stocky legs moving twice as fast as mine. "What's the plan? Remember, we either capture her or we kill her. We can't let her escape, though. Not a rabid Bigfoot."

I stopped and turned back to the sighting location. "When you saw her before, did you see which way she ran off?"

"I told you, I looked down at my phone to unlock the screen. When I looked back up, she was gone."

"It doesn't matter much," I said, mostly to myself, because Sasquatch didn't exist and this man hadn't seen a rabid one. "The plan doesn't change. You'll wait at the campsite. Don't worry about catching the creature on camera. Also, whatever you do, don't shoot it. We're going to capture Bigfoot alive. Okay?"

"What will you do?" James asked.

"When we see Bigfoot, Adam and I will fan out. I have two hunting nets back in the tent. We'll pinch Bigfoot and throw the nets at her. They're meant to tangle and restrain."

Earlier that day, before running to my apartment, I had stopped by a sporting goods store to buy hunting nets so that James wouldn't question my bogus plan. I had no intentions of throwing the nets at anything. However, I would include the nets in the itemized receipt sent to James Connors at the end of this investigation. He would reimburse me for the nets. So, no harm, no foul.

"What then?" Adam asked, joining our conversation. "Do we shoot her then?"

"We're not shooting anyone or anything," I said. "James, do you know of any cryptozoologist that live in Northern California?" I had found a few professors of the subject, but I hadn't searched beyond local colleges.

"I know a couple."

"You have a truck, right?"

"I do."

"Once we have Bigfoot netted, we'll hoist her into your truck, cover her, and drive her to whichever cryptozoologist you trust the most. They will know what to do better than us. If they decide to put her down, so be it... but the professionals should make that decision. Not us."

James stared into the ever-darkening forest for a second. "You're right."

"How do we plan on hoisting a Bigfoot into a truck?" Adam asked, crossing his arms over his chest and raising his eyebrows—being difficult for the sake of being difficult. We had discussed the situation in the car, on the three-hour drive out here. Bigfoot didn't exist, and everything I said and did was only to placate the customer until I solved the case. "How do we plan on getting a truck out here, or dragging the creature to the truck?"

"He brings up a good point," James said, wagging a finger at Adam. "She has to weigh about five-hundred pounds."

"James," I said, though I glared at Adam, "you're a hunter, right?"

"Yeah."

"If you shoot a buck or maybe a bear, how do you get them home with you? Do you just leave them lying on the ground to rot?"

"We usually gut them, quarter, and carry them out."

"Okay, well, that's not an option because we're not killing her."

"We'll all have to grab a limb and drag her then."

"There we go," I said. "That's what we're doing then. Dragging."

James yawned, stretching to the treetops. "I'm going to put on some coffee."

"That's a great idea," I said. "I can do with a pot of coffee."

James toddled off, disappearing into his tent.

I turned to Adam. "You don't have to make this harder than it already is. My job is twofold—solve the investigation by providing enough evidence for the person who hired me to prove their paranormal encounter doesn't actually exist. To break that down, I essentially make money by convincing people they're wrong and having them admit it. I know from experience, it's difficult to admit you're wrong to someone, but hardest to admit it to yourself. My job isn't just solving the case, but helping these people move forward with their lives."

"You think you're some kind of hero, don't you, saving these people from their own nightmares?" Adam scoffed.

"It's the job. I'm not a hero."

"I know you're not." Adam cleared his throat. "When I was in my sophomore year of high school, fifteen years old, I called you one night. Do you remember this?"

Like a leaf quivering in a slight breeze, I shook my head. The time he spoke of happened when the booze had led me far off track, and I was lost.

"I didn't think so. I called to check on you. Actually, I'm going to rewind. Mom and dad sat me down when they heard what happened. They didn't want me learning about the incident from someone at school or on the news. So, they sat me down and they told me exactly what happened." My little brother swallowed and blinked his eyes. "I called you that night. I needed to hear it from you, not from them. I needed to hear your story. You answered." Adam looked up at the sky.

He said nothing for a few seconds, so I jumped in. "I was sick."

"Don't make excuses… just don't. Admit you're wrong, to me and yourself, and move forward. Right? That's what you help this guy do, and all the others like him. Why don't you do it for yourself?"

"It's different."

Adam barked laughter. "How?"

I didn't have an answer for him.

"I was a fifteen-year-old kid worried about his older brother and calling to check on him, to see if you were okay. You answered the phone by saying, 'There's nothing worth living for anymore.' Dude, you said that to me, a kid struggling with his own insecurities and fear of the future. You said that to your little brother, as if I wasn't worth living for." Adam openly cried now, wiping his forearm across his leaking nose. "Guess what happened next? I didn't see you again until my graduation, and then I didn't see you again until Saturday."

"I shot someone last night," I said, blurting it out.

Adam's face froze. "What?"

"I shot a cop. He murdered someone, then he kidnapped two of my friends. I went after him and shot him. Once in his ribs, once in the shoulder, once in his chest. He's alive. Last I heard, he has some broken ribs, but nothing serious. Once he's discharged from the hospital, they'll transfer him to jail to await his trial." I swallowed, piecing together my thoughts. "One of my friends spent the night in the hospital, thanks to that man. I sat in the waiting room all night long, thinking about a lot of things. Do you know what never crossed my mind?"

Adam shook his head.

"Alcohol. I didn't want a sip. I don't remember that night you called me." I pursed my lips and shrugged. "I don't remember saying what I said, but it was the truth. I had nothing to live for because I cared for no one but myself. When you hate yourself, it's easy to believe everyone else hates you. I've learned that's not true, though. I've learned people care a lot about me, and I've learned to care for them, and through them, I'm learning to care for myself again. That's life, though... screwing up and making mistakes, learning from them and evolving and becoming a better person through failure." I stepped forward, arms spread wide. "I'm sorry for leaving you like that, for disappearing, but I'm trying to do better now. I am."

Adam hesitated for a heartbeat before diving into me, nearly tackling me. We hugged—maybe we cried.

James returned, breaking up our reunion. "Coffee is over there," he said, pointing back to his tent. A French press balanced atop a foldable table and two coffee mugs sat beside it.

"Thanks," I said, walking over and pouring myself a cup.

We all sat in a half circle, facing the spot where James had spotted Bigfoot. No one really spoke, rather we enjoyed the sounds of nature—the breeze rustling through trees, the birds, and the buzzing insects.

The sun fell behind the trees, and shadows devoured us. The moon stood in the sky, surrounded by a trillion stars.

"You don't believe in the paranormal?" Adam asked, nudging me with his elbow.

"I would like to, but I've seen no credible proof."

"Just wait," James said. "Just you wait a few more hours."

"I imagine," Adam said, "the paranormal exists like nature."

I cocked my head. "Explain."

"Well, in the city, we have insects, birds, wind, stars… but it's all hidden behind noise and light—unnatural noise and unnatural light. You know?"

"Yeah."

"I mean, if you think about it, people witnessed paranormal sightings far more often before technology existed. What if industry and technological advancement drowned our ability to perceive the supernatural?"

"The kid has an interesting point," James said. "People report, to this day, encountering the supernatural while outside of established civilization—the forest, the jungle, the ocean, or anywhere away from phones and street lights and technology."

"Exactly," Adam said. "Strip all that away. Maybe we can perceive the paranormal again, like we do the wind. Or hear it again, like we hear the birds. Or see it again, like we see the stars."

"Are you high right now?" I asked.

"I snuck an edible when you grabbed coffee."

"Does mom know?"

"It's legal now."

"Twenty-one and up. You're twenty."

"But if I drink, that's okay? Don't get me going on the alcohol scam. People, especially mom's generation of people—old, conservative, white people—have this strange aversion to marijuana from corporate brainwashing. It's actually healthier for your body and mind than alcohol, having way less short- and long-term adverse effects."

"Shh," James said, quieting us. He pointed up the hill to the spot where he had noticed Bigfoot. "You see that?"

I squinted against the shadows and the dark, seeing nothing but the sharp outlines of trees. "No."

"She's being shy," James whispered. "Don't say anything. Watch. She'll come out. You'll see."

Adam leaned forward, planting his elbows on his knees and furrowing his brow.

"I'm going to grab the nets," I said, carefully standing from where I sat, tiptoeing to the tent, and creeping inside. Once in there, I removed my cell phone from my bag, brought up the camera, and tapped the record button.

I had zero hunches or theories about this case, other than James had seen a black bear at night, and his paranoid, susceptible mind had allowed him to believe it was Sasquatch. To combat his ironclad faith in what he had witnessed, I had to provide contrary evidence. If the black bear returned, I had no intentions of throwing a net around it. Instead, I would record the creature and show it to James.

The minutes stretched forward, extending into an hour... two.

Adam remained angled forward, staring along with James into the shadows. I sat in the tent, on my cot, watching through the unzipped opening, recording the spot where Bigfoot would appear.

Three hours went by. Adam joined me in the tent, opening his bag and grabbing a mint box, though he didn't have mints inside it. He removed a couple of gummies. "Want one?"

"No," I said.

"I'll grab one for James then."

"I think he's sober, too."

"It's rude not to ask."

"I don't think so... but sure."

Adam returned to his prior seat. He offered the gummy to James, who raised a palm and declined. Adam popped it into his mouth, taking both of them. Great. Hopefully, Mom didn't ask if we went into the forest to get high, because I would inevitably tell her the truth. No, Mom, that's not why we went into the forest, but that's what happened while we were there.

My watch showed the time at nearly 0100hrs. Luckily, the coffee and my inability to sleep prevented me from dozing.

James also appeared wired, sitting upright in his chair, never once moving his attention from the money spot.

Adam, though, had dozed. He slumped in his seat, his cheek resting on his shoulder. At one point he snored, and James bumped him with his elbow, waking and shushing him.

Then, without warning, it happened.

James' entire body stiffened. He patted Adam's chest with an open palm, waking my brother again. The old man pointed directly at the spot.

Adam didn't react… not at first. After a second, probably as the sleep drifted away, he bolted upright, grabbing onto James' arm and looking back at me with wide, terrified eyes.

I saw absolutely nothing. There wasn't a black bear. There wasn't a raccoon. There definitely wasn't a rabid Sasquatch ravaging the tree.

"August," Adam said, whispering, though loudly. "Get the nets."

I situated my phone, making sure it continued to record in the correct location, and I collected the hunting nets, carrying them silently outside to James and Adam.

"Here." I divvied them out. "Adam, you go that way." I pointed to the left. "James, you go that way. Move slowly and quietly so you don't scare her away."

"Okay," Adam said.

"Wait," I said. "Hold on." I massaged my chin, wondering how to proceed. They both obviously thought they saw something that wasn't actually there. Did they see the same thing, though? "Adam, is that a blonde Sasquatch? It matters, too, the color of its fur."

My brother turned his head for another look. "Definitely blonde."

"What?" James said. "No. There's no such thing as blonde Sasquatch. She's brown."

"Dude, she's blonde."

"Adam," I said, "is she just sitting there, staring at you?" I purposely asked leading questions to manipulate his mind into seeing what I wanted him to see. A theory had finally formed, and I had to test it.

"She is sitting there. It's creepy. She's, like, cross-legged and staring right at us. Dude, she just waved. Should I wave back?"

"Are you high?" James said, raising his voice. "She's rabid. Look at her face, covered in foam and spit. And she's not waving, she's destroying that tree."

"Did you hear that?" I asked. "Is she singing a song?"

"Yeah," Adam said. My brother, who majored in music, hummed some tune I wasn't familiar with. "I love that song."

"No!" James yelled. "She howling and roaring. Are you mad?"

I shushed James. "You're going to scare her away. Hurry, take the net and capture her. Go. Now."

The two of them stood and ventured forward, neither of them listening to my suggestion of going left and right. Instead, they walked side-by-side, directly toward where they believed they saw a Bigfoot. I trailed after them to make sure they didn't hurt themselves.

"We'll throw them together," Adam said.

"Don't get too close," James said. "Remember, she has rabies."

"Rabies? I thought you said scabies."

"How would Sasquatch contract scabies? That makes no sense."

"Think about it," Adam said. "That's why we found fur on the trunk. It was scratching its back. I really thought you said scabies."

"Rabies."

"How does a Sasquatch even get rabies?"

"A rat or something."

"You think a rat is going to bite something so big and scary?"

The two dinguses stood about five feet from where they imagined seeing Bigfoot, arguing back and forth about what disease it had and where it had obtained that disease.

"Throw the nets," I said, not bothering to whisper.

Both Adam and James jumped at the sound of my voice, but they regained their wits enough to toss the hunting nets where they believed Sasquatch sat or thrashed. Both nets landed empty on the ground.

"Wow," Adam said. "Did she just... turn invisible?"

"No, she teleported," James said. "Invisibility doesn't allow you to phase through objects or for objects to phase through you. The nets would have captured her, even if she had turned invisible."

Adam stroked his chin. "Do you think Bigfoots can turn invisible, and that's why they're so hard to find?"

"I think they have some kind of natural cloaking trait, much like a chameleon."

"That's crazy. I mean, that's probably, like, why people think they see a Bigfoot, but then they can't find her. The Bigfoot just blends into the forest, you know? Is that what happened here? Because I don't see her anymore."

"I think so," James said. "She must have turned invisible."

"Or maybe she teleported," Adam said, now talking in circles. "What if Sasquatch couldn't turn invisible, but they could teleport? That's why they disappear so quickly and don't leave any traces behind. If they were invisible, they would still leave footprints, right? I mean, you said that whole thing about objects and phasing, so they would probably leave tracks when invisible."

"I think she teleported," James said. "That's what I think."

"Me, too." Adam scratched his head, ruffling his hair. "I can't believe I saw Bigfoot tonight."

I pivoted and returned to the tent, grabbing my phone and ending the recording. For the sake of everyone's sanity, I really hoped the video hadn't captured sound. I couldn't relive Adam and James going back and forth about Bigfoot and her imaginary abilities.

A few minutes later, the two twits returned, dragging the nets behind them. "Where do we put these?" James asked.

"Leave them there," I said. "I think we should tuck in for the night. We'll review the footage tomorrow morning."

"The footage?" James asked.

"I recorded everything, just to have proof of the encounter in case she escaped."

James tapped his temple with an index finger. "Smart."

"Let's get some sleep."

James Connors padded into his tent, zipping it behind him. A flashlight illuminated the fabric, and his silhouette showed against the glowing orange. He sat on the ground holding something, staring at it, and muttering. After a few dozen minutes, James must have knocked out, because the muttering finally ceased.

Adam collapsed onto my cot, mistaking it for his bed, and he instantly went to snoring.

I didn't sleep. Couldn't. I went outside and sat in a chair, staring at the stars and collecting my thoughts until the midnight purple faded into pink and the sun burned the horizon.

Saying Goodbye. Tuesday, April 26th. 0923hrs.

I sat in the stiff-backed hospital chair beside Glacia's bed. She was awake and lively, smiling at me. She ran her thumb up and down the back of my hand.

"What happened then?" she asked.

"Remember that story I told you about when I first stopped drinking? I hadn't discovered exercise yet, or abusing work. So, I couldn't figure out how to sleep."

Glacia chuckled. "The birthday card?"

"That dinosaur spoke to me! To this day, I refuse to buy greeting cards." I smiled, twisting my hand to grab hers and hold it. "As you informed me, severe sleep deprivation creates hallucinations. Sure, I still sleep nothing compared to your average person, but I sleep enough now to keep me mentally stable."

"Objection, your honor!"

"Sustained," I said. "I sleep enough to function at a basic level."

"Better."

"I don't think James Connors has slept since his wife's death. The human mind is very... susceptible to manipulation, especially when weakened and vulnerable. Bigfoot is popular where he lives. A tourist attraction. The town has statues and themed restaurants and... and all that. Bigfoot hunters come from everywhere to search the neighboring forests." I scratched my nose. "I think when he lost his wife and his ability to sleep, he needed to find something." I thought of my need to find proof of the supernatural. "The hallucinations gave him something he wanted—a story outside of his wife's death."

"How do you explain your brother seeing Bigfoot?"

I scoffed. "He was high. Again, the strain of marijuana combined with the late hour combined with the foundation of expecting to see Bigfoot probably created a shared hallucination between him and James. Except I shattered their shared illusion when I asked him leading questions. He saw what I planted in his head."

"Okay, Mr. Psycho-analyzer, why would James see Bigfoot as rabid?"

I shook my head. "I don't know. It was a projection of his diseased emotions. His unhealthy inability to move forward with his life. That's my best guess. You're the head doctor. You tell me what happened."

"I prefer listening to you come up with these explanations."

"You just like seeing me squirm."

"Guilty." Glacia reached to the nightstand and grabbed her iced water. She drank it through a straw. "Did your video evidence convince James? Did he pay you?"

"I recorded everything. He had no choice but to believe me. Especially after he watched himself argue with my brother for a solid two minutes before throwing a hunting net into thin air."

Glacia chuckled. "I wish I could have seen that."

"Um, you can." I grabbed my phone and pulled up the video, fast forwarding to the spot where James first noticed Bigfoot. "Watch."

"That's incredible," Glacia said, chuckling when the video finished. "Wow. Never erase that."

"I'll strategically edit it and send brief clips to Adam now and then. We have to rebuild our relationship somewhere. I figured ridiculing him is as good a place as any to start."

"You hit that nail on the head."

I bit my lip and cracked my knuckles, thinking of something to say that avoided what actually needed saying. My silence stretched into the territory of awkward.

"I want to buy your house." I raised my palms, gesturing for her not to interrupt me. "I know you saw my apartment and how it looked. I know you said you don't want Nana's home to degrade into that mess. But I'm ready to make changes and clean up my act. I think owning something with history and importance will keep me focused, too."

Glacia said nothing.

"Now, here's the thing. I can't afford it. I don't even think I can qualify for a loan. But I just solved three cases in as many days. I have another case pending. Fred said the phone is off the hook today. Maya is writing her big article, and she said she's going to feature Blue Moon Investigations heavily. Do you know what that means? Her audience will know my name, and her audience crosses with my audience. Not only that," I held up a finger, "but Alina noticed Fred sent Tempest Michaels the wrong routing address. That's why the seed money never arrived. We ironed that out, and we're expecting his investment soon. My old buddy from the police academy called me earlier, before I came in here. He mentioned something about the Sacramento Police Department contracting with me to help them solve unsolved cases. Things are turning around finally. If you lend me some time and trust, I'll pay for the house in full. I'll take care of it, too."

Glacia bit her lip and remained silent for a while. "My mom entered a rehab facility."

I exhaled, deflated at the change of subject. "I heard."

"She told me she wants to be there for me. For that to happen, she had to show up for herself. I knew those words weren't hers, though. My mom is a lot of things, but she lacks wisdom and self-awareness. So, someone held up a mirror for her to look into. When I asked her who, she said you."

"It wasn't my place. I know. I'm sorry."

"Thank you," Glacia said, squeezing my hand.

"What?"

"Whatever you said or did, thank you. For the first time in my life, I feel hope that I might have a relationship with my mom. You did more than rid Nana's house of the ghosts. You bridged a chasm I thought was far too wide to cross. I refuse to sell you the house, August."

I frowned, but nodded with understanding.

"I don't care how much you beg, argue, barter... it will not happen. Nana would never allow me to sell her home to someone like you."

"Well, I'm simultaneously feeling amazing and terrible about myself. It's a strange feeling, much stranger than being both hot and cold at the same time."

"You idiot, I'm giving you the house."

Her statement butted me in the gut, knocking the breath out of me. "What?"

"It's yours. My mom, my uncle, and Susan dirtied the money I could have made from selling it. Besides, I would rather you live there than anyone else. If you can't afford it, well, you can't live there. So, I'm gifting it to you."

"You can discount it. I mean, you don't have to give to me for free. That's ridiculous."

"No begging, arguing, or bartering. If you do, the deal's off. I'll sell it to someone else."

I zipped my lips.

"Good."

"What about us, then?" I asked, blurting out the question that really plagued my mind and heart.

"What about us?" Glacia asked.

"You're going back to Oregon, right?"

"I am."

"I'm staying here, in Sacramento. My business is finally growing, and I can't leave."

"You can't."

I lowered my chin and raised my eyes, shrugging my shoulders. "So?"

"So, what?"

"What about us?"

"We're not a couple," Glacia said. "You know that, right? In fact, I don't really think we're that compatible. I'm more of a girl who... well, I like my men more rugged. I think had someone not tried to murder me, twice since knowing you, we could have hooked up, and that would have been fun in a walk through the park kind of way."

"I prefer a rock concert kind of fun, if we're making hypothetical comparisons."

"Hooking up with you would have been fun, like going to an amazing, unforgettable rock concert. But beyond that…" she trailed off, shaking her head.

"Yeah, no, I figured as much. I mean, personally, you're not my type either. I like my woman taller than average, dark hair, dark eyes, independent, successful, funny."

"You're literally describing me." Glacia poked out her tongue, biting the tip, and grinning.

"I included funny in that description. You're not that funny."

"I'm hilarious."

"Yeah, you're right. You're pretty funny."

"What I said before, it was a joke anyway. You're a catch, but we wouldn't have worked out because you're really not that into me."

"What?"

"You like someone else."

"Don't even say Fred. I can barely stand that guy, especially when he eats chips. He chews with his mouth open, smacking and crunching, but only with chips. Nothing else. Why can't he close his mouth when chewing chips?"

"Maya."

I blew air through my lips in a half-exasperated, half-amused expression. "Please. Maya?"

"I'm heading back to Oregon tomorrow. We'll get the house in your possession within the next month or two."

"That's fine. My lease doesn't end for another three months, anyway."

Glacia squeezed my hand. "What next?"

Before I could answer her question, my phone rang. The unknown number who had stood me up flashed across the screen. "I think this is what's next." I stood and walked to the hospital window overlooking the beautiful parking lot, always brimming with cars. "August speaking."

"I'm sorry," she said, her voice timid.

"Claire?"

She cried through the phone, sniffling and choking on sobs. "I'm so scared."

"Claire," I said again, using her name to create a connection and build trust, "what are you scared of?"

"She won't leave me alone." The words sputtered off her lips in broken syllables. "She financially ruined me. She destroyed my marriage. I'm scared... so scared of what she'll do next."

"Who?" I asked, feeling my stomach knot.

Claire sucked in air. "Me."

The call ended. I redialed her number, but it went straight to her voicemail. I rotated around and leaned on the window, staring at Glacia.

"Who was it?"

"I don't know," I said.

"Did they need help?"

I popped my knuckles, cracked my neck, massaged my shoulders to relieve a little stress. "I think that she desperately needs help."

Glacia smiled at me with a sincere warmth. "She's lucky to know your number, then. I can't think of anyone better to help her than you."

Knocking on the Door. Tuesday, April 26th. 1133hrs.

Mr. and Mrs. Brooks lived in a two-story house on a cul-de-sac in Galt. Every yard in their small neighborhood boasted of pristine, well-tended care and attention. Green, manicured lawns and blooming, trimmed shrubs, and trees blossoming with white flowers.

I parked on the street in front of their home. Reaching to the passenger seat, I grabbed a bouquet and a card, placing them on my lap, and staring at their front door. It resembled any other door, but it represented so much more.

For me to walk up to that door, and for it to open up to me, held so much weight and power. It represented everything I despised about myself. It represented everything I feared in life. Opening it would signify the revelation of a new direction, an alternative path I could follow.

I stepped out of my car and exhaled slowly. Nerves pulled at my body, nearly lifting me off the asphalt and throwing me back into the vehicle. I pushed forward, though, heading up the sloping driveway to the front entry.

I had run this moment through my mind infinite times. I had practiced the apology, the explanation, and I had practiced reacting to their responses—anger, hate, forgiveness, love. Despite the many occasions I lived through this moment in my head, nothing prepared me for actually walking to the front door and potentially facing the parents of the kid I had murdered.

Still, I had to move forward with my life. No longer could I tolerate living in physical and emotional and relational filth. James Connors had shown me what obsession and sleep deprivation can do to the mind. Randall Fincher had portrayed the consequences of dependence. Peter Seed had helped me realize I had neglected myself and the world, living in ruin. Glacia had helped me understand I could exorcise the ghosts from my past.

Fear couldn't control my life anymore. I had to harness the ghosts haunting and terrorizing my soul.

I switched the bouquet from one hand to the other, along with the card—not a greeting card, of course. I had typed out a letter and sealed it in an envelope. So, I guess I had brought flowers and a letter. Either way, the note was simple, expressing deepest and sincerest apologies. The envelope also contained ten percent of the earnings I had made through my brief career as a paranormal investigator. As the note pointed out, I had founded this business to prove the supernatural world existed so that I could reach out to Aaron and apologize for what I had done. It was only appropriate that his parents receive a percentage of my earnings, and with it, they could do as they pleased.

I made a fist and raised it into the air to knock.

The End

Author's Note

Hello, Dear Reader,

I became apparent some time ago that my Blue Moon Investigations series was ripe for expansion. There were a couple of very good reasons to do so, not least of which was a desire to avoid repeating myself or risk allowing a popular series to go stale.

Alex Gates is an established urban fantasy author in his own right, and you will find a couple of his books on the following pages. Working with him has been a pleasure and the stories he had to tell within my constructed universe were … well, you just read the first book, so you already know how good they are.

There are more stories coming though Alex and I haven't worked out how many yet. I guess if people buy them, and Alex enjoys writing them, they could go on and on, much like mine have.

I published the first book, Paranormal Nonsense, in 2017, more than five years before this book graced the bookshelves. If you are now concerned that I might be retiring Tempest Michaels and his colleagues, you need not be worried for I have many more adventures lined up for the original team.

Sticking with the subject of new books, it may interest you to know that Alex is not the only new author writing stories in the Blue Moon universe, there are others. I'm not going to tell you any more than that right now, but if you want to hear more, you can sign up to receive my newsletter. There's a link on the following pages.

I'm going to leave it at that, but ask that you check out the final few pages to see all the other amazing stuff we have on offer.

Take care.

Steve Higgs

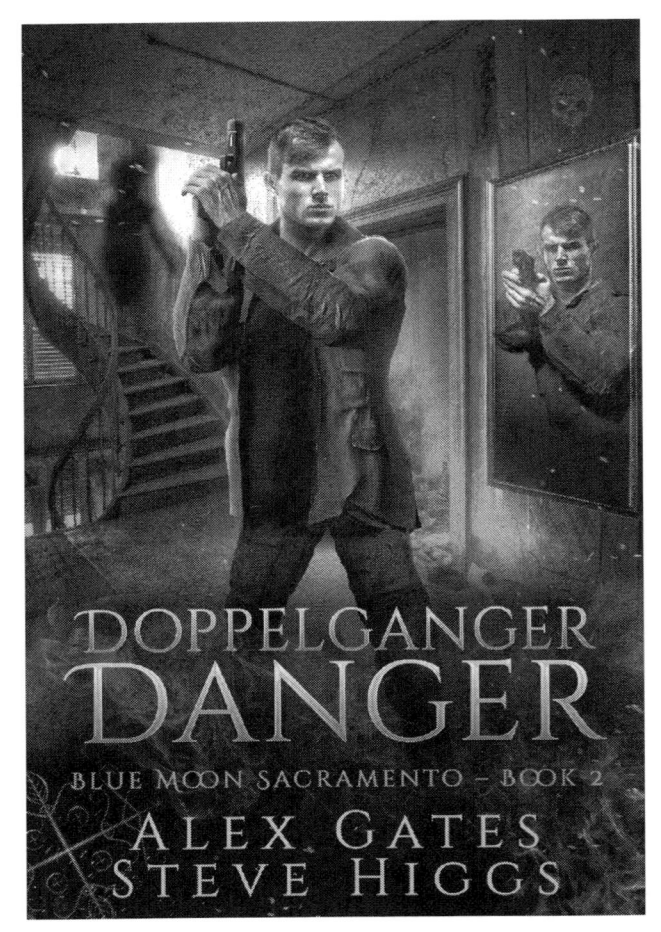

What's Next for August and Friends?

Investigate a murderous ghost, do battle with a shapeshifting demon, get ready for a date ... it's all in a day's work for Sacramento's only paranormal detective.

The ghost of a man's wife come to avenge her untimely death, a woman caught on camera stealing drugs from work when she wasn't even in town, and a family with a secret no one can ever know.

When August Watson takes on all three cases at the same time, it's not because he is short of work, but due to the worrying connection between them – they all point to impossible doubles.

Is there a shapeshifting doppelganger at work? It seems like the only explanation for the craziness ensuing, but as he gets closer to the truth, the long-hidden lies he disturbs come with a price.

His own life.

In a race to stop more deaths, August Watson will risk it all.

If only work was his biggest worry.

Books by Alex Gates

Dorian Miller, a private detective specializing in the supernatural, investigates a blackmail conspiracy involving the daughter of one of Sacramento's elite families who partook in a satanic ritual.

But the simple assignment soon turns un-deadly.

Zombies and golems rise around the city. The corpses of vampires are found slaughtered in a horrific manner. And rumors warn that a Revenant—the spirit of a dead Necromancer summoned back to this world—stands behind all the mayhem.

How much longer can Dorian run from Death before it catches up to him?

ALEX GATES

DARK PHOENIX SERIES
INHERENT MAGIC
BOOK ONE

Once struggling to make rent, Skylar must now use her budding magic to save the world...

As a child of abuse, Skylar Neveah knows desperation and terror from firsthand experience. But nothing in her past prepared her for a date ending with her getting sacrificed to a fallen angel. By blind luck and a touch of magic, Skylar escaped with her life. To do so, she murdered two wealthy, influential men.

On the run from the police and the supernatural world, a man approaches Skylar. He offers her refuge at a secret university for humans like her with magical powers. She hesitantly accepts his offer. But her problems aren't solved... far from it.

A cosmic war has kicked off. Somehow, Skylar landed in the middle of it. And the fallen angel has fixed his attention on her. He will stop at nothing to see her killed. Will Skylar stop running, learn to control her magic, and fight back?

Books by Steve Higgs

The paranormal? It's all nonsense but proving it might just get them all killed.

When a master vampire starts killing people in his hometown, paranormal investigator, Tempest Michaels, takes it personally ...

... and soon a race against time turns into a battle for his life. He doesn't believe in the paranormal but has a steady stream of clients with cases too weird for the police to bother with.

Mostly it's all nonsense, but when a third victim turns up with bite marks in her lifeless throat, can he really dismiss the possibility that this time the monster is real?

Joined by an ex-army buddy, a disillusioned cop, his friends from the pub, his dogs, and his mother (why are there no grandchildren, Tempest), our paranormal investigator is going to stop the murders if it kills him …

… but when his probing draws the creature's attention, his family and friends become the hunted.

UNTETHERED MAGIC
THE
REALM
OF
FALSE GODS
STEVE HIGGS

Today's tasks:
1. Escape from underground cell
2. Recruit snarky d-bag werewolf to help
3. Invade demon realm and rescue a girl

For wizard detective, Otto Schneider, magic has always kept him out of trouble. Now it's working in reverse …

… and he's just started the fight of his life. There's an ancient secret buried in the Earth's past and he just uncovered it.

Magical beings once ruled over us until their betrayed leader made a death curse with his final breath. Banished from the realm of man for over four thousand years, the curse is weakening, and these beings, these … demons, are coming back to rule the Earth once more.

They are powerful, immortal, and unstoppable, but they don't know everything.

They left some of their magic behind and their return has sparked an awakening.

Heroes will rise …

More Books by Steve Higgs

Blue Moon Investigations

Paranormal Nonsense

The Phantom of Barker Mill

Amanda Harper Paranormal Detective

The Klowns of Kent

Dead Pirates of Cawsand

In the Doodoo with Voodoo

The Witches of East Malling

Crop Circles, Cows and Crazy Aliens

Whispers in the Rigging

Bloodlust Blonde – a short story

Paws of the Yeti

Under a Blue Moon – A Paranormal Detective Origin Story

Night Work

Lord Hale's Monster

The Herne Bay Howlers

Undead Incorporated

The Ghoul of Christmas Past

The Sandman

Jailhouse Golem

Shadow in the Mine

Ghost Writer

Monsters Everywhere

Blue Moon Sacramento

Voodoo Blues

Doppelganger Danger

Nightmare Scare

Undead Dread

Patricia Fisher Cruise Mysteries

The Missing Sapphire of Zangrabar

The Kidnapped Bride

The Director's Cut

The Couple in Cabin 2124

Doctor Death

Murder on the Dancefloor

Mission for the Maharaja

A Sleuth and her Dachshund in Athens

The Maltese Parrot

No Place Like Home

What Sam Knew

Solstice Goat

Recipe for Murder

A Banshee and a Bookshop

Diamonds, Dinner Jackets, and Death

Frozen Vengeance

Mug Shot

The Godmother

Murder is an Artform

Wonderful Weddings and Deadly Divorces

Dangerous Creatures

Patricia Fisher: Ship's Detective

Fitness Can Kill

Death by Pirates

First Dig Two Graves

Rumble in Rio

Albert Smith Culinary Capers

Pork Pie Pandemonium

Bakewell Tart Bludgeoning

Stilton Slaughter
Bedfordshire Clanger Calamity
Death of a Yorkshire Pudding
Cumberland Sausage Shocker
Arbroath Smokie Slaying
Dundee Cake Dispatch
Lancashire Hotpot Peril
Blackpool Rock Bloodshed
Kent Coast Oyster Obliteration
Eton Mess Massacre
Cornish Pasty Conspiracy – the Killing in the Filling

Felicity Philips Investigates
To Love and to Perish
Tying the Noose
Aisle Kill Him
A Dress to Die for
Wedding Ceremony Woes
Something Stolen Something Blue

Real of False Gods
Untethered magic
Unleashed Magic
Early Shift
Damaged but Powerful
Demon Bound
Familiar Territory
The Armour of God
Terrible Secrets
Top Dog
Hellfire Hellion

[Demon Horde Gambit](#)

Raider and Rapier
[Graveyard Gods](#)
[Titan's Folly](#)
[The Stolen King](#)
[Where the Dead Float](#)

Free Books and More

Get sneak peaks, exclusive giveaways, behind the scenes content, and more. Plus, you'll be notified of Fan Pricing events when they occur and get exclusive offers from other authors because all UF writers are automatically friends.

Not only that, but you'll receive an exclusive FREE story starring Otto and Zachary and two free stories from the author's Blue Moon Investigations series.

[Yes, please! Sign me up for lots of FREE stuff and bargains!](#)

Want to follow me and keep up with what I am doing?

Join me on Facebook by clicking the link below

[Steve's Facebook Group](#)

Made in the USA
Columbia, SC
05 February 2023